BOOK ONE OF THE REBECCA BLACK TRILOGY

WHEN DIAMONDS BLEED

K.S. REID

ISBN: 978-1-960632-00-5

First Double Dutch Publishing Edition: May 2023

10 9 8 7 6 5 4 3 2 1

Dear Reader,

Please note that this book, **When Diamonds Bleed** by **K.S. Reid**, was previously published in 2016 as **Compliments of the Chef** by **Alex Crow.**

Minor content editing has been done, but the original story remains the same.

Prologue

"You don't have to do this. It's not too late to stop," Sara pleaded as tears cascaded down her cheeks.

The restraints burned into her wrists as she violently jerked her arms in a failed attempt to free herself. She gave up after only a minute, complete exhaustion overtaking her. Her body collapsed into the examination table, limp and drenched with a gruesome mix of sweat and blood.

The tears flowed uncontrollably now. "You can just stop."

He turned his head and stared deep into her eyes. His mouth formed a gentle smile. For a brief moment she thought she had finally gotten through to him. However, all hope dissipated as he slowly shook his head from side to side. And when he reached over her to cinch the restraints even tighter, she knew she wouldn't be walking out of that room alive.

He had been at it for hours. So had she. Begging, pleading, and crying to no avail as he continued to cut her over and over. He wasn't a sadist though. His repeated injections of local anesthetic proved that. She almost felt she should thank him for the courtesy. Imagine that. *Thank you, kind sir, for killing all my pain as you slowly kill me.*

Finally, he straightened and took a step back. He tossed a crumpled tube of Krazy Glue onto a stainless-steel tray. It joined an array of scalpels, syringes, gauze, and more empty glue tubes. All the ingredients needed to rearrange diamond-shaped sections of skin on a more-than-unwilling partner.

He then removed his blood-covered latex gloves and dropped them into a white trash bag. The white paper apron was next. Her eyes tracked him as he walked to the corner of the room and returned wheeling an enormous steel frame. Within the frame, a narrow six-foot mirror.

Sara squeezed her eyes shut. She knew where this was going, and she wanted no part of it. He swiveled the mirror within the frame and positioned it over her. It spanned the entire length of her body.

She refused to look at herself. She had made that mistake early on—hours ago when she still wanted to know what the hell he was doing to her. The sight had horrified her, and she learned right then and there that sometimes, knowing is worse. Her eyes remained sealed as she turned her head to the side.

She focused on the incessant buzz of the fluorescent light above her. The rhythm of blood droplets hitting the plastic tarp beneath her. The echo of her attacker's footsteps permeating the walls around her. The audible onslaught to her senses was too much for her to bear.

Her eyes fluttered open and darted around the room. Not for a potential escape—there was no option there—but instead, for any sight that didn't include the mirror positioned over her.

She remembered her first view of the room. She had regained consciousness and, for a moment, thought she was in a hospital. The white walls, floor, ceiling, cabinets—it was blinding. She had fought relentlessly with the bindings on her wrists and ankles, while the stench of antiseptic singed her nostrils. This was no hospital she wanted anything to do with.

And then *he* had walked in. Not as her savior, but as her executioner.

Now, she just wanted it all to be over.

As if hearing her thoughts, he strolled across the floor and stood at her head, looming over her. He held something in his hands. She craned her neck for a better view of the object. Two metal eyes, full of evil and malevolence glared back at her. She recognized it immediately. A tribal face of polished brass made up the handle. The three-sided blade was cold iron. *The Phurba Dagger.*

She squeezed her eyes shut as the realization hit her. She had been wishing for it to be over, but now that it nearly was...she wasn't ready.

His hand stroked her cheek. Softly. Slowly. He then cupped her chin and gently turned her head toward the mirror overhead.

"You truly are my greatest masterpiece," he said. "Open your eyes."

She did as she was told.

An audible gasp escaped her, followed by a deafening scream. It was her first visual of what he had been doing to her. The shock overtook her immediately and paralyzed her.

Diamonds.

An array of nonsensical thoughts raced through her head: *a jigsaw puzzle...a Harlequin suit.* But mostly, *diamonds...bloody diamonds.*

Over and over, the words repeated.

His work was done. He raised the dagger above his head and plunged it deep into her abdomen.

Diamonds.

Chapter 1

"He'll burn in hell for this," Rebecca Black said through gritted teeth.

Her body shifted incessantly in her seat at the back of the courtroom. She anxiously awaited the judge's return while simultaneously staring daggers into the back of the man sitting behind the defense table. His head of perfect black waves and his flashy smile did nothing to distract her from the monster she knew him to be.

Beads of anxiety-driven sweat ran down the back of her neck. The room felt like a furnace, but she knew it was all in her head. She gathered the long blonde tresses that hung down her back and twisted them up into a loose bun. A rush of cool air crossed her exposed neck. Unfortunately, it did nothing for the rage that boiled inside of her.

"I know you don't want to hear this, but I just don't think he's the one," Lexy said calmly, trying to diffuse her friend's rising anger.

"Are you kidding me?" Rebecca whipped her head around. "Are we talking about the same man? You've been right here with me the whole time. How can you not see him for the psychopath he is?"

"The evidence doesn't—"

"He butchered them! Case closed!" Rebecca glared furiously around the hushed courtroom, daring anyone to try to silence her.

"If it was that simple, we wouldn't still be here," Lexy said, clearly annoyed at the interruption.

Rebecca closed her eyes and drew a deep breath. Lexy had a point. The evidence was all highly circumstantial and didn't really prove a thing. It all pointed to him, but nothing was concrete, and his dream-team of lawyers made sure every person in that courtroom was aware of that fact. However, successfully hiding guilt didn't mean it wasn't there.

He was so sure of himself it was difficult not to believe everything he said on the stand. But it wasn't what he was saying that infuriated Rebecca. Instead, it was his mannerisms. His bold cockiness. His totally relaxed posture, as if he hadn't a care in the world. And, worst of all, the smile on his face and the twinkle in his eyes when the prosecution presented the crime scene photos. The rest of the courtroom flinched and turned away from the gruesome sight of the sliced bodies projected onto the screen. But that monster actually leaned in closer, as if to get a better look. These were not the actions of an innocent man. Rebecca wished Lexy could see him the way she did.

Lexy gave it one more shot. "Look, I know this is deeply personal for you, but you need to try to see it objectively, at least."

She paused and chose her words carefully. "I'm telling you this as your friend. You need to put your biases aside, just for now, and look at this with a clear head. Because if you don't, this whole mess is going to tear you apart. Not everyone is as 'sure' as you are...especially not everyone on that jury. They love him. They're hanging on his every word. It's written all over their faces."

Rebecca knew Lexy was right. Not about the man's innocence, but about her feelings being completely obscured by rage. But how could they not be? Four innocent women, murdered and dumped like garbage. And her sister, Sara, had been one of them.

As set as she was in her own judgement, Lexy had been her best friend for almost two decades, and Rebecca owed it to her to at least attempt her suggestion of objectivity. She closed her eyes and drew a deep breath. *No feelings. Only the facts.*

The first body had been found just over a year earlier, wrapped in plastic alongside a popular running trail within Rock Creek Park in Washington D.C. Exactly a month later, another body was found. The pattern continued every thirty days, like clockwork, until the body count reached four. Whoever had dumped the bodies had intended them to be found quickly. Such time and care had been taken to prepare them. He wouldn't have wanted them to be destroyed by animals, insects, or the elements.

The most horrifying sight came when the bodies were unwrapped. The victims were naked and covered with diamond-shaped lacerations. The edges were glued, either to keep the pieces from shifting or to stop the bleeding—maybe both.

The autopsies revealed the skinning was not the cause of death, and the victims had still been alive during that process. The cause of death came from a single stab wound to the abdomen, the one area where the flesh had not been removed. That kind of wound would have produced a lot of blood, but barely any was found. He had stabbed them, let them die slowly over several hours, and then cleaned them up before gift-wrapping and dumping them.

There was no doubt they were all victims of the same killer. If the surface mutilations and murder weapon weren't enough, his choice of victims was. His taste was specific. Tall slender brunettes with mid-neck wavy bobs, emerald-green eyes, and, of course, they were all stunningly beautiful.

Andrew Donovan had been questioned following the discovery of the first victim, as well as the second, third, and fourth. They had all been romantically involved with him at one time or another. He was the glaring connection between them all. The motive was not clear, but he was definitely linked somehow. His alibis placed him out of town at the estimated time of death of each woman. Suspicions had been high, but no hard evidence could put the knife in his hand...until the autopsy of the fourth victim.

The characteristics of the knife were inconclusive in the first three killings. Organs and tissue stretch and retract when impaled, which did not leave an exact impression of the blade.

However, the body of the fourth victim told a clearer story. With his most recent kill, the blade buried itself deep within the liver. And, being a solid organ, an almost perfect impression of the weapon had been retained—a three-edged triangular blade, similar to a tent stake.

Bruising caused by the impact of the knife's handle on the uncut flesh revealed the blade was nearly six inches long. Several days after the initial autopsy, more discolorations became visible. Intricate designs where the handle met the blade left patterned bruising and pointed investigators toward a very unique knife. One they had seen before...at Andrew Donovan's house during his previous questionings. The Phurba Dagger was one of a collection of ancient weapons he had acquired over the years and proudly displayed in his home office.

But why would he suddenly start killing off all of his exes? And why cut them up the way he did? As hard as she tried, Rebecca couldn't fathom a logical reason for it.

Once again, she closed her eyes and exhaled. And once again the horrifying images flooded her mind. She couldn't shut them out. Every day she tried, but they always returned.

The plastic cocoons lying at the side of the trail. The mutilated bodies that were revealed once the plastic was cut away. Their dead stares that seemed to look right through her. And the eerie similarities between the victims, as though Sara was being murdered over and over again. Rebecca shuddered as her memory randomly sifted through the crime scene photos. Diamonds, diamonds, and more diamonds.

A tear escaped down her cheek. The endless suffering Sara endured. The suffering all those women endured. Lexy passed a tissue into her lap, and Rebecca swiped it to the floor without a second thought. A superficial peace offering like that didn't erase the betrayal she felt. She didn't understand Lexy's thinking and why she defended him so strongly.

Again, her eyes bored into the man across the room. Mr. Perfect. Money, power, great looks, and charm. A very dangerous combination. She had never met him before, not even when he was dating Sara. But Sara had told Rebecca all about him. How amazing he was. How thoughtful and romantic and caring. Rebecca didn't buy it, though. Sara was under his spell, and there was no reasoning with her. A man didn't get to the top of the corporate ladder without being a master manipulator. The man was a flat-out wizard, with the way he could work people. And he had a pile of dead bodies behind him to prove it. All those women. They were all his, at some point. And none of them saw it coming. Yes, he was a very dangerous man. But why was she the only one to see it?

She gave a subtle glance to her right and immediately regretted it. The longing gaze in Lexy's eyes proved that she, too, was spellbound. Her long strawberry locks were likely the only thing saving her from joining the pile.

Rebecca's train of thought was broken as the crowd jumped to their feet. A hush fell over the courtroom as the judge took his seat behind the bench. Moments later, the jury marched in through the back courtroom door like a line of ants and shuffled into their box.

She glanced once more at the defense table. He looked confident with a subtle smile spread across his lips. He seemed to already know what the jury was about to say. And he did. He had known all along.

"We, the jury, find the defendant, Andrew Donovan...not guilty."

Chapter 2

Rebecca stormed down the front steps of the courthouse. She was absolutely livid. *The bastard actually walked.*

"Beck! Wait!" Lexy stumbled after her in her heels, struggling to catch up. She finally joined Rebecca at the curb, breathing heavily. "I know this isn't the result you wanted, but you have to accept it. He didn't do it. Game over."

"Why are you even here?" Rebecca shot back at her. "You're not here for me. You're not here for Sara. You're here for him!"

"No, that's not true!" Lexy replied. "I *am* here for you. To support you. But it's also my job to keep you level-headed, and right now, you're anything but that."

Rebecca's green eyes flashed with resentment. "She was my sister, Lexy. Maybe not by blood, but she was still my sister. We swore to protect her and keep her safe. I swore. And I failed!"

"You know there was nothing you could've done to prevent this."

"To hell there wasn't!" Rebecca lowered her voice, aware of the attention she was drawing from those passing by. "I knew there was something off about him. That pretty picture she painted of him...I read between those lines. I knew he wasn't as perfect as she was making him out to be."

"What are you talking about?"

"Don't you get it? She was his wife. They were all his wife. That's why he chose them."

"Being attracted to a certain look doesn't mean he's under the delusion that they're all the same person," Lexy said.

"Where is she, then? Where *is* Marie Donovan? Even the police don't know. She disappeared off the face of the Earth three years ago, and no one has been able to find her since. And you don't think it's strange that every girlfriend he's had since looks exactly like her?"

"That doesn't mean anything."

"It *does* mean something. It means *everything*. I bet he knows where she is. I bet she's wrapped in plastic somewhere in that park. She just hasn't been found yet."

"He didn't do it. He was set up,"

"It doesn't make a difference now anyway, does it? He's a free man. Free to kill again."

Rebecca looked deep into Lexy's eyes. She had never been this angry at anyone so close to her. Maybe that was why it hurt so much. Lexy had truly betrayed her. She was supposed to hold her hand, wipe her tears, and support her through this hellish trial. Rebecca's parents were far too distraught to even make it that far. They had stopped coming to the courthouse after the first week. She needed Lexy more than ever, and her best friend had let her down. The smile that spread across her face when the verdict was read infuriated Rebecca. Lexy was like family to her. In a way, she was her sister too. How could she be so clouded by a flashy smile? Countless people had been mesmerized and charmed by Andrew Donovan, but she had thought Lexy was smarter than that. She was wrong.

"You're clearly not as intelligent as you make yourself out to be," Rebecca said, knowing it was a low blow, but not having the willpower to contain it.

"Excuse me?"

"No excuses. You're not the friend I thought you were, and I just don't have the energy to put up with it anymore." Rebecca's eyes burned with the approaching tears, but she held them at bay as best she could.

She took two steps back to give Lexy some breathing room. With a heavy sigh her face softened. It was over. Her treks downtown to the courthouse, day after day. Her silent fight with Andrew Donovan. And worst of all, her friendship with Lexy.

"You can go now," she said, with as little emotion as she could.

Lexy stomped past her without a word and headed to the curb to hail a cab. Within a minute she was gone, and Rebecca felt truly alone.

She couldn't hold the tears back any longer. In an instant, the floodgates opened and they poured down her face. She'd been cruel to Lexy, and she hated herself for it. Her anger had been building for so long, and she simply couldn't contain it anymore. Without giving a damn about the scene she was creating, she dropped to her knees in the middle of the sidewalk and gave her tears free rein.

It took longer than she had hoped for her emotions to stabilize. She simply had nothing left. She was exhausted and dehydrated, and ready to get the hell out of there. Struggling to her feet, and shaking the pins and needles out of her legs, she decided to walk for a while instead of heading straight to her car. The sidewalk leading to the parking garage was flooded with press anyway, and she didn't want any part of it. However, she did pause for a moment as Andrew Donovan and his attorney exited the building behind her and were immediately ambushed by reporters. She watched him. He was absolutely beaming. And why wouldn't he be? He had won.

Chapter 3

J ust over an hour since leaving the bustling streets of downtown D.C., Rebecca steered her car down the quiet, shaded lane leading to her parents' house. Flowering cherry blossoms lined the curb on both sides and funneled her toward a destination she knew she was not emotionally ready for.

They would have already heard. The case had gained national attention, and the recent verdict was, no doubt, swamping every major news station with the story. She swallowed the rising lump in her throat and eased her foot off the gas pedal, trying to prolong the time before she would face them.

A physical pain throbbed deep within her chest. Her heart ached. She had been selfish those past weeks—consumed with feelings of guilt, sadness, and rage. She had put everyone else out of her mind, without the slightest consideration that although she had lost a sister, her parents had lost a daughter. A daughter who had officially entered their family only fourteen years earlier, but one they had assisted in raising since her birth.

Sara's single mother had been a regular fixture in Rebecca's life for as long as she could remember, and when she tragically lost her life at The Pentagon on September 11th, it was a given that the Black family would take in her only child and care for her as if she were their own. Rebecca and her older brother, Marcus, took great pride in healing the young girl's shattered heart and providing the light to pull her out of the darkness that had suffocated her. *But would she have been better off with a different family? In a different city?* Rebecca couldn't shake the feeling of responsibility for Sara's demise. She should have watched her more closely. She should have acted on her gut instinct that Sara wasn't being completely honest in her description of her relationship with Andrew Donovan. She could have stopped it. But now she was gone, and Rebecca had no idea how to quiet the screams echoing in her skull.

Approaching the house, her car creeped up the driveway and came to a stop. The face of the red brick colonial gave off a disheartening air as it rose into the graying sky. A storm was on its way, both inside and out, and Rebecca wasn't quite sure which one she would rather be caught in.

She stalled for a few moments more, taking in every detail of her beloved childhood home. She had never really looked at it from that viewpoint before. It was still in pristine condition, even after all that time. Gone was the broken window that highlighted Sara's first and last day of trying softball. Also gone were the dents in the garage door, sustained during Rebecca's failed attempts at teaching Sara how to drive.

Her eyes drifted to the pair of rocking chairs on the porch. So many evenings were spent in those chairs. Talking, plotting, laughing—even crying. It was during those moments that Rebecca and Sara's sisterly bond flourished. It was in those chairs that the name Andrew Donovan first left its bad taste in Rebecca's mouth.

The tears began to fall as they always did during recent trips down memory lane. Every joyful recollection came hand in hand with the realization that those moments were lost forever. She would never again sit on that porch, rocking away to the sound of Sara's dreams of the future and amusement at the past.

Rebecca swiftly pulled down the sun visor in front of her and flipped open the vanity mirror. She was a mess. She couldn't face her parents looking like that. They would need her strength to keep them afloat in the hell they were drowning in. She could barely keep her own head above water, but her self-loathing would have to wait.

Pulling a handful of tissues from her purse, she wiped away the black trails of mascara running down her cheeks and prepared herself for what lay beyond the front door. Her parents' house had always been a happy home, a symbol of a strong family that could beat any odds that fell before them. Not anymore. That family was broken, and no amount of positive thinking and optimism could fix it.

Rebecca rounded the corner to the living room and stopped in her tracks. The scene before her was one she had expected, but she was still not ready for what greeted her. Not that she ever would be.

Her mother sat on the sofa, her face red and swollen, half-buried in Marcus' chest. He hugged her tight and rocked her back and forth. The sounds of her sobs carried toward Rebecca's position in the doorway, and they cut her to the bone. It was a recreation of that day, a year earlier, when officers showed up at the front door to inform them of the body they'd found. However, the saving grace at that time was that it wasn't yet tangible. There was still hope that it wasn't Sara. It didn't last long, but it had been there.

Rebecca glanced over at her father, who painted a completely different picture. He was not the depiction of shock and denial as he had been that day. His large hands covered his face while his shoulders slumped forward and shook with each whimper that escaped through his fingers. She had never seen him like that, so frail and weak. As far back as she could remember, he had always been her rock. The epitome of strength, vigor, and hard work. He had been the one responsible for every ounce of her confidence and work ethic. Through him, she believed she could accomplish anything, no matter how daunting or impossible the task appeared. She had conquered everything she set out to do with her life, and it was all because of him. He was her Superman, but at that moment she didn't even recognize him.

Marcus' eyes met hers and that was all it took to strip away every morsel of composure she had been hanging onto. With half a dozen rapid strides she crossed the room and dropped to her knees in front of her father. The tears came hard and fast, streaming down her neck and soaking the collar of her blouse. She had no words. He was the one who always knew what to say. He was the one who had always filled her ears with the perfect line of encouragement, support, or advice. Right now, he needed her to show him the same strength, and she was drawing a complete blank.

She reached up and gently tugged his hands away from his face. The eyes that looked back at her were so full of grief that her brain switched off and her body reacted with pure instinct. She leapt to her feet and squeezed her slim frame into the armchair with him. Mimicking Marcus' comforting gestures, she urged her father's head to her shoulder and enveloped him tightly with her arms.

"Oh, Pop." Her words were barely a whisper. It was all she could manage, but it was all he needed. He wrapped his arms firmly around her waist and let out all of the anguish he had been trying so hard to hold inside.

She hugged him even tighter, hoping the strength in her arms would transfer into him somehow. How could she have been so selfish? All the time she had spent trying to avoid that moment, stalling as long as possible while her brother did all the heavy lifting. She glanced over at him, met his eyes, and mouthed her apology. It wasn't much, but it was all she had. He gave her an understanding nod before returning his attention to their mother.

The four of them remained huddled close together for the next hour, and the sobs began to quiet. Rebecca couldn't cry anymore. She didn't have the energy or the tears left to do so. She had always thought it a dramatic myth that a person could literally run out of tears. However, there she was...empty.

Chapter 4

Rebecca slammed her car door and stomped across the empty parking lot to the silver metal door. She caught her reflection and, for the first time all day, saw just how evil she could look. She had stayed at her parents' house until the exhaustion overtook them and they fell asleep. Her mother had made it to the bedroom, but her father didn't make it out of his recliner before drifting off. As dismal as the visit had been, it had felt good being with those who were going through the exact same agony. However, once she had pulled out of the driveway, the anger had reared its ugly head again and fueled her entire commute into work.

And here she was once more, about to be surrounded by people who had no idea of the hell she was in. She wasn't a good recipient of sympathy or pity; she didn't want any part of it. She was a strong woman and hoped to be treated as such. As shredded as her heart was, it was time to put her game-face on. After all, the distraction might actually be beneficial.

She calmed herself with a few meditative breaths and checked the silver mirror again. Better. Decked out in her chef's whites, she faked a smile and walked briskly through the back door of La Croix D'ior, an upscale French restaurant in downtown Bethesda.

It was her dream job; she had been head chef and co-owner for the past two years. Situated on a corner of Old Georgetown Road, it was right in the heart of Bethesda's so-called restaurant district. The area was known for its rich cultural cuisines: Thai, Ethiopian, Spanish, and, of course, French. With such a prime location and excellent menu, La Croix was constantly packed with diners, which was exactly how Rebecca liked it.

Unlike every other employee at La Croix, Rebecca was not French. However, she absolutely adored French cuisine and had an intense passion for it. After graduating from New York's French Culinary Institute, she accompanied her mentor back to France to learn from the masters in his Paris bistro. She had only meant to stay for a year, or however long it took for her to feel confident in her skills, but Gabriel had been too good to her. Four years had passed before she finally bid him adieu and hopped on a plane back to the States.

"Bonjour, mon amour," she chimed as she made her way into the kitchen.

"Bonjour, vous," replied the hunky twenty-year-old before her.

Peter was Rebecca's apprentice and also happened to be her business partner's son. She had been training him in the kitchen for the past eight months and recognized his special culinary gift, just as Gabriel had recognized hers. It was a natural talent that could not be taught, but she enjoyed teaching him how to refine it. Every day she marveled at his skills. They were no match for hers, of course, but Peter brought a youthful energy to the kitchen that she hadn't possessed since Paris. She was only thirty herself, but she felt ancient in comparison.

"So, I'm in love again," he said, grinning widely like a little kid at Christmas.

"Again? You were just in love last week. And, I think, the week before that," Rebecca pointed out.

"This time it's serious. She's the most amazing girl I've ever met."

"And what about the amazing girl you were in love with last week?" she asked.

"She's still here," he said as he over-dramatically slapped both hands over his heart. "And there's plenty of me to go around," he sang, opening his arms wide.

"Ahh...The French."

"And what is that supposed to mean?" He took a slightly defensive stance.

"Oh, relax. I'm just jealous. I wish I could fall head over heels in love every week." She gave him a little nudge as she sidled up next to him at the prep table and started slicing some carrots. She cherished their prep time. It would be several hours before the restaurant opened for dinner and the kitchen became a total madhouse.

Peter was totally adorable. It was no wonder his dance card was always full. What girl could possibly resist all that charm, delivered in that sexy French accent? He was quite a looker as well. Dark brown curls that he would swipe away to reveal deep brown eyes hooded with the longest eyelashes she had ever seen. Rebecca was not bad looking herself, although she never gave herself that much credit. She was very attractive, but not in a cause-a-car-accident-walking-down-the-street sort of way. Her long, honey blonde hair fell in natural free-flowing waves that would make any woman jealous. At five foot nine she was considered tall for a woman, and her love of sports gave her a strong and athletic, yet still very feminine, build. However, what mostly got men's attention was her smile. Thanks to years of high-school orthodontics, she smiled widely and often.

"Come on, my little French poodle. We've got a huge dinner rush to get ready for." She motioned for Peter to follow her.

Tugging hard on the chrome latch of the walk-in refrigerator door, she disappeared inside and immediately re-emerged with a butcher-wrapped beef rib roast. Making her way to the meat station, she placed the beef on the block and began to unwrap it. Peter trailed close behind her, but when she turned to look at him, his young, charming pep was gone. His smile had faded and the outside corners of his eyes drooped with concern.

"Are we ready to get real now?" he asked. "You can't fool me. I know you too well."

"Can't we just pretend for a little while longer?" Rebecca didn't want to face reality just yet.

However, Peter, who could switch back and forth between immature teen and wise guru in an instant, refused to let her off the hook. "You had quite a day today. It's been all over the news. They let him go."

Rebecca didn't respond immediately. Instead, she grabbed her favorite chef's knife in one hand and her honing steel in the other before merging them with repetitive earsplitting clashes. She knew it was only a matter of time before she would have to talk about Andrew Donovan. At least it was with Peter.

"Not enough evidence," she said, her knife gliding through the slab of beef with expert speed and precision. "It was all circumstantial."

"That shouldn't matter. People are convicted every day on circumstantial evidence."

Rebecca smiled. It felt great to hear someone else fight her battle.

"I thought the knife was his," he added.

"No blood on it. Or prints. His defense attorney said it was most likely a replica. And if it wasn't, then someone broke in, outsmarted his high-tech security system, stole the knife, used it, and put it back without anyone having any idea," Rebecca said sarcastically.

"Four separate times?"

"You know, I can understand how a jury can be conservative. It's a huge decision, sending a man off to die in prison. But Lexy? What's her reasoning? How can she be so gullible?"

"I'm sensing quite a bit of tension here," Peter said.

"She was there with me every day. She heard the same information I did. Evidence, testimonies, arguments. How can we draw completely different conclusions from each other?"

"Hmm...opportunity, motive, murder weapon, weak alibi. Check, check, check, and check. What's her story?"

"She believes he's being framed. Powerful guy, lots of enemies. Whatever."

"It *is* possible."

Rebecca whipped her head toward him and glared.

"I said it's *possible*, not likely." Peter saved himself.

"You should have seen him, Peter. When they showed those crime scene photos...he actually leaned in closer for a better look. It was disgusting. That is not the way an innocent man acts."

"So how are things with you and Lexy?"

"Not good. Not good at all."

"You should call her. Seriously. This man has already taken your sister. Don't let him take your friend too."

As usual, Peter made perfect sense. Rebecca couldn't just throw away an eighteen-year friendship over a misunderstanding. That was all it was. A misunderstanding. It had to be. Lexy just didn't see what Rebecca saw in that courtroom. She didn't see, she didn't hear, she didn't know. Since half a day had passed, and Rebecca had calmed down, she could explain it to Lexy in a more rational way.

The hours sped by, and Rebecca and Peter worked furiously to stay ahead of the dinner rush. Not another word was spoken about Andrew Donovan. Rebecca almost started to feel normal again, as if her heart hadn't been carved to pieces in the past weeks. But she knew her temporary feeling of peace was just that...temporary. She had to talk to Lexy.

When the last diner closed out their check, Rebecca tossed another pile of mixing bowls into the soapy water. She began scrubbing mindlessly.

A hand reached in from behind and took the sponge from her. "This is not your job," Peter said. "You have something more important to do. Go and do it."

She had been procrastinating, not looking forward to the task at hand. After a final walk-through of the kitchen, and a brief check on her manager, Rebecca left her safe haven and trotted across the parking lot, fishing her cellphone out of her purse. Settling herself behind the wheel, she dialed Lexy's number. A quick peek into the vanity mirror confirmed that she was in much better shape than when she had arrived earlier that afternoon. She hoped she would be able to keep her cool this time.

"Pick up. Come on, pick up," she mumbled to herself.

No luck. Lexy's outgoing message echoed in her ear and at that moment, she had no idea what to say. She ended the call and knew her window had closed. Lexy was never without her phone. Rarely did it ever make it to the second ring. Rebecca knew what it meant. Lexy was done with her.

Chapter 5

Rebecca pulled into her assigned parking space directly in front of a towering red brick townhouse. She turned off the car and paused for just a moment before slamming her forehead into the steering wheel. She winced at the pain radiating through her skull. She threw herself into it again. It had often been said that physical pain was easier to deal with than emotional pain. Not by much.

She exited her car with purse in tow and staggered up her front steps, holding her head to quiet the pounding. Blinded by the intense darkness inside, she stumbled twice before finding the light switch. She briefly thought of calling her parents and checking in on them, but it was late, and the best she could do for them was let them rest. After the day they'd had, they needed some quiet time. She kicked off her shoes, tossed her purse onto the sofa, and headed straight past the living room to the kitchen—and the liquor cabinet.

She grabbed the first bottle she saw. Tequila. That should do the trick. Her throat burned as she downed the first shot, but the feeling of calm was almost instantaneous. It was very likely psychological, but she didn't care. Whatever worked. All she wanted to do was forget everything that had transpired that day—even if only temporarily.

Just past the kitchen was the family room. She powered on the flatscreen on the wall and immediately tuned in to a marathon of *Friends* reruns. Grabbing her glass, she settled on the couch for a night of mindless sitcoms.

It took only a few minutes for the alcohol to begin taking effect. Unfortunately, the rush of brain-numbing endorphins brought a flood of emotion with it, and before long, she was a sobbing mess.

Once again, her thoughts drifted back to Sara. Rebecca felt sick to her stomach thinking about what her family had promised her when her mother died. They had promised to protect her and keep her safe from the cruel world they lived in. Not only had they failed in that regard, but the horrifying way in which she died was too much to bear. Rebecca wished it had been her. At least then she would be out of her misery and not totally consumed by guilt. Her tears continued to dilute the last drops of tequila in her glass. She rose and staggered to the kitchen to refill it.

She grabbed a lime off the counter, chose the biggest and sharpest knife she could find, and began hacking away at it. She winced and squinted as the acidic juice flew all over the kitchen. The poor fruit took quite the beating as she unleashed her fury upon it. She paused mid-swing as a breaking news bulletin flashed across the television screen. *Of course.* Would she ever be able to escape him?

Footage of Andrew Donovan leaving the courthouse, charming reporters and flashing that beaming smile that made Rebecca nauseous. She listened as he spoke about how harsh the world could be and how he would do anything he could to assist in finding the killer. He was good. He almost sounded sincere.

Having heard enough, she gripped the knife tightly in her fist and launched it clear across the room, where it lodged in the drywall next to the screen. Rebecca sighed. Her knife-throwing skills left much to be desired.

She walked back over to the sofa and sat on the floor in front of it with her full glass in one hand and a half-full bottle of tequila in the other. It was official. Andrew Donovan had destroyed her. Rebecca had become one of his victims and he had never even laid a finger on her. He had taken the one person that she truly felt responsible for from her. Sara was four years younger than Rebecca and so innocent in everything she did. She was only twelve when she lost her mother and she barely remembered her father.

Rebecca was sixteen at the time and, in the beginning, took on a mothering role. Even though they both had Rebecca's mother for that, she wanted that job for herself. She cared for Sara as if she was a bird with a broken wing.

Whenever Sara was troubled, Rebecca was there for her. Losing her mother so tragically and moving in with a new family had broken her. Rebecca's main goal in life had then become to fix her. She thought she had succeeded in doing so. The nights were the worst for Sara, and Rebecca moved Sara's bed into her room so she would never feel alone. Night terrors plagued her every sleeping moment, but Rebecca was always there to climb into her bed and hold her tight until she woke up. And there she would stay, to let Sara soak her pajamas with her tears.

As the months went by, it had happened less often. Little by little, Sara's grief began to subside. The passing of each season was marked by a new milestone in her emotional state. Before long, a year had gone by and her crying fits had all but disappeared. She was then able to cry over the petty things that normally affected teenage girls—drama, boy trouble. Rebecca was there for all of it, and it made her feel important, sharing her experience and wisdom. By that time, Sara didn't need her as a mother anymore. What she needed was a sister. A big sister. A loving, protective, glorious big sister. And that was exactly what she got.

Rebecca could barely see through the tears pouring from her eyes. What would Sara think of her now? How could Rebecca let her down so much that it had actually cost her life?

She remembered all the late-night chats about Andrew Donovan. Sara had dated him for about seven months. She was head over heels for him. Perfect in every way. Sara was devastated when he broke up with her and spent weeks begging him to take her back. It took so long for her to get over him, but as always, Rebecca was there to comfort her. Finally, she had accepted it and moved on. Rebecca was elated to find that she had raised her right. No man should control her emotions like that. Another milestone hit.

Rebecca had trusted it was all over, but she shouldn't have. She knew there was something Sara wasn't telling her. Why would Donovan have broken it off if everything was as perfect as she said? He had been out of the picture for over a year when her body was found. Just like the others. Dumped on the side of a trail in Rock Creek Park, the new gathering place for all those that used to belong to Andrew Donovan.

Rebecca's teeth clenched and the anger returned like fire shooting through her veins. Her trip down memory lane ended the same way it always did—with the realization that Andrew Donovan was truly the devil in the flesh. The empty bottle lying on its side on the coffee table told her what she already knew. Nothing could tame her rage against that man. Not even Tequila.

Chapter 6

It was late, and Rebecca could barely keep her eyes open. Her blurred eyes caught a glimpse of the knife still jutting out of the wall. She stood and steadied herself on the arm of the couch before crossing the room for a better look. Wrapping her fist around the protruding handle, she tugged hard and fell backward, the blade narrowly missing her brow as she and the knife crumpled to the floor.

She lay there, stunned for a moment, realizing the stupidity of her action. She couldn't distinguish whether she was still drunk or asleep, but the room began to spin and the tequila rapidly rose in her throat. Lacking the energy or balance to pull herself back onto the couch, she instead crawled to the nearest wall and sat herself against it. The nausea was steadily increasing, and she was losing the fight to keep the fluid down. In a last-ditch effort, she held up the knife still clutched in her hand and lost herself in its gleaming steel. Nothing could calm her quicker than her razor-sharp security blanket. It was her lifeline. Her stomach settled as her fingers slowly rolled the knife, casting flickers of reflected light throughout the room.

She was so captivated by the light show, that she didn't even hear the first knock on the door. The second knock rang slightly clearer, and by the third, she had risen and was on her way to uncover its source.

It didn't occur to her that it was 3 a.m. and quite late—or early—for a visitor. Hoping it was Lexy, coming over to accept her apology, she quickened her pace toward the door, still grasping the oversized chef knife in her fist.

She swung the door open and her jaw dropped. The color drained from her face.

"I don't believe it."

Under ordinary circumstances, she would have been thrilled to see such a gorgeous hunk of a man standing at her door at three in the morning. Not this time. Clad in blue jeans and a white dress shirt, Andrew Donovan's attire was casual but sexy. The black waves of his hair danced as the early morning breeze picked up. His blue eyes sparkled, but at the same time, were as cold as ice. They didn't coordinate with the blinding ear-to-ear smile he had planted on his face.

"I saw you at the trial," he said, as he eyed the full length of her. "You looked very upset, as naturally you would be."

Rebecca froze. Her brain screamed commands. *Shut the door! Call the police!* But she had zero control of her body at that moment. Her arms remained stiff at her sides and her bare feet rooted themselves firmly on the floor.

All that anger she had felt. Everything she told herself she would do to him if she ever got the chance. It was all easier said than done. Standing face to face with the object of every woman's nightmare, she was powerless. Her feet couldn't move a single step and her lips couldn't form a single word. There he was on her doorstep in the middle of the night and she knew, all too well, what he was capable of. Her trembling fingers gripped the knife tighter as it hung by her side.

"I looked you up and came over here to express my condolences for your sister." He glanced down at the knife she was clutching with white knuckles. "But I see you might have other plans for me."

He took an uninvited step through her doorway. Then another. Rebecca forced her legs to match his steps in reverse. Her eyes wide with fear, the courage and strength she had built her entire life on was, at that moment, nonexistent.

"You know..." He continued as he made his way even further inside, closing and bolting the door behind him. "I'm not usually into blondes...but if you're even half as feisty as Sara was...I think I can make an exception."

Through pure survival reflex, Rebecca spun around and began a sprint toward the back door at the far end of the family room. However, she had only taken two steps when she was suddenly yanked backward. Andrew turned her around to face him, his fist still clutching a fistful of her blonde locks.

"Where the hell do you think you're going?"

She raised her right arm and swung the knife as hard as she could toward his face. His hand flew up, caught her wrist, and halted her mid-swing, causing a sharp pain in her shoulder. He held her wrist there for a moment, the long metal blade hovering just over his eye.

"Well look what we have here," he said, grinning ear to ear.

Turning her hand over, he redirected the knife up toward her throat. She didn't know what to do. She felt helpless. He was big, standing over six feet tall and packed with muscle from head to toe. He felt even stronger than he looked. She tried to pull away, using every ounce of strength she had, but he didn't budge. He used her own hand to press the blade further into her neck as he grabbed her other wrist and drew her closer to him.

With his face just inches from hers, she could smell him. A hint of cologne mixed with Chardonnay and laced with utter amusement. She didn't actually think amusement had a specific odor, but if it did...that was it. She gasped as she felt a drop of blood trickle down the front of her neck.

He was still smiling at her. Was that image the last thing Sara saw before he skinned her alive? Is that how he got them in the first place? His smile? Rebecca didn't doubt it.

Her time was running out and she knew she had to do something...anything. She refused to surrender and allow him to torture her, even as he drove her hand and the knife deeper into her throat.

She made her move, bringing her knee up hard into his groin. Nothing. The man was made of steel. He gripped her wrists so tight she was sure her bones were going to shatter at any second. A shock of pain radiated through her hands followed by the clanging of the knife bouncing off the ceramic floor. At that, he dragged her back toward the sofa in the front living room and threw her onto it. She landed with a huge crack as the back of her head slammed against the wooden armrest. She let out an audible cry. It didn't last long as he leaped on top of her, straddling her stomach and knocking the breath right out of her. She gasped. She tried to scream, but nothing would come out.

He gathered both of her wrists together into his left hand and shoved them over her head. Again, she tried to scream, but no sound left her open mouth. She was suffocating; the weight of him on her stomach, the intense fear of what was going to come next. Again, she tried to muster up any noise she could. The only thing she could manage was a hoarse whisper.

He leaned into her, placing even more pressure on her chest. Nose to nose, he stared deep into her eyes. He held her wide-eyed stare for what seemed like hours. Finally, he sat up, still holding her wrists in place above her head. With his right hand, he reached toward the back of his jeans, pulled it out, and hoisted it high in the air. The three-edged blade glimmered in the dim light of the room. He ran his thumb over the tribal face, ornately carved into the handle, caressing every intricate detail. The Phurba Dagger—his weapon of choice. He leaned in again and brought the blade right up to her eyes and she stared into it. Wide eyes full of fear reflected back at her.

The tip of the blade began its slow journey down the bridge of her nose. Off the tip, outlining her lips, before traveling down her chin and drawing a center line on the front of her throat. Her breathing quickened as the hot metal forged on, following the path of her sternum into the valley between her breasts, which heaved as she fought for oxygen. It continued on its route, searing the buttons off the front of her shirt with barely any pressure at all. Beads of sweat dripped down her abdomen to pool into her navel. The blade followed. He stood the dagger upright with the tip deep in her umbilicus. Slowly he began to rotate it clockwise, bringing it into a slow-motion spin. Each revolution buried it deeper and deeper into her.

She jerked violently, trying to knock him off balance, fighting hard against the enormous single hand that held her arms. He ignored her physical protests and kept the blade spinning, drilling deeper into her abdomen. Her larynx was paralyzed, preventing a single peep from escaping her. She felt the pop as the blade broke through her abdominal wall and came to rest deep within her. With disbelief, she looked down at her stomach just as a fountain of blood spewed from the puncture. Her head throbbed as blood pulsated through her brain, matching the rhythm of the ringing in her ears. Ringing louder and louder.

Chapter 7

S uddenly her hands were free. She slapped them over her ears to stop the ringing that was shattering her skull. Her eyes flew open and she realized she was still on the floor of the family room. She looked at her stomach. Nothing. Glancing around the room, her eyes fixated on the wall, the handle of her favorite chef knife protruding from it.

There it was again. The ringing. Rebecca leaped up and raced into the kitchen to grab the cordless phone off the counter.

"Hello?"

"Rebecca! I've been trying to call you for the last half hour!"

"Marcus?" Still dazed from her near-death experience, which still seemed all too real, she carried the phone around, searching each corner for any evidence that Andrew Donovan had been there.

"Rebecca...are you still there?"

"Yes, I...I'm here."

"Dad's in the hospital."

"What! What happened? When?" Rebecca's head began to spin as she felt a growing sense of dread in the pit of her stomach.

"He woke up after you left and started freaking out. It went on for hours." Marcus paused, hoping she would make a guess so he wouldn't have to say it. "He had a heart attack. A bad one. It's critical."

Rebecca didn't know how to respond. Her mind was still fuzzy, trying to figure out what was real and what wasn't. Andrew Donovan hadn't tried to kill her in her house...he was trying to kill her dad in his.

"Where is he?"

"Shady Grove. He's still in surgery. There were complications." Marcus' voice began to get more and more frantic. "Look, Mom's going crazy...you've got to get down here. We're on the fourth floor. Hurry!"

"He did this," she said, her voice a combination of fear and fury. "Andrew did this."

She slammed the phone down and began pacing the floor in a frenzy. Her emotions were a whirlwind that sent her mind spinning out of control. The guilt washed over her once again. *I shouldn't have left him. Neither he nor my mom had been in any condition to be left alone. Why hadn't I seen that? First, Sara, and now, Dad.*

She collapsed down onto the sofa. She just needed a minute. She didn't know what to do. She didn't know how to feel. For just a brief moment her thoughts shifted their course and attempted to make sense of the frightening, illusory encounter she was still reeling from. For months she had wanted to kill Andrew Donovan. Then, when she actually had the chance, she froze. She knew she hadn't really had a chance, but it had felt so real, and in that split second of opportunity, she panicked.

It wasn't the first time he had visited her in her dreams, which always turned into nightmares. This time it was different, though. It was a real experience. She really had felt she was going to die. That look in his eyes chilled her to the bone. She couldn't imagine what Sara had gone through, looking into those eyes, knowing he was about to kill her. She couldn't imagine what any of those poor women had gone through, even though she felt as if she had just experienced the same thing. It definitely was *not* the same thing.

For the past year her feelings had ricocheted between grief, anger, sadness, revenge, and more grief. She had thought the trial would give her closure, but she had expected him to be found guilty. Because of the jury's decision, he was free to live the rest of his life as if none of it had even happened. The thought sickened her, but it was a thought she had no time to entertain. Her father's life was in grave danger, and as much as she blamed Andrew Donovan for that as well, it wasn't the time to spend precious moments hung up on it.

Without wasting another second, she hopped up, grabbed her keys, and headed to the front door. She didn't make it that far though. The spinning in her head sent her crashing into the wall and onto the floor, bringing a hailstorm of framed artwork and broken glass down with her.

She lay motionless for a moment before summoning the strength to pull herself toward the wall and prop herself against it. She closed her eyes in an attempt to slow the room's merry-go-round, but that just made it worse. Spotting her phone amidst the rubble by her feet, she clumsily pulled up the number for the cab company and sent for her ride.

She knew she would die if she tried to drive herself in her intoxicated state, but sitting there on that floor while her father was fighting for his life...it appeared the outcome would be the same.

She flipped over her wrist and checked her watch. The waiting was excruciating. Her heartbeat sounded like a drumroll and the wave of heat rising to her head sent beads of sweat trickling down her neck. She checked her watch again. Anything to keep her mind from facing the reality of what was happening. It was no use. The face of the broken man she had left earlier that day continued its dance in front of her eyes.

The muscle in her jaw tingled, saliva pooled in her mouth, and she lunged for the closest trashcan she could find, emptying her mind and her stomach of their contents.

The cab finally turned into the parking lot and pulled up to the curb. There had been a lot of cars on the road considering it was four in the morning and the drive took much longer than expected—also due to her need to pull over twice. It had helped though. Her stomach had settled and the spinning had ceased.

She paid her fare and bolted out of the vehicle and into the ambulance bay. The bright lights blinded her as the double doors opened and summoned her inside. Rushing past the emergency room triage desk, the nurses were silenced as she flew by them, disappearing just as quickly as she had appeared. She slipped sideways into a closing elevator and hit the button for the fourth floor.

The slow jazz escaping the elevator speakers calmed her. She was proud of herself for directing the cabbie into the hospital parking lot instead of Andrew Donovan's driveway. Or disappointed—she couldn't decide which. Such violent thoughts had run through her head for months, but when the time came to take action, she ran away with her tail between her legs. All talk. Not that she had a clue what she would have done if she had actually gone to Andrew's house to confront him. Yell at him? Call him a liar? Hack his penis off with a machete? Rebecca failed to keep the subtle smile from curving her lips at that last thought.

The doors opened, and she saw her mother and Marcus slumped over in waiting room chairs. They clung to each other, eyes red and swollen. Her smile vanished, and she made her way down the corridor and kneeled in front of them. No words were spoken, but four arms enveloped her and pulled her close. After several minutes, her mother finally broke the silence.

"That man..." she said, her voice strained and broken. "He got away with it. Your father...he was up all night crying. His heart couldn't take it."

Seeing her mother like that, Rebecca's heart couldn't take it, either. She looked completely defeated. Her mother and father were perfect. As was her brother, Marcus, and her sister, Sara. A typical Norman Rockwell painting. Family was everything to them. They were an impenetrable wall. Until one of them was taken in the most awful way imaginable, leaving each of them to break down, one after the other.

"He can't get away with it," her mother said, looking deep into Rebecca's eyes.

"He won't," she replied with such certainty that she almost believed it.

Marcus stood and took Rebecca by the arm. Slowly, he walked her toward the other side of the room, out of earshot. "What's going on with you?"

"He won't get away with this. He won't." Rebecca lifted her shoulders and puffed out her chest a little.

"Let it go. I don't want to lose anyone else to him." he said. "Look where we are. He can kill people without going anywhere near them. Let it go."

Rebecca hung her head and let out a deep sigh. He was right. She knew he was. There really was nothing she could do *about* Andrew or *to* Andrew. So why was she suddenly fighting with everyone who even dared to speak to her? All she had done since Sara's death was cry. And all she had done since the conclusion of Andrew's trial was seethe…and cry. Was keeping her anger fueled ever going to make her feel better? No. Was she ever going to make him pay? No. She wouldn't even know where to start, even if she did falsely convince herself she would go through with it. Marcus was right. She needed to let it go, for her own sake and for the sake of the family she had left. Her father wasn't dead yet. And if he survived that night, that would be her victory over Andrew Donovan. Right then, she needed to be there for him and for her mother. That's what Sara would have done.

"I'll try," she said.

Marcus smiled. "I know you will. And I know you'll succeed. You don't know how to fail."

If only he knew just how much she had failed already.

Marcus hooked her elbow and walked her back to the empty chair next to their mother. She looked so tired. Rebecca put her arm around her and gently directed her mother's head onto her shoulder. That was what it was supposed to feel like. In an instant, Rebecca's breathing slowed and the hostile thoughts dissipated. She sank into the chair and let Marcus' calm and patience infect her. Her eyelids became heavy just as he shot up from his seat. Snapping awake, completely alert, she followed his eyes to a bearded man in blue scrubs walking toward them.

A lump caught in her throat and her eyes widened. She studied him as he came closer, looking for some sort of indication as to what his news would be. His gait was slow and his shoulders slumped. Marcus ran to him, stopping him thirty feet from where Rebecca and her mother sat, wide awake and clinging to each other. She was glad her brother took the initiative. She didn't want to hear what the surgeon had to say. She didn't need to anyway. Her brother's reaction spoke for itself.

Chapter 8

It had been seven days since Andrew Donovan had been declared innocent. Seven days since her last Donovan-themed nightmare. And seven days since he killed her father. Rebecca had promised Marcus she was going to make a valiant effort to release her anger and find peace within the memory of Sara's life, not her death, although she hadn't expected to piggy-back her father onto that promise as well.

It was hard—one of the most difficult tasks she had ever undertaken. Her mind had just that—a mind—and altering the thoughts that ran through it took more discipline than she knew she had. Thoughts of Sara and of her father were with her every second of every day. She would never want to change that, but it was the tone of her thoughts that hurt. She had to keep reminding herself that she couldn't change the past. Those she had lost would have cringed at the ugly notions that had previously ruled her brain, and Marcus' mantra rang loud inside her head and she took every opportunity to repeat it to herself over and over. *Let it go.*

She stepped out onto her front step, closing the door to the brick Kensington townhouse behind her. Clad in spandex shorts and brand-new top-of-the-line running shoes, she was going all-in with her new appreciation-of-life attitude. She inhaled a deep breath of crisp morning air, skipped down her front steps, and trotted down the street in a light jog.

The Andrew Donovan headlines had waned. Her mind was clear during the day and even clearer at night. She felt as though she was finally stepping off of the emotional rollercoaster she had been riding for the past year. The restaurant was booming, and she finally had the peace of mind to enjoy it.

Jogging aimlessly through the neighborhood streets, she didn't remember taking a left onto the paved path that ran alongside Beach Drive. Her mind was so filled with positive thoughts of the future that she also didn't notice veering off the pavement and onto the dirt trail at the entrance of Rock Creek Park.

About a mile and a half in, her breathing began to become unusually heavy. She gasped for air, confused about this sudden onset of fatigue. Lumbering along, hoping it would pass, the trail turned, and suddenly, it all made sense. Slowing to a walk, she stepped off the trail and made her way a few feet to a large, ornately painted wooden cross. Her legs had involuntarily brought her to the one place in the world she wasn't yet ready to be. Her knees hit the ground hard and the rest of her body followed.

The tears came, hard and fast. Uncontrollably. She had been doing so well, putting Sara's death out of her mind and pretending she was simply out of the country on vacation. Her mind was getting stronger every day, but it was not yet strong enough to come to terms with the scene in front of her. She needed more time, but she had no choice. Somehow, she had brought herself here subconsciously. It was time to face the tragedy head-on.

Remaining on her knees, Rebecca composed the rest of her body, put her hands together, and closed her eyes. She wasn't a very religious person, and couldn't remember the last time she truly prayed, but it was what Sara would have done if the circumstances were reversed. Stumbling through how to start, she finally decided to just talk to her sister herself.

"I'm sorry. I'm sorry I couldn't protect you from him. I'm sorry I didn't go with my instincts and know that something was wrong. And I'm sorry that when the first and even the second victim was found, I didn't put the pieces together and force you out of town. You are the last person on this Earth that should have gone through that ordeal. Of course, none of those women deserved it either, but you..." Rebecca's voice cracked and she took a moment to recompose herself. "How could anyone hurt you like that? How could anyone cause you to suffer that way?

"I was so angry. I wanted to kill him. For a while I thought I actually *would* kill him. There's always the hope that new evidence will come up, or maybe some piece of God-inspired fate will swoop in and find justice for you and all of us. Maybe God *is* the one I should be talking to right now." Rebecca chuckled a little. She knew she was awful at it, but she knew Sara never judged her for her horrible way with words. "Maybe while you're up there with Him, which I know you are, you can ask Him to send a little bit of wrath down here to make Andrew Donovan spontaneously combust." Smiling again, she simply shook her head. "I shouldn't be saying all of this. This is the exact opposite of what I promised Marcus I'd do. I'm supposed to actually *try*. I will never forgive him, just so you know. But I will try to forget him. I'll never forget you, though. You were everything to me. You still are and always will be every—"

"Hey there."

Rebecca sprang up into a defensive stance, eyes wide and fists clenched.

"Sorry. I didn't mean to startle you." A young twenty-something man in too-short running shorts stepped off the trail and started toward her. "I heard you talking and, nosy as I am, had to check it out."

Rebecca took a couple steps back until she felt the wooden cross press into the back of her heel.

"Look, I'm not here to hurt you or anything." He flashed his open palms. "I heard all the stories on the news about what happened here. Did you know her?"

"She was my sister."

"Whoa." His eyebrows arched in surprise. "Uh...I'm really sorry. This must be horrible for you."

Her brows cinched together. He seemed like a nice guy, but she couldn't help thinking it a bit rude of a complete stranger to interrupt someone kneeling and praying at the foot of a memorial.

"If you don't mind," she said as she turned slightly back toward the wooden marker and lowered to a crouch, keeping the stranger in her periphery. She didn't want to completely turn her back to him, but she did want to get the point across that she was done with the conversation before it even started. Unfortunately, the man didn't take the hint.

"So I heard he got off. Scott-free. What do you think of that?"

"What the hell am I supposed to think?" Her head snapped around and her cheeks burned as they filled with blood. "He's a killer and a liar and the luckiest son-of-a-bitch I've ever seen." Her battle with silence was officially lost. The man was obviously ignoring her desire to be left alone. She surrendered and hoped the quicker she answered his questions, the quicker he'd move along.

"How many more do you think he'll get away with before they catch him...if they catch him?"

Her annoyance at the man suddenly lessened and her chin rose to attention. It was the first time since the trial that Rebecca had thought of it in that way. All that time she had been fuming over what he had done to Sara, wondering how she could get revenge...make it right. She hadn't even thought about the fact that he was still out there and free to do it again. He *would* do it again. They always did.

"I don't know how you can stay so calm with all of this. If some maniac tortured and killed my sister in such a gruesome way I'd—"

"You'd what?"

"I'd kill him. March right into his office and shoot him dead. End up with life in prison for it, but it'd be worth it."

"Men are so stupid," Rebecca said, turning back to the marker and outlining the cross with her fingertips.

"Stupid? For seeking vengeance?"

"Stupid for going at it so guns-blazing like that. It's too direct."

"So how would you do it?" he asked.

Rebecca paused, staring at her fingers, which were beginning to bleed. Drops of blood smeared across the coarse, splintered wood. Standing up, she glared at him but continued her silence. Wiping her bloody hands on her shorts, she pivoted and took off at breakneck speed through the woods. *Who the hell does he think he is? What random guy comes across a crying girl in the woods and taunts her like that? Asshole.* He didn't think she had the guts to do anything about Andrew Donovan. He was wrong.

Leaping out of the brush and landing on solid pavement, Rebecca stopped and glanced over her shoulder at the new path she had just blazed through the dense thicket. Luckily, He hadn't followed her. Panting heavily, she continued along Beach Drive at a brisk walk. The corners of her mouth curved up into a slight grin, which grew into a wider smile with each stride. Her feet quickened and she launched herself into an all-out sprint.

Sorry, Marcus. I'm going to have to let you down again.

Chapter 9

Rebecca emerged from the door of Alexander's Hair Salon. The sun felt warmer and looked brighter; the air was clearer, though she wasn't convinced the weather had improved that much in the two hours she was in the chair. She knew her new state of mind was responsible for the change. The fresh new way she saw the world. A world that was ready to assist her in her new mission. She would no longer be afraid. She would no longer sit by and see justice ignored. It was her turn.

She turned and faced her reflection in the large glass front of the salon. She didn't recognize herself. He wouldn't either. Her long blonde ponytail rested carefully in a zip-loc baggie in her purse, ready to be shipped off to whichever hair donation center wanted it. All kinds of good would come from this.

She tossed her head a little and smiled as dark chestnut strands swiped her cheeks. She admitted to herself that the new short tousled bob made her look a little exotic. European. Chic. Maybe she should have chopped it off years ago.

However, as confident as she was in everything she did, her hair was something she just wouldn't mess with. It was the main thing she had going for her. When she wore her hair up, in a loose bun or ponytail, she hardly received a second look. However, she was blessed with gorgeous golden, natural waves that she grew more than halfway down her back. When she wore it down, she really wore it down. Lexy had always said, "You've got to flaunt what you've got." The thought of chopping it all off almost made her sick, but not as sick as the consequences of not doing it. She was all-in, this time, and the stunning beauty that looked back at her agreed wholeheartedly.

"I'm ready for my close-up," she sang to herself.

Digging into her purse, she fished out her phone. She paused for a moment, closed her eyes, and drew a deep breath. Exhaling slowly, her eyelids lifted and revealed a look of total determination. Her fingers slid across the screen before she pressed it to her ear.

"I'm on my way."

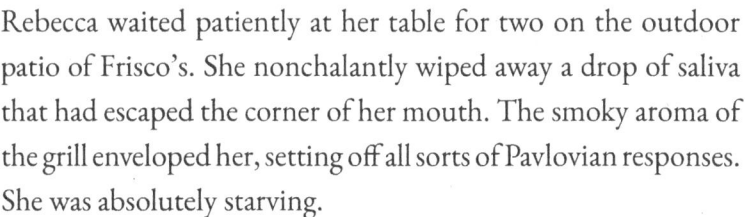

Rebecca waited patiently at her table for two on the outdoor patio of Frisco's. She nonchalantly wiped away a drop of saliva that had escaped the corner of her mouth. The smoky aroma of the grill enveloped her, setting off all sorts of Pavlovian responses. She was absolutely starving.

The day had completely run away from her. She had forgotten to stop for lunch during her manic running of the most unusual errands, though she had felt like a celebrity for most of it, sporting big bug-eyed sunglasses that complemented her new look. Even her walk had morphed into a casual sexy strut. She received coveted second looks. Lots of them, from everyone she passed. She was sure not to smile back at them, though. *That is not how A-List international actresses behave. Or am I a runway model?* She had the legs for it, although critics would say she wasn't skinny enough. Her athletic build was toned and shapely. She would never have passed for a runway model. *Okay, then. Actress it is.*

The sun began to set behind the tall office buildings that lined the street across from her, and she could finally remove her sunglasses, which were so dark they were more like a blindfold. Her sight returned and she realized it wasn't as close to nightfall as she had thought.

The steady flow of traffic on The Pike made it feel even hotter than it actually was. She couldn't feel the heat pouring out of their tailpipes, but she knew it was there.

Her mojito arrived with perfect timing. Just when she thought she was approaching heatstroke, the young waiter set the glorious ice-cold drink in front of her. She reached for it immediately and drained the glass completely, letting it chill her from the inside out. The waiter had only taken a couple of steps and was still watching her. His eyebrows shot into high arcs as she set the empty glass back on the table.

"Another, please."

"Right away, Miss."

Ooh, Miss. I like the sound of that. Although it was true. She was single, and thirty definitely wasn't yet old enough for "ma'am." Was it? Well *she* wasn't ready for it yet.

Rebecca was quietly having a great time, flirting with young waiter man-boys and receiving glances from other diners who seemed to think she was someone famous, but not really knowing who. She lounged on the restaurant patio with nowhere to be, just enjoying her own company.

Her second mojito arrived, and she vowed to take that one a little slower. She had an air of class to uphold...and she had to drive home later. She hadn't been able to relax and have a nice cocktail in over a year. Recently all her drinking was done in misery, grief, or frustration. Never celebration. Not until then.

While watching the river of shoppers pass by on the other side of the short patio fence, she saw another young man-boy approaching her. She couldn't flirt with that one, though. He weaved throughout the other tables and came to a rest in the empty seat across from her.

"All good?" Rebecca said

"I have them," he said, his accent barely noticeable as he set a large padded envelope on the table and slid it toward her.

Rebecca pulled the envelope into her lap and took a peek inside, rifling with her fingers. A Maryland driver's license, which featured the photo he took of her earlier against the blue wall in his apartment, and a pair of Maryland license plates.

"They look great," she said, closing the envelope and stowing it in her bag. She pulled out two crisp hundred dollar bills and discreetly slid them under the basket of bread, nudging the basket toward him. "Our little secret, right?"

He grinned. "This is not a drug deal, you know." As obvious as ever, he lifted the basket and scooped up the bills.

"No, I don't know. I've never done this before." Rebecca's eyes shifted nervously around the patio.

"I see," he said, stifling a laugh. "So why can't Peter know about this?"

Alex was a friend of Peter's and shared a bachelor pad with him and several other young hopefuls. They hung around La Croix often, and it wasn't long before Rebecca overheard many conversations regarding their lucrative side business.

"You seem to be forgetting our agreement." Her eyes narrowed at him. "No questions asked, which also means no statements told...or something like that."

The puzzled look on his face urged her to go on. "If Peter or anyone else *doesn't* find out about this...then cops *won't* show up at your door wondering what a houseful of French immigrants are doing with a fake ID business."

His confusion faded as her light threat hit home. She didn't have much to worry about with him anyway; having a successful illegal business meant he was good at keeping secrets. Even still, Peter was one of his housemates, and Rebecca didn't want to involve him in any way.

With his business finished, Alex rose to leave. As she watched him vanish through an oncoming party of eight, she finally exhaled the deep breath she had been holding for most of their conversation.

She was glad that part was over with. She didn't really know Alex, and although she trusted him, because Peter did, she couldn't help feeling very tense around him. It must have been the fact that he was a criminal. They had a way of keeping people on edge.

She allowed herself to relax. She nursed her drink, which had become distastefully diluted by the ice, and waited for her dinner to arrive. She rarely had the opportunity to enjoy a good meal, cooked and served by someone else. La Croix kept her busy—very busy—and most of her meals were eaten standing in the back of the kitchen, right before the dinner rush. Saturday nights were the craziest, and she should have been working, but she couldn't risk Peter showing up at his house while his friend was making her a fake ID.

In fact, it had turned into a great opportunity to give him more responsibility in the kitchen. She had great kitchen staff, and Peter always jumped at the chance to lead the kitchen on his own. He was so young, yet so gifted, and Rebecca had aspirations to expand. When the time came to open a second restaurant, Peter would be at the top of the list to take over the chef duties at La Croix. She needed to know he was capable, and the small doses of responsibility she often threw at him only increased the faith she already had in him. He was a natural. Too good to her...and too good to be caught up in any of her misdeeds.

Chapter 10

Rebecca sat patiently in her car across the street from Chadwick's Coffee Shop. It was lunch hour, and The District was hopping with people coming and going all along Pennsylvania Avenue. It was a familiar sight to her. She had sat in the same spot for the last week. Waiting. Watching. She learned that every Monday, Wednesday, and Friday, at 12:45, Andrew Donovan got his caffeine fix after his lunchtime run around The Tidal Basin. Her watch read 12:30. There was still enough time to talk herself into it...or out of it.

That day was supposed to be *the* day. The day she would meet him. The day she would look directly into his cold murderous eyes. It would also be the day he would fall in love with her...and seal his fate.

She had no real idea how she would do it, though. His attention, she would definitely get. Her stylist had made sure of that. Glancing in the rear-view mirror, she carefully inspected her new look. She was a shoe-in for his type. But a few questions still ate away at her. Was she the type he liked to love, or the type he liked to kill? Both? Sara was both. His mysteriously missing wife was also probably both. Who was she kidding? All of them were both.

The longer she sat there, trying to come up with her lines, the more she thought of the consequences if she couldn't pull it off. She had never done anything this crazy in her life. Sweat began to pour down her neck as she checked the time. 12:38. She had two minutes to decide whether or not she would cross the street and walk through that door. Her heart beat out of her chest. She could still turn back. She could just drive away and come back another day...or another week. However, once he laid his eyes on her, it would be too late. But he hadn't seen her yet. She could still quit.

What if he recognized her from the trial? She knew that was impossible. She didn't even recognize herself, and she had always sat at the back of the courtroom. He never once even looked her way. What would Marcus say if he saw her new look? He would know she was up to something and would never let her out of his sight from then on. What about Lexy? She probably wouldn't care at all.

Rebecca had a long list of reasons she shouldn't do it, but only one reason why she should. And that one reason was the only one she needed. He must be stopped.

She took one more long look in the mirror. Her emerald eyes almost glowed with determination. Her cropped hair looked even darker...more sinful...more evil.

"Rebecca Black could never do this. But you are no longer Rebecca Black. You are now Amanda White. And you *will* get your justice."

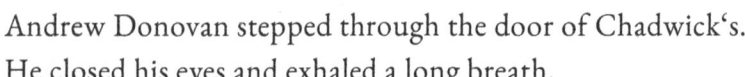

Andrew Donovan stepped through the door of Chadwick's. He closed his eyes and exhaled a long breath.

"Thank you, God, for air conditioning," he said as he grabbed a handful of napkins from the windowsill and began wiping his face and neck. His blue track shirt was soaked through and every inch of exposed skin glistened with sweat.

He had thought he would become more acclimated to running in the summer heat, but after every lunchtime run he stumbled into Chadwick's the same way, choking on the thick, humid air and gasping for breath. His legs quivered, weak and barely functional enough to hold him upright. He eyed the shiny leather couches in the far corner of the shop—empty, very rare for lunch hour. How amazing it would feel to collapse face-first into them and sleep for the rest of the day. He would never dare do it, though. As wet as he was, he would most likely slip right off, leaving quite a disgusting slug trail behind.

That was how he always felt after summer runs. Near heatstroke. But he had always gotten over it. It was nothing that a steaming hot cup of coffee wouldn't fix. *Ironic*. He dragged his attention away from the welcoming sofa and opted instead to take his place in line.

"The usual, Mr. Donovan?" asked the chipper barista-boy behind the counter.

"Absolutely." Andrew flashed his winning smile as he dropped a twenty into the tip jar. Good service always followed good tips, and Andrew always demanded the best of everything. Life was too short to waste time on frustration or irritation. Pay well and you would be treated well, it was as simple as that.

He moved down to the pick-up counter, careful not to swipe the glass with his sweaty arms. He always tried to destroy the stereotype of power executives; having money didn't mean you had to treat people like dirt.

His office was filled with those stereotypes, as were his power lunches. Pompous, conceited, arrogant assholes who got their hard-ons by disrespecting everyone beneath their status level, badgering the waitstaff, their assistants, secretaries...baristas. The same people those jerkoffs couldn't function without. Pathetic. They basked in the delusion that they were the higher class, yet they treated people in the most classless way. Assholes.

Andrew swore he would never be that way. He'd worked hard to get to where he was; the only thing that was handed to him was a life insurance check, and he'd worked his ass off to turn that into a multi-million-dollar company. He didn't need to belittle the working class to feel good about himself. He already knew what he was made of. And he didn't want to risk giving them a reason to piss in his coffee.

Shuffling down the counter a little more, he leaned against the painted stone wall, far away from the sparkling glass and the other patrons who didn't need his musky sweat scent mixing with the rich aroma of their lattes. He had a panoramic view of the entire shop from where he stood. He loved people-watching. He loved trying to figure them out from a distance—studying them. All sorts came into the coffee shop during lunch. The pretentious suits that needed their over-priced caffeine to make it through the rest of their miserable lives. The hemp-wearing hippies that just loved the atmosphere, man...and the free Wi-Fi. The young teenage socialites who always looked for the most expensive anything to charge on Daddy's credit card. Their white chocolate mochas didn't even pass for real coffee. They could have just as easily been drinking a chocolate milkshake from McDonald's, but they would never have been caught dead at a McDonald's.

"Medium dark roast with two shots, two sugars, and two creams," the barista-boy said as he set the tall cup on the top of the glass.

"Thanks, Simon."

Andrew leaned himself and his coffee back against the wall. He wasn't quite ready to go back out into the summer heat yet. The air conditioning vent was right above him, and he simply didn't have the will to walk away from it. He took a sip, leaned his head back against the wall, and closed his eyes, letting the cold air dry the last remaining sweat droplets from his hair.

Several minutes passed before he opened them again. His attention immediately fixated on the woman giving her order at the counter. His heart stopped. She was stunning, and the resemblance was uncanny. Marie. The love of his life. She had been everything to him, and when he lost her, he lost his mind. He had tried and tried to replace her, tried so hard to find that feeling again. There were several that had the potential—the look, the smile, the eyes—but they could never compete with Marie. The others...they were all *almost*...but *not quite*.

He continued to watch the woman at the counter. The muscles in his neck twitched as he tried to look away. He couldn't. Blood rushed to his head and then pumped furiously throughout his entire body. It could have been the coffee, but it wasn't. It was her. He couldn't go down that road again. After everything he had been through, he couldn't do it again. But he also couldn't *not* do it. She was the closest he had ever seen. The likeness was startling. She was the one. After her, there would be no more. There wouldn't need to be.

His gaze morphed into a creepy leer. Thankfully, she didn't see him. Her attention was buried in her phone as she waited for her order. His eyes traveled the length of her. He tried to size her up. To study her like he did with everyone who walked through those doors. His mind drew a complete blank. His objectivity fled. She was too close to Marie. It was her. It wasn't really...but it was.

Simon popped his head above the glass. "Amanda? White chocolate mocha?"

White chocolate mocha? Seriously? He didn't even care. She could drink whatever she wanted. He already was powerless against her.

The woman began her walk toward him, toward the pick-up counter. Her eyes locked with his and held him there. Stiff. Unable to move. She came to a stop right before him. The staring contest continued. He tried to speak, to say something—anything—but he was paralyzed. All of his confidence was gone, and he felt like a peasant before her.

She was waiting. Waiting for him to say something. He had nothing. Her right eyebrow lifted and she broke away from him. Turning her attention toward Simon, she took her cup from him and headed toward the door. Not a word out of her...not even a second glance. She was gone.

Chapter 11

An intense heat wave, rare for late June, had hit the east coast, and the sun was high and hot, scorching the tip of every blade of grass it touched. Rebecca plodded along, her legs struggling to keep from giving out altogether. She had only just begun her lunchtime three-miler around The Tidal Basin, but the heat recreated the sensation of hitting the wall during her last marathon.

Approaching the entrance path, she was thankful to be leaving the streets and entering the large oasis on the southwest side of the city. The nausea that had popped up in her stomach during the short walk from her parking spot began to subside. The competing smells of taco street vendors and taxi cab tailpipes never sat well with her.

She picked up her pace slightly to further distance herself from the noise and odors of the city streets. Turning onto the paved trail, she was half-blinded by the intense light reflecting off the water. Her legs were still dead weight, and the soles of her shoes stuck slightly to the hot pavement with each step. The shaded section of the trail arrived just as she began to give in.

She was a great runner and prided herself on her ability to complete multiple marathons, but intense heat had always been a problem for her. The shade from the perimeter wall of Cherry Blossom trees lowered the temperature by a good ten degrees and she was able to get herself back on track. She needed to work up a good sweat if Andrew was to believe that she was a regular runner there.

The last three weeks had been exciting and quite fun. Her first moment with Andrew in the coffee shop surprised her. She didn't expect to strike him speechless. The arrogant and conceited man-whore that he was, she fully expected him to dish out some creative pick-up lines and immediately invite her into his bed. That didn't happen. He was completely frozen and shocked, which, in turn, had handed all the power to her and she loved it. She had full control over him. She wasn't exactly sure what it was that had affected him so strongly; was it that his next victim had fallen into his lap when he least expected it, or was it her close resemblance to his missing wife? He had looked at her as if she was a ghost; it made perfect sense. From the photos she had seen of Marie Donovan, Rebecca admitted that she did pull off quite a convincing impersonation. It wasn't just the hair or the airbrush tan she had applied to achieve that olive, Mediterranean look. It was most likely her eyes. From what she could tell, his wife possessed the same deep emerald eyes as Rebecca. Whatever the reason, her plan had worked. He was hooked.

Rebecca enjoyed the new-found confidence that came with her new alter ego. She was able to be a totally different person, and she took full advantage of it. Leaving him hanging like that was exactly what she needed to do to ensure she haunted his every thought for the days to come.

She had stopped back into Chadwick's a couple of days later, and there he was again, sitting at a table with his coffee as if he was waiting for her. He was. He wasn't speechless that time as he approached her and introduced himself. It was difficult for her to admit, but he was rather charming. Electric in the way he looked at her. She kept up her act, though, leading him on with a few smiles but nothing else. She left that day refusing to give him anything more.

Andrew Donovan was a hunter and he needed to hunt. Without the hunt there would be no interest for him. She had already gotten his attention, but now she needed to keep it. She had let him find her there several more times, and even humored him with some brief conversation, but not recently. He needed to miss her before he would realize how much he really wanted her. That was why she chose to run that day—a new location. He would think fate had brought them together again. It wasn't fate, it was her stealthy stalking abilities...but he didn't need to know that.

She slowed to a walk as she approached the half-mile mark. It was less crowded than usual, the heat surely discouraging many. She scanned the length of path as far as she could see. Her view of the opposite side of the reservoir was unobstructed, but it was simply too far away to make out the figures. He would be trotting her way any minute if he stuck to his schedule. Andrew

Donovan was nothing if not punctual. Picking up her jog again, she continued. He couldn't catch her resting; that would show weakness and conflict with the iron-strong epitome of woman that Amanda White was, or who Rebecca was pretending to be.

Another mile covered but still no sign of him. How could he be so late? She could set a clock to his habits. He never wavered from his schedule, at least not during the last month she had been watching him. She stopped and looked at her watch again, then back down the path. He wasn't there. Perhaps he was also turned away by the heat. Perhaps he had skipped his run and gone straight to Chadwick's for his coffee. There would still be time to catch him there. But looking like she did then...no make-up, hair a total mess, soaked with sweat... The trail was the only place she could allow him to see her like that.

She turned and started a brisk walk back in the direction she had come, choosing the shaded route back instead of continuing the loop in the open sun. That was when she spotted him, shuffling along at a pace way too slow for him. He was too far away for her to be able to make out his face, but she knew it was him. She had watched him for too long to not be able to pick him out in a crowd from that distance. He didn't see her standing there, camouflaged in a pack of speed-walkers diverting around her. He was too distracted by the leggy redhead flouncing along next to him. Who was she and why was he paying attention to her? She wasn't even his type.

Rebecca stared hard as her view of them became closer, clearer. He was laughing. He wasn't just distracted by her, he was with her...they were together. It had only been a week since she last saw him. Had he lost interest that quickly and already replaced her with another? It didn't make any sense. That woman didn't even come close to being the type he went for.

Snapping out of her daze, Rebecca knew she had to make a move. He couldn't find her just staring at them dumbfounded in the middle of the path. She spun around and started off down the path. She quickened her pace slightly to create a little more distance before settling down into a slow jog to match them. They followed about thirty yards behind her, still chatting it up, she assumed. Her mind raced through possible scenarios of what to do, how to pull him back over to her. Maybe she needed to put his hunt on hold and appeal to the softer side of him...if he had one.

She saw her opportunity and veered toward the trio of terriers headed her way. The fierce yapping and lunging began immediately as the owner clenched the leashes and yanked the dogs off the left side of trail. Rebecca countered with an exaggerated sidestep that sent her stumbling off to the right and face-planting into the grass.

"Oh my God! Are you okay?" The dog walker started toward her, his face wrenched with worry.

"I'm fine. You can go ahead." Rebecca waved him off. "I can't be near dogs."

Confusion spread over his face. Not allergic, not afraid of, just simply couldn't be near them. In truth, she loved dogs, but that dog walker was not the hero she needed to rescue her and he needed to be on his way...quickly.

Dragging herself further off onto the grass, she shot him a stern look as he continued to wait. "Go!"

Sitting up, she brushed the grass clippings off her legs and examined them. She was a better actress than she gave herself credit for. She meant to have a soft grass landing, but her falling stunt was a little too real. She had skimmed the pavement on the way down and her knee honestly burned a little from the impact. Nothing was more convincing of an injury than actual oozing blood. Bending her knee for a closer look, she began to pick out the loose gravel that was embedded in her raw flesh.

"Amanda?"

Perfect. Rebecca winced and looked up with the best pitiful, injured face she had. His tall frame was just a dark silhouette against the bright sky. Shielding the sun from her eyes with her free hand, she gasped in surprise.

"Andrew?" she asked, faking total surprise at seeing him there. Oh where was the Oscar she so deserved right then?

Andrew dropped to his knees beside her, his forehead wrinkled with concern. One hand under her knee and the other under her thigh, he began flexing and extending her knee, checking her range of motion. As far as she knew, he didn't have a background in orthopedics, but he was pulling off his assessment quite well. She winced here and there, to exaggerate her pain and keep his warm hands moving over her legs. As much as she despised him, she couldn't ignore the fact that he had a phenomenal healing touch.

The redhead he was with did not enjoy his examination nearly as much as Rebecca. She stood behind him with arms crossed, rolling her eyes every few seconds and being as unhelpful as she possibly could. Not that her help was welcome anyway. The loud sighs she added as an attempt to draw Andrew's attention also failed. His focus was one hundred percent aimed at Rebecca and her knee, and nothing else.

Rebecca gave the woman a slight wink and a smile just to get her unspoken point across. At that, the color of the woman's cheeks began quickly approaching the color of her hair. Her entire body stiffened as her mouth let out an offended gasp. She gave one last huff before flipping her hair to the side and trotting off down the path alone. Point successfully taken.

Andrew did not seem to notice the absence of his earlier companion as he stood to help Rebecca to her feet. "I'll carry you to your car," he said as he lowered himself to scoop her.

"No, no, we don't need any of that," she said with half a giggle as she took a step away from him. "I'm okay. I can make it."

His head lowered as he took a step away from her.

"I meant, with your help I can make it to my car."

He regained his posture, his face brightened, and now she was beginning to understand him. He was like a fragile puppy, not knowing what was right or wrong. He didn't know where he stood with her. He wanted her to want him. He needed her to need him. His lack of confidence was an entirely new side of him that Rebecca hadn't expected and didn't know what to do with.

With her arm tight around his shoulders, she gingerly limped the rest of the way around the loop. They stopped at a bench near the entrance and took a few minutes to catch their breath. He stared at her hard as they sat, not saying a word. It made her feel a bit uneasy, but she couldn't figure out why. Did he simply not know what to say to her? Was he waiting for her to make the first move? Or was he trying to estimate how many diamonds he could slice her into? She was a good three inches taller than Sara was. Maybe her increased height was throwing off his calculations.

Snapping herself out of her morbid thoughts, she bottled up her rising fear and threw it into a deep corner of her mind. She was Amanda White, and she feared nothing. That silent declaration lifted her mood in an instant. She was going to really enjoy screwing up his plans for her.

"How about Chadwick's for a cup of coffee? I'm parked right over there," she said, motioning toward the street beyond the trail entrance.

"That's exactly what I was about to say." His mouth turned upward into a spreading smile. "As long as it comes with a bag of ice and some Band-Aids," he added, nodding toward her swelling knee.

Rising from the bench, she assumed her position and threw her arm over his shoulder and together they lumbered off in the direction of her parked car.

Chapter 12

T he black Audi tore down 16th Street before coming to an abrupt halt at the red signal. Traffic was abnormally light for a Monday night, and even though it was well after rush hour, there still should have been more people out and about on a warm summer evening downtown. Maybe it was just too warm.

Rebecca glanced over at the man behind the wheel. He caught her eye and gave her that smirky smile that so many women were such suckers for. She had finally agreed to his request for a date, although she didn't expect it to be that very night. Andrew had taken great care of her earlier after her intentional wipeout. He practically carried her into Chadwick's, set her on the corner sofa, and meticulously tended to her injured leg. Retrieving a large bag of ice from the barista, he wrapped it around her knee and secured it with plastic wrap.

The light turned green and they were on their way again. She opened her clutch purse and took out a bottle of ibuprofen. The coffee shop ice treatment worked, but at the time she was only keeping up the appearance of what she thought was a fake injury. Eight hours later, she realized she wasn't faking it at all.

She really had injured herself and had the swelling to prove it. It was worth it. She'd needed something drastic to pull him away from that redhead and she'd been able to do just that.

Andrew pulled up in front of The Winslow Hotel, which housed the extravagant Kingfisher's restaurant inside. She knew the head chef there and had assisted him the year before, when Kingfisher's was used as the venue for a large presidential campaign banquet. Andrew had great taste. The food there was exquisite. Although, taking her there for their date most likely had less to do with his taste for fine food than it did for him simply wanting to show off his money. It was no secret that it was the place to be for anyone who was anyone.

The valet opened her door and took her hand. Half stumbling out of the passenger seat she realized right then that stiletto heels and lower extremity injuries did not mix well. Andrew instantaneously appeared at her side with a firm arm around her waist, holding her steady. Regaining her balance, she hooked his arm and together they followed the doorman into the hotel entrance.

Although she had been there many times before, Rebecca always took a moment or two to marvel at the majestic architecture of the hotel's lobby. The domed ceiling towered above them with thousands of recessed lights and chandelier crystals spilling their glow onto all the smiling faces below. Enormous white columns ascended out of the floor and disappeared into the elaborately carved moldings outlining the dome. Black and pearl diamond-shaped tiles filled the lustrous marble floor. Diamonds. How appropriate.

They ventured farther into the lobby until Rebecca stopped dead in her tracks. She caught a glimpse of a female photographer off to the left, shooting photos of a bride and groom draping themselves over the hotel's gleaming grand piano. As the woman turned to adjust her tripod, their eyes locked. A shudder traveled through Rebecca's body. As much as her appearance had changed, she would still be recognizable to those that knew her well, especially with the man standing next to her as context.

The photographer hoisted the neck strap of the oversized camera over her head and began her aggressive approach across the lobby floor. She covered the space between them in just a few seconds, strawberry blonde curls bouncing with every rapid footstep. Coming to a stop just six inches away, her fiery eyes bore into Rebecca so hot she felt as if her bones were melting.

"Lexy. I wasn't expecting to see you here."

"I'll bet you weren't," Lexy said as she turned her glare onto Andrew.

"Seems you two know each other," Andrew said as he extended his hand. "I'm Andrew. It's a pleasure to meet you, Lexy."

His hand remained untouched as Lexy turned her attention back to the target of her anger. "You have got some nerve," she said through gritted teeth.

Rebecca felt dryness in her mouth and swallowed hard in an attempt to relieve it. Her entire plan could go straight to hell if

Lexy said another word in front of Andrew. She turned to him and gave him a strained smile. "Why don't you go on in, and I'll meet you there in a minute."

The two women stood there silently, waiting for him to leave them. He finally withdrew his still outstretched hand, shrugged, and headed off through a large arched doorway leading to the restaurant.

Lexy was the first to break the silence between them. "You've hit a new low this time, Rebecca."

"It's not what it looks like."

"Really? Because it looks like you changed your appearance to match your dead sister so that you could date her ex."

Lexy's words burned through her like fire. Yes, that was exactly what it looked like, and it was exactly what she'd done, but not for the reasons Lexy thought. Not that she could tell Lexy her true motivation. Rebecca took the easy way out and lowered her eyes to the floor, not saying a word.

"So you're not even going to deny it? You were so sure he was a serial killer. You wanted him to burn in hell, remember that? And now you're on a date with him!" Her tone got harder and louder with every word.

"All I can say is that it's not what you think. I can't explain it all to you now, but I will at some point, okay?" Rebecca had no idea how to diffuse the situation and keep Lexy from going on a total rampage.

"No, it's not okay!"

The concierge stepped from his small booth and began to walk softly yet swiftly in their direction. Lexy waved him off.

"Rebecca Black, you utterly disgust me," she said as she spun on her heel and headed back across the lobby to resume her photo shoot.

Rebecca's eyes stung as she attempted to blink the tears away. A deep pain developed in her gut and spread throughout her chest. Lexy's words cut her to the bone. She could handle words like that coming from anyone else...but not Lexy. Rebecca was officially broken.

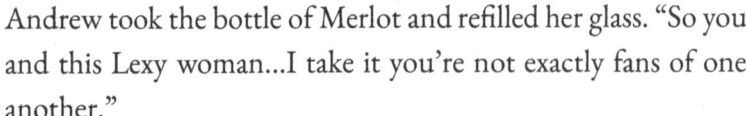

Andrew took the bottle of Merlot and refilled her glass. "So you and this Lexy woman...I take it you're not exactly fans of one another."

Rebecca thought hard for a response. She knew she was going to have to explain that scene in the lobby, but she hadn't thought of how. She had raced right into the restaurant, desperately needing to hide away within her alter ego and put everything Lexy said out of her mind. She should have taken a few minutes to get her story straight before she did.

"We go back a ways," she finally responded.

He leaned forward placing his elbows on the table and clasping his hands together under his chin. His intrigued expression told her he was not going to let it go.

"We were roommates in college and had a falling out."

"And?" he said, pushing for more detail.

"It's no big deal really." She shrugged. "I had a serious boyfriend and she spread a lot of lies about him, and me, and both of us, and it caused a lot of drama, and that's it," she added, trying to be as vague as possible.

He continued to study her, his eyes probing her for more.

"And that's it," she said again more firmly, taking a sip from her glass to affirm the point that she was done talking about it.

He seemed to take the hint as he relaxed his shoulders and leaned back into his chair. It only lasted a moment. He leaned forward again, his piercing eyes boring into her. "So, I have another question," he said.

Rebecca shifted uncomfortably in her seat. She didn't know what to expect from their date, but she had been hoping for more mindless chit-chat, like their coffee shop conversations. The serious look in his eyes told her he was ready to get down to business.

"You're a local gal. I doubt you've been in a bubble the last few months, so I'm sure you've caught the news at least once or twice." He paused, as if waiting for some kind of reaction. When he didn't get one, he continued. "Why would you want anything to do with me after what I've been accused of...especially looking the way you do?"

Rebecca's heart thumped hard in her chest. She knew it would come up at some point but had hoped it somehow wouldn't. She couldn't play dumb to it. She wouldn't be able to pull it off and she needed to gain his trust.

"My boyfriend in college was accused of rape."

Andrew perked up. "Do tell."

"He didn't do it." She emptied her glass, buying a little more time to spin her story. "He was with me the whole time. Evidence was planted, but it wasn't enough. Although that didn't stop the rumors from completely destroying his reputation. His parents were devastated. His privacy...our privacy...was opened up and poured out for everyone to see. He lost his internship. He lost everything. It's all anyone would talk about for the entire school year. He eventually couldn't take it anymore and dropped out." She casted her eyes down, trying to draw on her deep well of painful emotions. Her eyes began to gloss as they met his again. "It was Lexy. She did that to him."

Andrew's mouth slacked open in surprise before it curved into a sly smile. "The plot thickens," he said.

"So I do know a thing or two about false accusations," Rebecca said, feeling victorious.

His face said it all. He believed her. He trusted her. He thought he had finally found a woman who understood exactly what he had been through. Men really could be so stupid.

Their entrees arrived just in time. Rebecca needed a break from her interrogation. She felt she had done pretty well up to that point. The hard question had been asked and she was able to explain Lexy, although she wasn't keen on the fact that he could now link Lexy to her. She didn't want him knowing anything about her real life or the real people in it. All she could do was pray that he and Lexy never crossed paths again.

They spent the next several minutes enjoying their meal and commenting about how great it all was. Of course, Rebecca had to dumb herself down a little when she gave her review of the food. She was not supposed to be that highly educated on the topic of fine cuisine. Not too dumb, though; Amanda White was still a classy, confident woman with great taste. She just had to forget her background and pretend she was eating that dish for the first time...not that she had spent a hundred hours learning to prepare it from the man who practically invented it.

She did her best to concentrate on the food and Andrew and nothing else. However, it was becoming increasingly more difficult to ignore the stares. To silence the whispers. She could see them out of the corner of her eye. All of them. Every patron dining in that restaurant had given them *the look,* followed by hand-shielding whispers to their companions. They all knew the story, who he was, and what he had done. Unless they had been living completely off the grid in the Appalachian backwoods...they knew the story.

She knew what they were thinking too. *Run! You're next!*

Rebecca didn't like the fact that all of those people had suddenly become witnesses to her relationship with Andrew Donovan. Her act of superior confidence was beginning to crumble. Maybe they were right. Maybe she should have taken the advice written all over their faces and just run. Or maybe she should have slipped into the kitchen and poisoned them all so there would be no witnesses to link her to him. Intriguing dilemma, but who was she kidding...she wasn't a killer.

Chapter 13

Rebecca raced into the parking lot of Bethesda General Hospital. Throwing her car into park, she grabbed the small duffel from the passenger seat and leaped out, slamming the door behind her. The short beep of the horn signaling the remote locks echoed as she dashed across the lot and through the emergency room doors. She tried to keep her speed at a steady "fast enough to get there quick but slow enough to not draw attention" pace.

She headed for the elevator on the far side of the waiting room. Once inside, she pulled out her phone and sent a quick text: *Running late. Be down in 10.*

The elevator doors opened at the third floor and she quickly jumped out and raced down the hall to the women's restroom. Thankfully, she was alone. She cringed as she caught a glimpse of herself in the mirror. It was okay. She was supposed to look like hell.

The handicapped stall gave her just enough elbow room. Her hands were shaking and fumbling with the zipper on the duffel bag, but finally came through. She pulled out an unflattering pair of light blue scrubs and quickly began shedding her clothes.

The past three weeks had been a whirlwind for Rebecca. Dating Andrew Donovan had left her completely exhausted. Lunchtime jogs followed by Chadwick coffee cool-downs. Late night movie dates that ended at two or three in the morning. It turned out that Andrew liked romantic comedies just as much as she did, or he pretended to, at least. Social time with him, in addition to her evening chef duties had completely drained her. It amazed her that he could keep up, considering he ran a multi-million-dollar company.

It relieved her that he was taking their relationship slowly. It meant she didn't have to get too physically close to him. However, he was getting more and more serious with her, and that day could come at any time. And she didn't know how she would handle it when it did. It worried her that she wasn't as thoroughly disgusted at the very thought of him as she once was. The more time passed, the more she caught herself seeing him as a regular guy. A super-attractive, super-charming, and super-rich guy. So not very regular at all. She couldn't lose sight of what he really was—a tortuous butcher who just happened to also be an Oscar-worthy actor. He could add that to his regular-guy resume.

Her knee slammed into the side of the stall as she struggled to pull on the scrub pants while still wearing her shoes. Why hadn't she simply changed at work? It most likely would have been quicker that way. But she knew why. Explaining to Peter and the rest of her staff why she was moonlighting as a nurse would have been even more awkward than the confines of that stall.

It was the perfect cover-up. There was no way in hell she could let Andrew know where she was actually working every night. He would find out her true identity in a second, and that would endanger everyone she had any connection with. An operating room scrub nurse in the cardiac unit was genius. He could never witness her working. Visitors were not even allowed on the cardiac floor unless they were the family of a patient. It explained the late hours and weekend work as well. She just hoped no one ever had a medical emergency on one of their dates. She could wield a knife like a surgeon, but that was the extent of her medical knowledge. Although, if Andrew was the one having the emergency...nature just might do her job for her.

Rebecca quickly cleared her mind of those sinister thoughts. She was not trying to kill him, just catch him. Send him to rot in prison for the rest of his life. And most importantly, put an end to any more "Sara Wilsons" that family members needed to identify in the morgue.

Andrew Donovan paced back and forth across the expansive lobby of Bethesda General Hospital. After checking his watch once again, he finally took a seat. He had gotten her text, but his nerves still made him restless. He always felt that way in the moments before seeing her. It confused him. He was used to taking control and being the alpha. How was she able to knock him off his game so easily? There was something about her, something different that brought about a touch of anxiety he didn't even know he had. Something. He just couldn't pinpoint what it was.

The elevator doors at the far wall opened and Amanda bustled out first. She speed-walked across the lobby toward him. She was definitely cute. The scrubs she wore hid her athletic curves, but that made it even sexier. Her hair was a tousled mess and her cheeks flushed pink. He breathed long and slow as an excited calm fell over him. With a sly smile, he rose as she approached him.

"Sorry. I was running so late and I didn't want to take more time by changing." She glanced down at her frumpy hospital attire. "Is this okay?"

"Absolutely," he said, extending his smile. "It's just a movie. It'll be dark."

She breathed a sigh of relief, relaxing her shoulders.

"Come on. We still have time to smuggle in some drive-thru." He took her duffel in one hand, her arm in the other, and steered her toward the front door.

Arm in arm they crossed the tile floor, starting a wave of heads turning in their direction. He saw the stares from almost everyone they passed; they knew him. Everywhere they went, the looks followed them. He knew Amanda saw them too, but she remained unfazed.

She truly was special. She accepted him and all the baggage that came with him. It couldn't be easy, being with a man like him. A man she couldn't take home to Mom or introduce to her family. A man she couldn't double-date with her best friend. A man that couldn't be involved with any social aspect of her life without harsh judgement from those she was closest to. However, she accepted him regardless of it all.

Maybe she really was the one. Maybe all the others were just practice. She was the one he had been waiting for. If only she knew that. What would she do? Run? Or stay and fulfill her destiny...her purpose.

He could barely wait. He had been taking it slow and nursing their relationship...pun intended.

Soon. It would be soon.

Chapter 14

The red Honda creeped along the never-ending driveway. She was stalling, not yet ready to take the next step. However, she needed to, whether she was ready or not. This would be their first time. Not sex...she wasn't ready for that and was hoping she would be able to wrap up her plan before she needed to be. No, the firsts that would come that evening were much more terrifying. The first time at his house which could have likely been the very location he used to cut those women to pieces. The first time meeting his son. How could she look him in the eye knowing her goal in life was to lock up his dad for the rest of his life? But what chilled her to the core was that it would be her first time being in private with him. She was relieved that his son would be there, but it was a big house and teenagers were known for not wanting to hang around the adults any longer than they had to. What would happen when dinner was over and Andrew wanted to retreat to a different room in the house for some alone-time? The house was immense. Anything could happen.

The driveway took a left turn when it reached the front of the house and opened into a giant parking pad that led to a huge four-car garage. Rebecca parked and took a moment to calm her nerves. The summer sun had just begun to set and the shades of orange streaking across the sky almost made her forget she was walking right into the lion's den. How could evil show its face on a night like that?

A soft knock on her window startled her and shattered her daze. She didn't know how long she had been sitting there, but it was long enough for Andrew to come out and greet her. He opened her door and extended a gentlemanly hand to help her out.

"You seem nervous," he said. "I hope it's not me you're scared of."

An anxious giggle escaped her lips, and she heard the shakiness in her voice. "No, of course not," she said, forcing confidence and strength into her vocal chords.

His brows narrowed as he gave her a drawn-out sideways glance. It amazed her that he could go from being so charming to scaring her to death with a single sentence.

"I just want him to like me," she said, explaining away her trembling. "Kids can have a really hard time accepting their parents' new relationships. I don't want him to feel threatened by me."

"You are the one that should feel threatened by me," he said with a devious grin.

There it was again. What did he mean by that? Second thoughts raced through her mind as they moved closer and closer to the front door. It was her last chance to pull out. She could have faked stomach cramps...or suddenly fallen and twisted her ankle. She had already played that card, though. And with either one of those excuses, he would have taken her inside and administered his expert first aid. The only way out would have been to simply bolt, right then, with no explanation. There would be no coming back from that. If she was going to go through with her whole plan, going through that front door was the only way.

They headed toward the wide flagstone porch, and her eyes scanned the enormous front of the tasteful French colonial before her, its sandy brick broken up by tall arched windows. Rounded bushes and potted spiral shrubs stood symmetrically on either side of the towering French doors. He reached forward to push one open and lightly pressed the small of her back to usher her inside.

There she stood, stiff and motionless. Her eyes were drawn up to the elegant glass chandelier that hung over the expansive two-story foyer. Dropping her gaze, her reflection stared back at her from within the gleaming white marble floors. There was so much to take in; she didn't know what to focus on first. More than a few recessed niches housed various culturally diverse vases and small sculptures. It wasn't quite what she had expected from a single father and teenaged boy, but the level of feminine elegance displayed made it clear to her that this was his wife's design. Marie's former job as a historical art curator explained the abundance of foreign artifacts that peppered the foyer's decor.

The staircase curved up to the left to the second level. Rebecca's eyes followed it and her panoramic view revealed an open hallway that encircled the vast marble foyer beneath it. Large arched doorways lined each wall on the main level, and the rooms beyond were brightly-lit with the exception of a single room just to the right of the front door. The doorway was narrower than the others and appeared rather dark in comparison. The smallest of them all, it was the room that most piqued her interest.

She gave Andrew a quick look, realizing she had forgotten about him for the moment. He was still there next to her, watching every move she made, causing her cheeks to redden.

"I'm sorry," she said. "It's so beautiful. I've never been inside a home like this."

"It's just a house. Not quite a home, anymore." He took her wrist and gave her a gentle tug.

He tossed his keys into a glass bowl sitting atop a small circular table in the middle of the foyer as he led her forward, through the center massive arch, down a short hallway, and into an enormous gourmet kitchen. Rebecca was in heaven. Her eyes widened in awe as she looked over the entire room from floor to ceiling. It was, by far, the most professional kitchen she had ever seen in a private home, even rivaling those of some of the small bistros she had worked in while living in Paris. As much as she tried to stay focused, and remember that Andrew was the bad guy, she couldn't help but be extremely impressed by him at that moment.

Granite and stainless steel stretched as far as her eyes could see. Four barstools were parked along the central island and resting on it was a single burning candle that transmitted the sweet scent of vanilla throughout the room. The kitchen opened into a breakfast area with a large round table and beyond that, an immense living room that led back toward the front foyer. At the rear of the kitchen, a gorgeous plush sunroom housed towering bay windows that looked out over the backyard.

Another minute went by before she realized how she must have looked to him. Standing there, wide-eyed as if she had been kept captive in a dirty basement her entire life. She picked her jaw up off the floor and turned toward him, smiling.

"You have exceptional taste," she said.

He gave her a quick wink and grabbed two wine glasses hanging from the bottom of one of the cabinets and placed them on the counter in front of her. "What can I get you? Red or white? Sweet or dry?"

He was obviously relieved that her home inspection was complete, at least for the moment. "A little Chardonnay would be great, if you have it," she said, as she took a seat on one of the high bar stools at the counter across from him.

She watched as he reached down below and came up with an ice-cold bottle dripping with condensation. Purely by reflex, Rebecca leaned back to look under her side of the counter. "What else do you have hiding under there?"

"All of my deepest darkest secrets," he said with a smug smile.

With minimal effort, he uncorked the bottle and poured two glasses, handing her one. Raising his, he toasted, "To my deepest darkest secrets...may you learn them...and accept them...and show me yours, of course."

It was quite an odd toast, considering it was his dark secrets that had gotten him tried for murder in the first place. She would have preferred a simple "Cheers," but it was too late for that.

He clinked her glass and leaned so far forward across the counter she could see her reflection in his eyes. Still smiling he took a sip. "I know you have them."

"Have what?" she asked, taking a sip of her own.

"Secrets. I can see them." He leaned in even further, his smile slowly fading. His head tilted slightly as his eyes pierced right through hers. "You're hiding something."

She coughed as her subtle gasp sent her sip of wine straight down her windpipe. "What do you mean?" Wiping the corner of her mouth with her thumb, she tried her best to appear unfazed by his suspicious words. "What am I hiding?" she asked him, calling his bluff.

"Everybody is hiding something." He continued to stare her down, his ever-present smile still absent.

What seemed like hours had passed, even though it had only been a second or two. She wasn't sure how much longer she could keep her strong Amanda-face on. The tension had built to the point of being downright awkward. Leaning forward, she planted a soft kiss on his lips. His smile returned just as quickly as it had left.

"Time for you to meet him," he said, putting down his glass and disappearing back through the hallway.

Rebecca took a few deep breaths, more than a few sips of wine, and waited patiently for Andrew to return with his son.

Chapter 15

Rebecca tucked her hair behind her ear, straining to decipher the mumbling she heard making its way down the staircase. As hard as she tried, she was unsuccessful. A moment later, Andrew entered the kitchen with a tall handsome teenager lagging behind him.

The boy was blessed with his father's good looks, there was no doubt about that, but she couldn't help thinking how much more attractive he would be if his face wasn't contorted into such an angry sneer.

"Amanda, I'd like you to meet my son, Spencer."

Rebecca left her stool and closed the distance between them with an outstretched hand. "It's so nice to finally meet you," she said with the warmest smile she could conjure up.

Spencer stood there, unmoving. A nudge from his father forced his hand to reluctantly take hers in a half-hearted grasp. His touch sent an icy chill coursing through her. His hand was cold, but that wasn't the reason. It was his eyes. They were the same cerulean blue as his father's, but their gaze was much more sinister. His brows were dark and furrowed, and they cast such a shadow that his eyes appeared to grow darker with each passing second. Her warm smile dissipated as she drew her hand back. She had heard of the angsty teenager cliché, but Spencer seemed far beyond that.

"Can I go now?" Spencer asked, turning his head toward his father. Not waiting for an answer, he turned and stomped loudly down the hall.

Andrew quickly chased after him, catching him as they both reached the foyer. They were out of view but not out of earshot.

"Who the hell do you think you are?" Andrew's voice was low but stern and filled with ire. "How dare you disrespect my guest like that? You are my son, this is my house, that is my girlfriend, and you will treat her with respect."

"Stop acting like this is something new...like she's the first!" Spencer's voice bellowed through the house much louder than his father's. It was evident that he wanted her to hear what he had to say.

"You better choose your next words very carefully, son." Rebecca could hear the words grated through gritted teeth.

"Or what?" Spencer asked defiantly. "We go through this every time. Every time you bring home another carbon copy of Mom."

Rebecca trembled as she heard the heavy footsteps returning to her. Spencer reappeared in the kitchen archway, seething with hate.

"You can't replace her!" He yelled at her, saliva spraying from his lips. "No one can replace her!"

The shockwave from his voice startled her glass out of her hand and sent it crashing to the floor. The fire in his eyes was so intense; the chill she felt in him earlier was now replaced with the searing heat of rage. Once again, he turned and stormed down the hall. That time she heard his footsteps scaling the stairs without any interruption from his father.

She expected to hear something from Andrew, but nothing but silence came from his direction. He didn't return to the kitchen. He didn't chase Spencer upstairs. Nothing.

Several minutes passed and Rebecca began searching the cabinets for a towel to clean up the wine and broken glass from the tile. She needed to do something; waiting in silence was killing her. After many unsuccessful tries, she finally found the lower cabinet that housed the dish towels. She picked up the glass pieces one by one instead of searching for a broom. First, because she had no idea where to find one, and second, because she wanted to be doing something whenever Andrew did come back in. She worked slowly, drawing her task out as long as she could. Far too soon she heard footsteps coming back toward her. She remained in her crouched position, pretending not to hear them. She felt his presence behind her. Out of the corner of her eye, she saw the brown leather of his shoes planted just three inches off her back heel. Still, she feigned obliviousness. Finally, he crouched down next to her, and she could ignore him no longer.

"I got this," he said softly.

His calm had returned, and she stood up to give him some space. She didn't know what to say to him. He apparently didn't know either. Piece by piece, the glass shards disappeared from the tile and filled the towel, now lying open in his hand. Not another word was spoken between either of them.

Finally, he stood, throwing the wine and glass-filled towel into the garbage can. Grabbing a clean towel from the pile she had brought out, he slowly began wiping his fingers, one by one. He hadn't yet made eye contact with her. She studied him as he continued to clean the same fingers over and over. Was he ashamed? Embarrassed? The vulnerability she saw in him was something very new to her. He *was* human after all. He *did* have feelings. As much as she wanted to stay focused on her mission, she couldn't help feeling sorry for him. Raising a teenager was tough, but Spencer seemed to be off-the-charts tough.

Slowly his head lifted. With his eyes closed he drew a long deep breath. When they opened, she saw the pain inside. He was broken. It amazed her how a single child could completely destroy one of the most powerful men in the tri-state area.

"I'm sorry. I'm so truly deeply sorry." His voice was soft and it cracked on every other word.

"It's not your fault," Rebecca said. She reached down and took the towel from his hands and replaced it with her own gentle touch.

"It is. He's been through so much since his mother..." His voice trailed off as if he realized, just in time, the conversation he was about to start. "I need to go talk to him." He paused as if waiting for her permission.

"Absolutely. I'll be fine here." Rebecca was looking forward to exploring a little, and she couldn't do that with him hovering over her.

With a quick kiss on her forehead, he turned and was gone. Taking a new glass from under the cabinet, she filled it, waiting for enough time to pass before she could safely venture out of the kitchen.

Chapter 16

T he sunroom off the back of the kitchen overlooked the vast expanse of his property. There had to be nearly three acres in the backyard alone. A stone patio stretched the entire length of the back of the house and led down to a large amoeba-shaped swimming pool, complete with a stone waterfall, a grotto, and of course, a hot tub. The waterfall poured out of a bridge of boulders extending across one of the outstretched amoeba arms, allowing someone to swim through the waterfall and enter into a small private cove on the other side. Her high vantage point from the sunroom was the only reason she even knew it was there. Otherwise, it would have remained completely hidden. Rebecca imagined all the women Andrew had most likely taken to his hidden cove. It was very probable she would need to play that part as well at some point.

Rebecca turned from the window and walked back through the kitchen on her way to the family room to begin her tour.

The sound of her footsteps was muted by the luxurious carpet. Getting her first full look at the room, once again she was in awe of its size, as well as the tasteful decor. A television almost the size of a movie theater screen hung on the wall over a fireplace with a massive U-shaped sectional sofa in front of it.

Rebecca continued through the room, pausing at the array of framed photographs sitting atop a large buffet cabinet. They were all different variations of the three of them: Andrew, Marie, and Spencer. A couple of the photos were professional portraits, complete with stiff posing and coordinating colors. Most of them, however, looked to be from many trips to Europe and Africa, possibly due to Marie's job with the museum. Judging from Spencer's age in the photos, the trips spanned at least ten years.

The backgrounds of pyramids and architectural ruins were intriguing. However, Rebecca's attention was drawn more to Marie's body language. She held Spencer close in every picture they were featured in together. She did the same with Andrew in what looked to be the older ones. A picture-perfect family that belonged on a greeting card. However, as Spencer's height increased, so did the distance between Marie and Andrew. The differences displayed along the photographic timeline was unmistakable. He held a possessive arm over her shoulder while she leaned slightly away from him, clutching Spencer tighter and tighter. An ear to ear full-faced smile became a forced disinterested grin. The earlier sparkle in her bright green eyes replaced with what seemed like actual fear. Rebecca was amazed at how obvious it was to see the subtle changes when she had something to compare them to.

She glanced up at the large mirror that hung in front of her. Looking back and forth between the mirror and the photo she held in her hand, Rebecca finally realized what a great job she had done with her transformation. She could clearly see why it didn't take much effort to get Andrew to notice her. It wasn't just the hair and the clothes. She really did bear a resemblance to Marie, right down to the bone structure in her face.

The muffled voices she heard coming from upstairs refocused Rebecca's attention. She didn't know how much time she had, but she knew she had spent too much of it on the photos. A wide archway transitioned the family room into the formal living room. The carpet was gone and the clack from her heels echoed against the hardwood floor. The couches looked stiff and uncomfortable, as if they weren't actually meant to be sat in. A white grand piano in the far corner made her wonder if it had ever even been played, and more family photos showed the same decrease in affection she had seen earlier.

Moving through the room as quickly as she could, Rebecca emerged in the foyer where she had first entered the house. She could hear the conversation between Andrew and Spencer clearer than she could before, but still not clear enough to make out any actual words. She didn't really want to hear what they were saying anyway. She just wanted to make sure she still had time to snoop around.

She had noticed the darker room with the narrow doorway when she first came in through the front door, and she headed

WHEN DIAMONDS BLEED

straight for it, trying to minimize the clacking of her heels on the marble as best she could.

The room was not as dark as it appeared from the outside. The walls were made up of darkly-stained built-in bookshelves. Books filled every inch of the shelves, floor to ceiling. A library.

"Hello."

Rebecca jumped and turned in the direction of the voice. A large walnut desk sat in front of a small window at the far end of the room. A single desk lamp was lit and made it difficult for her to make out the figure sitting behind it. As she moved closer, she could see it was a boy roughly the same age as Spencer. Confused, she moved even closer.

"Hi. I'm sorry, I didn't know anyone else was here," she said.

"I'm Tyler. Tyler Maddox." The boy stood and extended his hand to her across the desk. "You must be Amanda."

She gave his hand a firm shake. "Do you live here too?" Rebecca didn't like the idea of another witness to her presence there, although Tyler seemed much more pleasant than Spencer, so she went along with it.

"On occasion I dwell here. I'm Spencer's friend," he said as he sat back down behind the desk and picked up a pewter hooked blade. He held it up to the light and examined it closely as he turned it over.

She took several cautious steps backward.

He gave her a sly smile and a slight chuckle. "It's okay. This isn't for you."

Her eyes were wide as she took another step backwards. His eyes remained locked on hers, as his free hand slowly reached beneath the desk and reemerged holding a pale yellow polishing cloth. Her shoulders relaxed and a strong gust of air escaped her lips. He was toying with her. Her brow furrowed, letting him know she was not impressed by his little game.

His chuckle grew louder. "You're a skittish one, aren't you?" Without taking his eyes off of her, he leaned back in the chair and began moving the cloth in tiny circles over the length of the blade. "I'm the only one he trusts with this."

"What do you mean?"

"His collection." Tyler waved an arm at the six-foot-high glass display cabinet against the wall beside him. "He won't even let the cleaning lady touch them."

"What about Spencer?"

"Not these days. Spence has been way too wound up lately." His head lowered slightly and his voice became softer...even seductive. "These babies need a special touch."

"And you have that touch?" She could tell he was flirting with her, and honestly, he wasn't doing a bad job.

"Oh yeah. I've got that touch." His gaze never left her, although it did travel up and down the length of her a few times. He coordinated it with a few long strokes of his cloth along the blade for an added effect.

Feeling a little too exposed, Rebecca pulled a chair over and sat. This wasn't the first time she had been hit on by a teenager, but this was the first time she had been knocked off-balance by it. Tyler was quite a good-looking young man. His blonde hair was cut clean and short with a little extra on top that allowed for some expert styling. He smiled often, which he obviously knew was his money-maker. The way he looked at her was a little creepy, but she couldn't help being mesmerized by his charm and confidence.

She broke his gaze and looked toward the display cabinet. Almost two dozen knives of varying size, shape, and age hung in rows of four. Some were silver, gold, some were even wooden, but all of them uniquely shaped with ornate handles depicting the area and time they were from. Some appeared ritualistic while others were obvious weapons of war. The collection was like nothing she had ever seen outside of a museum. The one knife she would have recognized was not present, however. There was an empty space in the second row, which she could only assume was the spot reserved for the Phurba Dagger. Still resting comfortably in an evidence locker downtown, it was very likely that knife would never return to its bed behind that glass door.

She looked back at Tyler, whose smile had vanished and eyes bore into her intensely. He knew what she was looking at and what she was looking for. His boyish charm was gone, replaced with a mistrustful and suspicious aura. Her breath caught in her throat as she tried to think of something to say. The silence between them was uncomfortable, and too much time had passed for her to play the naive card. It had only been seconds, but it felt much longer. His head cocked slightly to the side as he waited for her to speak.

"There you are." She spun around in her seat as Andrew entered the room.

His timing couldn't have been better.

"I see you've met Tyler," he said, as he rested his hand on her shoulder. "He's a regular fixture around here. You'll get used to it."

Her eyes once again returned to Tyler. A smirk and a wink from him were all she needed to rise from her chair, take Andrew's hand, and follow him toward the doorway. The click of the cabinet door closing prompted her to turn and see that Tyler was on his way behind them.

Chapter 17

"He has a hard time when I date," Andrew said as he slathered the beef filets with garlic butter. "He still misses his mom every day."

"That has got to be difficult for him. How long has it been?" She knew exactly how long it had been since Marie vanished into thin air, but she tried to appear as though she didn't know every detail of Andrew's history.

"Three years. Just gone. Without a note...a phone call...nothing."

Rebecca immediately regretted continuing the conversation in that direction. Andrew had been the prime suspect in her disappearance, although nothing came of it. He was right, one day she just disappeared. With no evidence of any foul play, and no trace of her body alive or dead, she simply became an unsolved missing person case. Rebecca didn't believe, however, that she had just up and left, and neither did the investigators. Marie had a son, her only son. No matter how bad her marriage with Andrew became, how could a mother just disappear and leave her son without letting him know why...or even if she was okay?

The silence between them became awkward, but Rebecca had no idea how to break it. She lowered her head and resumed her carrot-cutting, hoping the conversation would simply fix itself.

"Tyler has been super helpful." Andrew peered over his back shoulder at Tyler, who was making quick work of setting the dining room table. "He keeps Spencer in check. Makes sure he doesn't go off the deep end."

"Is he here a lot? You said he practically lives here."

"He comes and goes, but mostly comes. Let's just say he's here more often than not. He lives a mile or so down the road. A good kid...good student...hard worker. He went to school with Spencer, and his father worked his fingers to the bone to afford the tuition."

"What does his father do?" she asked, starting on the zucchini.

"He owns a landscaping company. It's small, just a few guys, but they do incredible work. Tyler works for him in the summer to pay for his car and his phone." Andrew opened the oven and slid the seasoned steaks inside. "Nothing is given to him. He works hard for everything he has. Great work ethic, that kid."

The respect Andrew had for Tyler was unmistakable. He was definitely a man who respected hard work.

"I try to help him out as much as he'll let me, which isn't much. The boy has a lot of pride. No handouts allowed. They're both graduated now, so he'll be working for me starting in the fall. Spencer, on the other hand, wants nothing to do with me or my company."

She could see the hurt on his face as he leaned against the counter, facing her.

"Maybe he just needs a little more time. He'll come around," she said.

"Maybe. But it doesn't look like it'll be any time soon." Andrew glanced down at her cutting board. His eyebrows rose in disbelief. "Wow. You've certainly done this before."

She followed his eyes down to the vast array of cut vegetables in front of her, julienned into piles of perfect identical pieces. A flush creeped over her cheeks. She went through those bags too fast and her work was too perfect. After all, she was supposed to be a nurse.

"I'm addicted to cooking shows," she said.

His smile broadened. "Then next time...you're cooking." He leaned in and gave her a quick kiss. "Deal?"

"Deal."

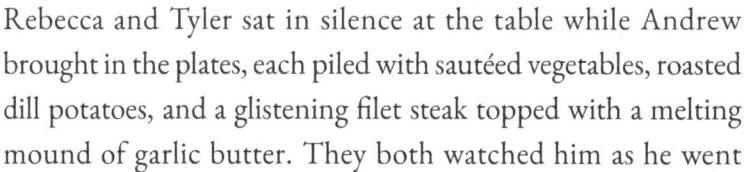

Rebecca and Tyler sat in silence at the table while Andrew brought in the plates, each piled with sautéed vegetables, roasted dill potatoes, and a glistening filet steak topped with a melting mound of garlic butter. They both watched him as he went into the foyer and called up to Spencer to join them for dinner. Rebecca caught a glimpse of Tyler and the wink he sent her way. Shifting uncomfortably in her seat, she was relieved when Andrew returned to sit across from her.

"Is he coming down?" she asked.

He let out a long sigh. "Who knows."

"So are you a cook or a nurse?" Tyler piped in. "You looked pretty handy with that knife in there."

Rebecca's pulse quickened. She wasn't aware her skills were that obvious. "I'm an OR nurse at Bethesda General...but I dabble."

Andrew sliced off a generous piece of meat. "Cooking shows, huh? I know exactly how addicting those can be," he said as he popped the piece into his mouth.

"I'm always super impressed by those hibachi chef guys and how they throw those knives around." Tyler made frantic slicing motions in the air with his knife and fork. "I can clean 'em, but I can't work 'em. Not like that, anyway."

"It just takes practice," Rebecca said, giggling slightly at Tyler's air ninja moves. She couldn't get over how complete opposites he and Spencer were. An unlikely pair of best friends. She knew Spencer had gone through a tough time over the past several years. Losing his mother and not knowing whether she was alive or dead...his father's parade of girlfriends...the lengthy trial that should have landed his father in prison for serial murder. Any one of those by itself would have a detrimental effect on a teenager. Even still, Tyler appeared the polar opposite of Spencer in every way.

"So what's your favorite? Cooking style, I mean."

Andrew's question jarred her back to the conversation going on around her.

"French usually." She didn't see any harm in being honest about that particular interest in her life. "Although I do love a good steak," she added out of respect for the meal in front of her.

"Have you ever been to France?"

Not anticipating that her responses would come back to haunt her so quickly, she racked her brain thinking back to the lengthy talks she and Andrew had during their dates. She couldn't remember her time in France ever coming up. She would have lied about it anyway.

"No. Never been. I just love French food."

"As do I," he said with a sing-songy tone. "What's your favorite dish to make?"

"I think it would have to be Coquilles Saint-Jacques with a slightly chilled Chablis."

"Oooh...scallops."

"You know it?"

"One of my favorites," he said, his eyes growing wider with his excitement. "There's a place downtown on Connecticut that has the best Coquilles Saint-Jacques dish I've ever had." He kissed his fingers with classic French flair.

A loud groan came from the end of the table. She had been so busy trying to keep her story straight with Andrew she had almost forgotten Tyler was still there.

"Not a fan?" she asked.

"Definitely not. I don't eat anything I can't pronounce." Seemingly happy to be back in the conversation he rapidly switched gears. "So where did you get your degree?"

"My degree?"

"Your nursing degree. You have one, right? Please tell me you're not practicing without a license...harvesting organs during surgeries and selling them on the Black Market."

A nervous laugh escaped her lips as she entered back into her alternate persona. "Not anymore. The French restaurants I used to sell the organs to couldn't afford me anymore."

"And that is why I stick with food I know," he said, digging into his pile of potatoes.

"So where *did* you go to school?" Andrew asked the question again, confirming she wasn't getting away with not answering it.

She had made the mistake of not coming up with an in-depth backstory she could stick to. "Georgetown." She answered with the first school she could come up with that she knew had a nursing program.

"Really?" Andrew shot upright in his seat. "A guy I ski with is a Urologist at Georgetown. I'm sure you did a Urology rotation. Dr. Maxwell Brandon?"

Her anxiety was increasing by the second. Why had she picked a local school? "Sounds familiar."

"I hope so. The guy is a legend."

Rebecca knew she needed to end this line of questioning as soon as possible. She jerked her head upward as if she had suddenly heard something from the floor above her. Andrew and Tyler both followed with the same motion, straining to hear a noise that wasn't actually there.

"He's not going to come down, is he?" she asked.

"I don't think so." Andrew shook his head slowly as his smile faded.

"Would you mind if I went up and talked to him alone?" As much as she was dreading the thought of looking into those angry eyes again so soon, she wanted to get a read on him without his father around.

Andrew hesitated for a moment, studying her eyes. Rebecca couldn't tell whether he was trying to protect her or if he suspected an ulterior motive.

"You don't have to, especially with the way he treated you earlier. But if you want to give it a try..."

Without giving him a chance to change his mind, she took a large bite and stood up. Andrew and Tyler stood up as well. Glancing down at her still full plate, she felt a little guilty that she had barely eaten. Not that she had a chance with the interrogation the two had just put her through.

"I'll be back for that," she said, pointing to her plate.

As she turned and headed for the foyer and the staircase, she heard Tyler's voice behind her. "Be careful up there. There's a reason those that preceded you aren't here now."

Her head whipped around at Tyler's warning. Did he mean here in this house or here on this Earth? Was that a warning or a threat—or both? Second thoughts circled through her head, making her wonder if she actually should have ascended those stairs and found out exactly what he meant.

Chapter 18

R ebecca reached the second floor, and it dawned on her that she had no idea which room Spencer was in. The landing was a large square that wrapped around the entire foyer below. Three-foot-high white rails were the only thing preventing her from plummeting fifteen feet onto the marble floor beneath her.

From her position at the top of the stairs, she could see that two corridors extended toward the rear of the house. One on the left and one on the right. She scanned the closed doors, searching for a hint that would tell her if one belonged to a teenaged boy. No such luck. Looking back and forth between the two corridors, she did an eeny-meeny-miny-moe in her head to choose which one to venture down first. Heading off to the left, a low whistle from below halted her.

She took a couple steps back and peered over the railing to the foot of the staircase. Tyler stood below, shaking his head and signaling a different direction. Throwing a single nod back at him, she pivoted and headed off toward the right.

Entering the hallway, her pace decreased as she took in the numerous works of art lining both walls. A closer look revealed assorted puzzles that had been assembled and framed. The sizes varied, as did the colors and themes of the puzzles. A chill traveled up her spine as visions of diamond-cut flesh ran through her head. Human jigsaw puzzles was how the prosecution had described the bodies.

She came to a stop in front of yet another closed door. She gently pressed her ear to it, listening for an indication that she had the right room. Nothing. She had expected to at least hear something, perhaps music blaring from a stereo or sounds from a television. Even a string of profanities with her name sandwiched in between would have been something.

Inhaling a deep breath, she gave a light knock on the door. After thirty seconds of more silence, she knocked again, harder that time. She looked back down the hallway in the direction she had come, hoping Tyler would have come to her aid again. He didn't, and she couldn't go back downstairs without at least making a valiant effort. She reached for the brass knob in front of her and gave it a slow turn.

It wasn't locked and the door creeped open just wide enough for her to peek in. She saw him there, half of him, sitting on the edge of his bed. He was leaning over, his elbows resting on his knees. She opened the door further.

"Spencer?"

His head turned and his eyes rose to meet hers. He remained silent, his glare fixed in her direction. He was fiddling with something in his hands, but she couldn't see what it was. His fingers kept twirling as his eyes remained locked on her.

"I know we got off to a bad start, and I know I'm the last person you want to see right now...probably ever." She waited for him to respond.

His lips parted to reveal clenched teeth, but still no sound came out of them. She hadn't expected that. He was so vocal earlier and that was what she was prepared to face. She didn't know what to do with silence.

"Maybe you could just give me a chance?"

Feeling bold, or maybe just wanting to elicit some kind of reaction from him, she took two steps into the room and closed the door behind her. He released her from his stare and went back to his fiddling. Taking another step, she finally saw what he had in his hands. The light from his lamp reflected off the stainless steel and shimmered as he rocked the blade back and forth into his thumb. A crimson droplet ran off the end of his thumb and landed on the folded newspaper between his feet with an audible spatter, the growing red target seeping toward the edges of the paper, made Rebecca aware he had been at it for quite a while. Probably since he stormed up to the room over an hour before.

He was using a surgical scalpel in the exact manner it was intended—to cut through flesh. He was trying to scare her. To have her run out of the room screaming, without him having to say a word. However, she refused to give him the satisfaction. If she was going to do her job, she needed to be able to handle a whole hell of a lot more than a self-inflicted wound to his thumb.

Ignoring his bloody attempt, she wandered across the room to a large drafting table next to the side window. Her gaze swept over an uncompleted puzzle of a cloudless blue sky speckled with colorful hot air balloons. She guessed there were over a thousand pieces. He was more than halfway done, leaving the most difficult part for last. Several hundred identical-looking blue pieces were scattered across the bottom of the table. The slightest change of shade and hue was barely visible to the naked eye. She had attempted puzzles like that before, but always gave up when she got to that part. She simply didn't have the patience to try all four sides of each piece in every single spot.

Rebecca resisted the urge to look his way. He was still driving the scalpel deeper and deeper into his thumb. The rhythmic spattering of the blood droplets rang in her ears. She remained calm and chose her words as carefully as she could.

"You hate him for it, don't you?" She eyed the puzzle pieces one by one, giving herself a reason not to look at him. "The way he keeps bringing new women home that remind you so much of your mom?"

She never took her sight off of the puzzle, but out of the corner of her eye she could see his head turn in her direction. The tempo of the spatter slowed.

"It doesn't necessarily mean he's trying to replace her. Maybe he misses her just as much as you do. Maybe he would rather have the reminder of her than not have her at all."

She paused and listened. It had gone. The ticking of blood droplets had ceased, and she could feel his eyes on her. She was getting through to him, or at the very least, he was letting her try. A subtle smile crossed her lips. She felt triumphant. Reaching across the table, she picked up one of the blue pieces and unsuccessfully tried to fit it into the top left corner of the sky.

"Don't touch that!" Spencer jumped to his feet. "You just can't help yourself, can you? Always gotta jump in and fuck with everything!"

The tiny piece of blue cardboard dropped from her hand as she took two quick steps away from the table. Frightened by his sudden outburst, she backed up toward the door, cowering beneath his enraged glare.

He crossed the room and stood in front of her, waving the bloody scalpel in front of her face. "You need to leave me—and my dad—alone," he ground through gritted teeth.

A drop of his blood flew off his thrashing hand and landed on her upper arm. Reaching behind her for the doorknob, she refrained from turning her back to him. She didn't trust what he would do to get his point across. She opened the door just enough to slip through it backward into the hallway. The door slammed shut in front of her.

She stepped back and leaned against the wall behind her. Wiping the blood off her arm with her free hand, she was relieved that no one was waiting in the hall, witness to the disaster. She didn't rush to return downstairs. She needed a moment alone. Alone. That was all Spencer wanted from her. To be left alone. And for his dad to be left alone. Unfortunately, that was the one thing she couldn't give him...wouldn't give him. Someone in that house was a killer, and she was not going to leave anyone alone until she found out which of them it was.

"How'd it go?"

Her moment of solace was gone. She breathed a deep sigh. "How did it sound?"

"Like you went to battle..." Tyler eyed her up and down. "...and you survived." He took a spot next to her against the wall.

"So are you here to rescue me from him, or him from me?"

"Both." His charming smile returned. "Actually, Mr. Donovan sent me up here to check on you. He didn't want to come up here himself. Thought it would just make it worse."

"It probably would have." Gazing up at the wall of puzzles in front of her, Rebecca recalled how violently Spencer had reacted the second she had laid a finger on the one in his room. "He's really into these, isn't he?"

"Puzzles? Him, not necessarily, but his mom...obsessed. These are all hers," he said, gesturing at the wall. "One word to describe Mrs. Donovan...puzzles."

Rebecca's eyebrows lifted in surprise. "Really?"

"Yeah. It's the one thing that makes Spence feel close to her. It was their thing. She would do most of it, of course, but she'd always leave big chunks of easier pieces for him to do. Spencer never had much patience."

That surprised her even more. "I wouldn't have guessed that. He's working on a puzzle in there right now," she said, pointing to the door. "Even though he's left the hardest for last, that puzzle is huge. Even the so-called easy sections take an enormous amount of patience."

"Between you and me, I think that's why he does them." Tyler's voice lowered to a whisper. "It's as if he's proving to her, wherever she is, that he can do it. Pull his weight. Do his part. You should see the garage."

"What's in the garage?"

"More. A lot more."

"Puzzles? Like these?" She honed in and focused on the puzzle directly in front of her. It was a night painting of a grey wolf...stalking...staring right back at her with keen eyes of amber.

"Yep. Glued and framed, hanging all over the walls. He rotates them." Tyler moved his fingers in circles. "Same time, every month. He'll take the ones off of these walls and switch them out with ones from the garage walls. Even if part of the frame is broken or scratched, he'll still hang it."

"Huh. He has unconditional love for these," she said, running her palm over the smooth glass surface of the frame. "He has unconditional love for her." She moved closer until her reflection stared back at her from within the glass. "To him, these puzzles *are* her." The reflection of her eyes lined up with those of the wolf, animating them. It appeared as if the animal would leap out of the wall at any moment. "It must eat him alive every time his father brings home a new 'Mrs. Donovan.' And this month it's me."

Chapter 19

It was Monday afternoon and Rebecca parked in her designated spot in front of the row of brick townhouses. She refrained from getting out of her car right away. The restaurant was closed on Mondays, and she had nowhere she needed to be, though she would have cancelled even if she did have somewhere to go. All she wanted to do right then was sit and do nothing at all.

She was overwhelmed. Anxiety washed over her and sucked up every ounce of energy she had. The dinner the night before at Andrew's hadn't been what she had expected at all. The possibility that his son might not be into the idea of his dad moving on with his life hadn't occurred to her. How could he be, when Andrew's pining was so obvious? She had expected it would just be the three of them. Even though Tyler had done a lot to ease the awkwardness of the whole situation, he still was another person she had to worry about. Another witness to her relationship with Andrew. Another person she had to hide herself from.

She missed Lexy. Badly. Lexy was the one that always kept her straight, kept her thinking logically. Rebecca desperately needed to talk things through with someone. She thought she had planned everything out, but the conversations that occurred at dinner had given her the realization that she was pretty much going in blind. What was her endgame, anyway? She wanted Andrew caught. She wanted to find proof that he killed those women. But how? The only way she would get that proof was if he tried to kill her. She had thought of that before, but not in any detail. She was confident she wouldn't become a victim, because she wouldn't let her guard down. She would expect it, see it coming, and would be prepared. But *how* had she prepared herself? The truth was that she hadn't. And as the night unfolded, she had been forced to entertain the idea that maybe Andrew wasn't who she needed to prepare herself for.

Rebecca took her cell phone from its cradle on the dashboard. As she scanned through her contacts and selected the number, she wondered if she should even open that door.

It became too late to close the call as Lexy's voice came on the line. "Yes?"

"Can we talk?" Rebecca asked, not sure what answer she was hoping for.

"I'm working from home today if you want to come by."

Her tone was cold; nearly emotionless, yet calm. Not at all like the Lexy she had last encountered. It was too late to turn back, so Rebecca finished the call and reversed back out of her spot.

She arrived at Lexy's apartment a half hour later with two Starbucks in hand. She needed a peace offering, and it was too early in the day for a bottle of wine, even for them. Lexy opened the door and let her in without saying a word. The calm she exhibited over the phone remained, but Rebecca still wasn't sure how to approach her. Instead, she simply handed over the coffee and took a seat on the plush sofa.

Lexy didn't join her. She opted for the matching loveseat opposite. Pulling her feet up next to her, she gave Rebecca her full attention and waited.

"I'm sorry." The words caught in Rebecca's throat, but she forced them out anyway. "I'm sorry for losing my temper after the trial and the way I acted at The Winslow."

"I understand why you were so upset at the courthouse," Lexy said, her voice low and steady. "What I don't understand, is why you were so upset at *me*."

"I just—"

"You yelled at me. I sat in that courthouse with you every single day, not because I didn't have anything better to do—because, believe me, I did—but because you needed me. I was there for you throughout that entire mess and you ripped me to shreds afterwards."

"I felt betrayed." Rebecca's voice began to rise with her growing defensiveness. "You took his side. You believed him."

"And you don't? Now? Was that not a date the two of you were on the last time I saw you?" Lexy's calm had vanished and she matched Rebecca's tone. "And what the hell is with all this?" Her hand extended and motioned up and down, indicating Rebecca's new look.

Rebecca stopped herself from retorting. She really did have a lot of explaining to do. Lexy was right to be angry and confused. Rebecca's behavior didn't make any sense. Counting to ten in her head, Rebecca regained her focus and reminded herself of the reason she was there talking to Lexy in the first place. She needed her friend. She wanted to tell her everything, but at that moment, she realized that could be a huge mistake.

Taking a deep breath, she regained her composure. "I think you may have been right. He might not have done it. I wanted to give him a chance to convince me."

"Out of the blue? You just suddenly decided to give the guy you think killed your sister a second chance? Why?"

"It wasn't exactly out of the blue. I ran into him a couple times. Downtown, while I was running. He didn't recognize me from the courtroom and... he seemed different."

"Since when do you go downtown to run?"

"Since I needed a change of scenery. You might not believe this, but it began to get a little sickening running by body dump sites and makeshift memorials every day on the trail...including the memorial I made for Sara." Her irritation was returning, but she held it at bay. "I needed a change."

"And your hair?"

Rebecca hesitated a few seconds before answering. "People cope in different ways. I know it seems stupid now, but at the time, it made sense. I went to her stylist, and to be honest with you, it helped. Seeing this reflection in the mirror every day actually helped." The lies were coming easier. She didn't want to keep lying to Lexy, and had gone there with the full intention of coming clean, but she wasn't ready. Not yet.

Lexy seemed to accept her reasoning. She backed down and took a slow sip of coffee. "You realize this is why he's dating you, right?" Her hand gestured again. "He may not have killed those women, but he did date them. He still has a type."

Rebecca frowned at Lexy's inclusion of Sara in her generalization of "those women."

"And that type was targeted. Beck, you could be in very real danger!" Lexy popped her feet onto the floor and shot up off the loveseat. "Is it really worth it? For whatever reason, some maniac is targeting his girlfriends, and you've just put yourself on the hit list." Lexy's eyes were wide and her hands moved frantically as she displayed true fear for Rebecca's safety.

"That's the thing. I don't think it's just some maniac. I think it's someone he knows." Rebecca leaned back into the corner of the sofa and calmly swirled her coffee container. "I think it's someone in his house."

Chapter 20

Rebecca loved fireworks. She hadn't been able to attend a true Fourth of July fireworks display in years, but that year the fourth fell on a Sunday, and the restaurant closed at five on Sundays.

As a child, Fourth of July celebrations had always been a major event. Her parents would pack up the car with coolers of food and cold drinks and their family of four would head down to the National Mall bright and early to secure their spot on the Capitol lawn, right in front of the stage.

As an adult, Rebecca had lived out of the area most of the time, but even in the three years she had been back, her work life had been too busy to celebrate. Her heart filled with excitement when Andrew suggested a remote viewing area along the Mount Vernon Trail. It wouldn't be the up close and personal experience she remembered as a child, but with his recent media situation, she was pleased by the privacy.

Silence filled the car as it sped down the GW Parkway. It was the first date they'd had since the dinner at his house; she didn't count the times throughout the week that they had met up for lunchtime runs at The Basin.

He hadn't spoken much of that night or Spencer's behavior, though he had apologized. As much as she had wanted to dig deeper, and learn more about the relationship Spencer had with his mother, she didn't dare. She knew it was a touchy subject and left it to Andrew to bring it up, which he only did rarely and in small doses.

It was good to be with him away from the house where there wasn't an unstable teenager lurking in the shadows. She wondered if Andrew was thinking the same thing. That night couldn't have been easy for him, either. His repeated apologies were testament to that.

But she couldn't help thinking of Lexy's words. Rebecca *had* made herself a target. She had known that from the beginning, but she hadn't thought about how obvious it would be to others and how she would explain being that stupid. Anyone that really knew her wouldn't believe she was blind to the dangers of being involved with Andrew Donovan. But *he* might believe it...and that was the crucial part.

She stared out the window at the line of parked cars along the side of the road. Traffic was surprisingly light, and after about a half mile the cars along the shoulder became less dense. Andrew finally pulled the car off the road and parked it in the grass. Throwing her a quick smile, he got out and almost instantly appeared at her door. She followed him back to the trunk, where he unloaded a small cooler and a folded fleece blanket.

Taking the blanket from him, she turned and crossed the paved trail on her way to the river bank. "I'm so excited," she said over her shoulder.

"Whoa, little lady. Not here." He hooked her arm and guided her back onto the trail and further up the bank.

"What do you mean?" She glanced around. "Are we not watching them from here?"

"Give me a little credit." His teeth glowed with the reflection of the setting sun. "I have a better spot."

They walked along the trail for a few more minutes before heading back down toward the river's edge. She looked ahead and saw a man slouching in a bright red camping chair. In the water in front of him was a small fishing boat tied to a wooden post that rose out of the ground. He heard their approach, dropped a lit cigarette into a bottle next to him, and rose to meet them.

"All set?" the man asked.

"Yep." Andrew handed him the cooler, which he then placed inside the boat. Andrew stepped aboard and extended a hand for Rebecca, helping her to join him. "We can take it from here," he said to the man standing knee-deep in the water, holding the boat steady with both hands.

"You got it." The man backed up to the post and untied the tether before returning to give them a push-off.

They floated away from the bank for a few seconds before Andrew yanked the starter cord, bringing the boat's small motor to life with a loud roar. He took his seat at the back and stretched his right arm behind him to grab the lever controlling the rudder. Off they went, puttering along at a leisurely speed that preserved the glassy surface of the water.

The sun dipped low in the sky behind them, casting a fiery glow across the Potomac. They still had plenty of time. The show wouldn't begin until every trace of color was gone from the sky, and that wouldn't happen for at least another hour. Their speed, as slow as it was, still whipped her shortened curls against her face, but she welcomed it. The past few days had been so muggy and the air so still. The long-absent sensation of actual wind invigorated her. Her eyes closed as she tilted her chin upward, exposing her neck to the coolness of the air rushing past her.

The initial odor of gasoline that engulfed her when Andrew had first started the motor dissipated into the air behind them. It was quickly replaced with a mixture of scents: smoky charcoal wafting out of portable grills along the riverbank, the earthy scent of lush vegetation blanketing the small island in the distance, and of course, that burnt gunpowder smell from the drugstore bottle rockets going off around them. Signature Fourth of July. Her smile stretched from ear to ear as the smells brought her back to some of the most exciting times of her childhood.

The river was wide open. Only a handful of small boats accompanied them on the water, and they were so dispersed she couldn't even tell how many people were in them. She glanced behind her at Andrew, seemingly enjoying his role as captain of their small vessel. His lids lowered into a slight squint as he gazed lazily off into the distance. The wind was doing miraculous things to his hair, as well as his half-open shirt. His skin was afire with a reddish-gold hue cast off of the setting sun and reflected in the water. Beautiful.

They continued upriver, closer and closer to the forested landmass. As they approached the sliver of beach on the island's perimeter, Andrew gunned the motor and ran the boat halfway up the sand. Rebecca lurched forward as they came to a sudden stop. He cut off the engine, stepped past her, and leaped off the front of the boat. She took her cue and followed him before he had the chance to turn and offer his assistance. With both of them ashore, he gave a forceful tug and pulled the rest of the boat onto land.

"This place is amazing." Rebecca turned a full rotation to take in the complete panoramic view. "Why is no one else here?"

As far as she could tell, they were alone. There was a lot she couldn't see, with the dense trees obstructing her view inland, but there definitely wasn't anyone else close by.

"Most people go the bigger island on the other side. It has a pedestrian bridge to get across the river. This island is only accessible by boat."

"But still...there are other boats out on the water."

"And they may or may not decide to dock them for the show. It's more likely that they'll just come a little closer to land and throw an anchor. The view is just as good out there as it is here. Actually, it's better."

"Then why don't we stay out there?" She pointed out toward the water. Rebecca felt she was way overdue for a good firework show. It was a new spot for her, and she wanted the best experience possible.

"Because," Andrew came up behind her and slid his arms around her waist. "I can't touch you out there the way I can here." He buried his face in her hair and nuzzled her neck. "Not without tipping the boat, that is."

She laughed and leaned backward into his chest. His skin was hot and her bare shoulders burned against him. Her shoulders relaxed and her head tilted back, offering him ample neck to plant his kisses.

Her pulse quickened. It could have been her excitement, but she knew there was more to it. Anxiety was rearing its ugly head. They had been taking it slow for a month, but the grace period was coming to an end. She knew he wasn't the type of man that would allow himself to be strung along. She could feel it too...pressed into the small of her back. He had been a complete gentleman from the beginning, but she couldn't deny what he really was and had always been: an Alpha. That trait was what made him the man he was. The success. The power. The confidence. He knew what he wanted, and he went for it. He didn't wait for it. Alphas never waited.

She had thought about sex with him...even fantasized about it. She just didn't know if she could actually go through with it. There was too much she didn't know about him. Too many unanswered questions. Questions she didn't dare ask. Questions she wouldn't get an honest answer to, even if she did ask. And then there was the moral dilemma of him being her sister's ex.

His trail of kisses traveled down the side of her neck and across her shoulder. "You taste so good."

Rebecca lurched forward and spun to face him.

"Was it something I said?" His smile indicated he was still having fun, but his eyes showed complete confusion.

"Let's set up our camp." She trotted over to where the blanket rested, crumpled on the sand. Giving it a couple harsh shakes in the air, she laid it flat, tugging on the corners to smooth the wrinkles and bunches.

He gave a half shrug before heading toward the boat to retrieve the cooler, as well as a small waterproof tote bag from beneath the front seat. She was already sitting on the blanket when he returned. The bag contained three pretreated fire logs. He threw one on the sand near the blanket and lit it. Instantly, flames poured out and shot toward the darkening sky. The fire wasn't for warmth; the temperature was still hovering around eighty degrees, even with the disappearing sun. Extra heat was the last thing they needed, and one log wasn't enough to make a substantial campfire anyway. Its sole purpose was for ambiance, and maybe to keep a mosquito or two away.

He grabbed a bottle of wine and two crystal glasses from the cooler and joined her on the blanket. It was turning out to be quite a great night indeed, if only she could get over the fact that it was still possible he was a murderer.

The last remaining streaks of orange fled the sky as Rebecca rambled on and on with fake Fourth of July memories, careful not to resemble any stories Sara might have shared with him. He added in a few of his own before they were both hushed by a huge boom that echoed across the water. The raining droplets of light silhouetted the Washington Monument and The Capitol building, forming a breathtaking view of the DC skyline. She felt as if she was directly in the middle of the show as the lights from the sky reflected on the water and completely engulfed them. For the next half hour, they sat in silence, mesmerized.

The finale lit up the sky as if it was high noon. Rebecca's heart pounded in her chest and her eardrums pulsed with each explosion. Then it was over. Loud applause and cheering enveloped them from all sides, urging them to join in.

"Wow. That was amazing." Rebecca clapped until her hands hurt, but she was alone in her celebration. She looked at Andrew and caught him giving her a sideways glance coupled with a truly wicked smile. "What?"

"Nothing. Just enjoying the show." He rose and threw another log onto the pile of glowing embers in front of them. The fire reignited as he sat back down on the blanket.

"Are we not leaving yet?"

"What's the rush? The parkway will be all backed up with everyone trying to get out of here," he said as he reclined onto his back and placed both hands behind his head. "We've got plenty of time." He grinned and looked up at her from his position, his eyes twinkling in place of the smoke-covered stars.

His hand emerged to tug on her supporting arm, bringing her down next to him. With one swift motion he was on top of her, pinning her beneath his weight. She didn't struggle. She told herself it was because she couldn't risk rousing any suspicions of her. And there was truth in that. But, there was also a side of her that was enjoying it.

Supporting his weight on one forearm, his other hand lightly brushed a wayward tress from her cheek. She gazed up at him as the fire cast a warm glow across his face. His eyes twinkled with help from the dancing flames. His thumb gently traced her lower lip as his mouth formed a seductive grin. Her lips parted and he wasted no time taking her up on her silent invitation. He lowered his head and melded his mouth with hers. A tingling sensation ran from her lips down to the deepest part of her belly.

It became clear to her that, regardless of which side she took—the undercover femme fatale, or the gullible fool that was actually falling for him—her decision for how that night would end remained the same. *All in.*

Chapter 21

Rebecca awoke alone and disoriented. Her sleepy eyes fought hard to focus as she slowly cast an eye over the room. The window drapes were open on the far wall, and she could see treetops she recognized in the backyard. Sunlight poured into the room, forcing her to squint her still-adjusting eyes.

She flopped back into the soft bedding, vigorously rubbing her hands over her face to rouse her senses. She had no idea how late it was. She couldn't see the sun from where she was, but the amount of light coming in through the windows told her it was at least 8:00. Turning her head, she caught a glimpse of the alarm clock on the nightstand. 9:22. She wasn't surprised at the late hour. It had been well after three in the morning when she finally fell asleep. The fact that the bed was the most comfortable she had ever slept in added to her comatose state throughout the night.

She spotted a blue Post-It note stuck to the nightstand in front of the clock. Andrew had left for work and she was to make herself at home and call him later. *Very trusting of him.* She

WHEN DIAMONDS BLEED

rolled back onto her side, pulled the down-filled duvet up over her shoulders, and sank the side of her face into the pillow. The room was cool, considering the sweltering heat outside. His air conditioner had been working overtime, making it that much harder to crawl out from the warmth of the bedding. Her legs were sore and she stretched them out into a scissors pose. The movement triggered a deep ache between her thighs, reminding her of what had happened the night before.

She recalled the foreplay on the beach. Fortunately, foreplay was all it was. Her relief was short-lived however. They eventually headed home, to *his* home, where they would have complete privacy. Spencer was off camping with Tyler and some other friends for the night, and they had the house to themselves until Spencer was to return the next day.

The drive was both too long and too short for her comfort level. The awkwardness she felt made the minutes feel like hours, yet, when they finally pulled into the garage, she had wished to God she had more time. She wasn't ready. Her mind spun with anxiety and questions and fear. Her gut had told her she could trust him. However, as recently as a week earlier, her gut had told her he was a killer.

She didn't want to anger him with her suspicions. Perhaps that was the downfall of those before her. Or perhaps he had nothing to do with their demise at all. She had just needed to get through the night and then reevaluate.

It had begun in the pool, in the secluded waterfall cove she had spotted from the kitchen window. Even back then she had

139

imagined that was where he took his women to seduce them, and she was right. No swimsuits meant no barriers, and it wasn't long before he had taken full advantage of that. For round two, they relocated to the bedroom, leaving a trail of wet footprints behind them.

Rebecca had turned it off...her fear...her defensive instinct. She had to. He needed to trust her. He needed to believe she wanted to be there, and once she had muted the paranoid voice in her head, she *did* want to be there. Her untamed thrashing and primal screams were testament to that. Perhaps it was the essence of danger that surrounded him, or the highly-experienced lover that Andrew was, but he had unleashed a side of her that even she hadn't seen before.

Rebecca remained in bed for a few more minutes, contemplating the night before and what it had meant. She could not allow herself to develop feelings for him. She had a job to do, and whether she succeeded or failed, it was going to change his life, or hers, or both. What happened between them the night before was simply a vacation from reality. It wasn't real, and the two of them would never have a real relationship. When she was done, someone would be in prison or someone would be dead. She was, of course, hoping for the former, but either way, neither of them would come out unscathed.

With her motivation back on track, Rebecca rose and gingerly crossed the room. She paused in front of the window and peered at the pool below. She spotted her clothes from the night before in a crumpled heap on the deck. Her brows furrowed. *Well that's inconvenient.*

Ducking into the master bathroom, she washed up and yanked Andrew's robe off the hook on the back of the door. With her nakedness covered, she proceeded to take a slow lap around the bedroom, exploring the closet and peeking in drawers. Tidy, organized, and boring. There were no secrets hiding under the bed or in the closet as far as she could tell.

The rumbling in her stomach put a stop to her fruitless detective work. She was famished. Cinching the robe's belt tight around her waist, she slowly opened the door and peeked out before stepping into the hallway. She made her way toward the front of the house and stopped at the top of the staircase, one foot dangling over the first step. She listened. She didn't know when Spencer would return from his camping trip, but she was pretty confident it wouldn't be that early. Still, her breaths slowed as she cocked her head, listening for any sign of life besides her own coming from within the house. No sound from a television, no clanging from the kitchen, no footsteps anywhere.

She looked over her shoulder. The hallway leading to Spencer's room was quiet and still, lit only partially by the sunlight beaming through the large foyer window. Her pulse quickened as she looked out the front window to the deserted driveway leading away from the house. She listened again, tucking her hair behind her ear to eliminate any impedance. Turning away from the stairs, she darted down the hall before she had a chance to change her mind.

Standing with her ear to his door and her hand on the knob, she inched the door open little by little until she was sure the room was empty. Once inside, she stood motionless with her back against the door, scanning the room left to right. The blackout shades were raised and natural light filled the room. The drafting table by the window was empty and clear. The unfinished puzzle that had last cluttered it was intact and hanging on the wall above the bed, secured tightly in a poster frame.

She hadn't noticed it the other night, but now, looking around, Rebecca learned that although Spencer was not as tidy as his father, he was still far neater than she had expected a teenaged boy to be. The bed was roughly made, but made nonetheless. A sock and shirt or two littered the floor directly in front of the hamper. The top of his dresser was cluttered with track trophies, half-full water bottles, and piles of spare change. Other than that, the room was relatively clean.

Rebecca's sense of urgency returned and she immediately dashed toward the desk across from the foot of the bed. He had taken his laptop with him, evidenced by the rectangular void on the desk surface accompanied by a power cord hanging unplugged off the side. Rolling the office chair away, she stepped in and opened the top drawer. Assorted markers and pens, a calculator, a ruler, and other typical school supplies.

She then plucked out a hard plastic blue box with a hinged lid. Expecting to find it filled with art pencils, her eyes widened as she opened the box and a glimmer of light escaped. Neatly secured within were an array of stainless steel surgical tools. Varying sizes of scalpels, tweezers, scissors, and alcohol wipes indicative of an anatomy class dissecting kit. She had owned a similar one in high school. The outward design had changed over the years, but the contents were the same.

She snapped the lid shut, put the box back in the drawer, and continued her search, rifling through the remaining drawers. Amidst the array of random scrap paper and spiral notebooks, a thick forest green folder grabbed her attention. She lifted it out of the drawer, careful not to disturb the reddish-brown smudge on the lower right corner. Opening the folder, she gasped at its contents. Rebecca pulled out a collection of news articles printed off the internet. Estimating roughly fifty or sixty sheets, she spread them across the desk surface.

Large inkblot shapes of dried blood blocked out most of the type on many of the articles. She recalled the last and only time she had been there in his room, and from that she knew exactly what he had been doing while reading them. She pushed the papers around with her fingers, examining them as quickly as she could. The articles covered everything...the murders...the investigations...his father's arrest.

She shuffled them around again and tears pricked her eyes and spilled over when she saw Sara's eyes staring back at her. It was all too real. Rebecca had done her best to bury her sister's memory, at least when she was with Andrew. She needed to stay focused and unemotional. But seeing her like that, with spatters of blood framing her beautiful face...the floodgates opened, and Rebecca collapsed on the chair in a sobbing mess.

Nearly fifteen minutes passed before her cries were interrupted by the sound of a door slamming shut. The front door. She froze. Her breath caught in her throat and she threw her hands over her mouth to stifle the gasping cough that followed. She heard the clang of metal against glass—specifically, a set of keys landing in the bowl in the foyer. Shooting upright out of the chair, she quickly gathered up the sheets of paper and stuffed them into the folder, unaware if they were originally in any particular order. Shoving the folder back into the drawer, she gently rolled the chair back in place and made it to the door in three giant strides. She sidled into the hall and pulled the door closed, holding the knob to avoid a loud click as it latched. Hurrying down the hallway, her bare feet were inaudible on the plush carpet. She turned the corner and stopped in her tracks at the sight before her.

"Where are you running off to?" Tyler seemed larger than she remembered him as he blocked the sunlight coming in the front window. "Or maybe a better question is...where are you running *from*?"

His gaze ran the length of her, much like the first time she met him in the library, only slower. A hungry grin grew on his face as his eyes paused and lingered on her chest. She followed his eyes and saw that the robe had opened slightly and a part of her left breast was peeking out. She pulled the edges together with both hands and overlapped them tightly. She took a step to the side in an effort to move past him, but he placed an outstretched arm against the wall, blocking her exit. His eyebrows arched in question as he remained there, waiting for her answer.

"Sorry. You scared me," she said with a nervous giggle. Running possible excuses through her head, she stalled for more time. "I'm in a robe."

"I can see that." He didn't budge and also didn't seem to care how uncomfortable she felt talking to him as underdressed as she was. In fact, it was obvious he quite enjoyed it.

"I slept over last night."

"I know."

Rebecca fought hard to control the shaking that had taken over her body. "How did you know? I thought you and Spencer were out camping or something."

"That was the plan." He removed his hand and leaned his back against the wall. His foot rose and planted on the opposite side, still managing a successful blockade. He wasn't subtle and didn't try to hide the fact that he was holding her there, whether she liked it or not. "It was too hot. We aborted the whole camping thing and came back here hoping to swim instead."

Her chest began to heave. She was sure no one was home when they returned from the fireworks. "And you couldn't?" She knew the answer even before she asked.

"Nope. The pool was already occupied." His smile broadened as his gaze, once again, toured over her body.

She felt sick. The color drained from her face as she replayed the previous night's events in her mind. She and Andrew were in the pool when Spencer and Tyler got home. They were having sex. They ran naked through the house to his bedroom. She was mortified. Her color returned as a wave of heat rushed over her cheeks.

Standing upright, Tyler moved closer to Rebecca, but she stood her ground. He was trying to rattle her, and was doing a damn fine job, but she refused to let him know that. Another step closed the distance between them and he began to trace a lazy finger along the edge of the robe where it met her sternum. She slapped his hand away as her fear morphed into anger.

"Oh…feisty. That's fun," he laughed. "Come on. I've already seen what's under there anyway."

His behavior was shocking to her. He hadn't been like that before. She had left after dinner the other night with the notion that Tyler was the most gentlemanly teenager she had ever met. Her savior, even. Her mistake had been thinking of him as a teenager in the first place. He was only seventeen or eighteen years old, but he had the build of a full-grown man. She had never considered him a threat. He was just a kid, after all. Wrong. Andrew's absence had emboldened him to an extraordinary degree.

He ceased his advancement and displayed his palms. "Okay. I get it. You're not ready yet. But just remember…" His brow narrowed and he dug his thumb into his chest as he leaned in. "…*I* get his leftovers."

Rebecca's hands trembled as she cinched the robe tighter. He took a step back, finally giving her room to breathe.

Crossing his arms across his chest he said, "You never answered my question. What are you doing here?"

"I told you. I slept over."

"Here. What are you doing *here*?"

She had forgotten how suspicious she appeared, standing outside of Spencer's room when Spencer wasn't even home. "I was just looking at the puzzles." She turned from him and gestured further down the wall. "I didn't get a good look at them before and...they're really quite amazing."

"Uh huh." He tilted his head back and looked down his nose at her.

He didn't believe her, and she didn't care. All she wanted to do was get away from him as quickly as she could. She wasn't all that worried about him running off and telling Andrew about her suspicious exploration. Actually, she was rather confident that he wouldn't want Andrew to know about their encounter at all. He thought too highly of Tyler, and Tyler wouldn't want to do anything to jeopardize that. And as much as he implied that Andrew was okay with sharing, she knew better. There was a reason that Tyler was respectful and full of manners when he was around. Andrew was an Alpha...and Alphas didn't share.

At that, Tyler stepped to the side, allowing her an exit. Rebecca scurried past him and never looked back. Her hunger could wait. What she needed more than food was to get the hell out of there.

Chapter 22

The black Audi rumbled slowly over the long gravel driveway. Every pebble the tires kicked out into the car's undercarriage brought more and more peace to Rebecca's swirling mind. The loud pings of rock against metal echoed through the vehicle's interior and made Andrew wince and grimace, but to Rebecca, it was the sound of sweet freedom. Freedom from the utter madness that inhabited the Donovan house.

She hadn't been back since her run-in with Tyler. All week she had made excuses about why she couldn't go back to the house. She told Andrew she was picking up extra shifts at the hospital due to several nurses being on vacation. It had sounded like a fool-proof plan, until he texted her from the hospital lobby one day, asking if she had a free moment to help him eat the take-out lunch he had picked up from across the street. Luckily, nurses' schedules were known to be chaotic and unpredictable and he didn't have the clearance to get up to the surgical floor to check for himself. He had reluctantly accepted that she couldn't see him and went on his way. However, she knew her luck would run out at some point. He was clearly frustrated, thinking her avoidance of him had something to do with their Fourth of July lovemaking.

She hadn't told him about Tyler and had no idea if he knew that they were being watched that night. Either way, her head was spinning and she needed time away to think. Not necessarily away from him...just away...which was why his suggestion of a weekend at his lake house was music to her ears.

They had been driving for almost two hours, deep into Virginia, and the further away they got, the more her mind cleared. When they finally pulled off the paved road and onto gravel, she could hardly contain her excitement. Rebecca hadn't taken a full weekend off since she took over co-ownership of the restaurant with Peter's father. La Croix D'ior was her baby, and she could have never entertained the thought of leaving it in someone else's hands until now. She had trained Peter well and had full confidence in his skills. He had run the kitchen without her several times recently and had proven himself to be more than capable. A deep sigh escaped her lips as she put Peter, the restaurant, and all of her responsibilities out of her mind.

They came to a stop in front of a beautiful brick rancher with a wrap-around porch. Andrew turned off the engine and leaned back into his seat, his head tilting upward against the headrest. He closed his eyes and inhaled deeply. She watched him. It appeared as though he needed the trip just as much as she did.

"Ready?" he asked as his eyes fluttered open.

"More than ready." She smiled broadly, flung open the door, and jumped out, not even waiting for him. Her hands stretched upward as far as they could reach and she gave a quick twist of her torso.

"Go ahead and explore. I'll get the bags," Andrew said from behind the open trunk.

She didn't need to be told twice. She took off further down the gravel path at a quick trot as it bent around the back of the house and toward the dock. As she neared the water's edge, her pace slowed and she stepped onto the forty-foot pier. Halfway along, the wooden walkway expanded into a square landing. A large pavilion roof shaded five Adirondack chairs circling a small portable fire pit. Rebecca ran a relaxed finger across the back of a chair as she strolled past and imagined sitting out there on a cool night with a glass of wine. After she came out from under the roof, another ten feet of pier extended into the water. She stepped up and leaned over the guard railing, peering into the dark water. Even with the low visibility, she still managed to spot two or three small fish swimming around the pier's support legs.

Her eyes rose and she gazed off across the water. The lake stretched as far as she could see. Only two houses were in her range of sight, and both of them were a good distance away and shrouded in greenery. It was quiet, the only sound coming from birds far off in the distance. The water was still and motionless, with not a single boat to send a lonely ripple her way.

She was fully aware of the oddity of the silence surrounding her. It was late morning on a Saturday in July. The lake should have been buzzing with people. She attributed the water's emptiness to her location. Andrew's house rested within one of the long arms that jutted out from the lake's main body. With only two other houses in the immediate area, the lack of activity might not have been that odd after all, especially if they were currently vacant.

She turned back toward the house. The rancher sat atop a gentle slope about fifty feet from the water. Towering oaks and dogwoods formed an impenetrable canopy while still leaving the ground area uncluttered. Just then, the doors off the patio slid open and Andrew emerged, trotting down the path in her direction. Leaning back and resting her arms on the railing behind her, she lifted her face to the sun and savored its heat as she patiently waited for him to reach her.

"Nice, isn't it?" he said as he sidled into the space next to her.

"Peaceful."

He mimicked her by draping his arms over the railing and also tilting his face to the sun.

"Why is it so quiet? Where is everyone?"

"This part of the lake doesn't get much action...which is exactly why I chose it."

Rebecca cracked one eye to steal a glance at him. His neck glistened with sweat, dampening the collar of his gray V-neck. The observation brought to her attention just how hot it was out there next to the water and away from the coolness of the shaded canopy. A wave of heat suddenly washed over her and her legs became wobbly.

"Let's get you out of the sun," he said, noticing her sinking frame and vacant expression. Throwing her arm around his neck, he walked her forward to the shade of the pavilion and lowered her into a chair before taking a seat himself.

"I'm usually fine with heat. I don't know why it's affecting me like this." She immediately felt better and the droplets on her arms caused her skin to tingle as they cooled. She took a deep breath and followed it with a forceful exhale. "That came out of nowhere."

"Maybe it's because you're hungry."

She *was* hungry. She didn't realize it until he had mentioned it, but she was actually famished.

"We need to hit the grocery store anyway." He stood and extended both hands out to her. "Are you okay to move? The sooner you eat, the better you'll feel. We can get an early lunch in town before grabbing some dinner items for later."

She held his hands tight as he lifted her. "Are we eating in tonight?"

"Of course. The restaurants around here aren't that great and..." He flashed her a sideways grin. "...you promised to one day make me some scallops."

"I did?" Rebecca asked, confused.

"Yep. Coquilles Saint-Jacques. Your specialty, I believe."

"Whoa, I just said I knew how to make it. I didn't promise anything."

"You are just so adorable when the heat fries your brain. I distinctly remember you saying, 'I would love to make Coquilles for you. Anything for my man.'" He laughed as he kissed the side of her forehead.

His falsetto impression of her left much to be desired. Under any other circumstances she would have probably been a little offended, but she looked forward to a good meal and knew that no one in that little vacation town could cook like her. His lie didn't go unnoticed, however, but he was practically drooling and it was the least she could have done.

"Coquilles, it is then," she said, pumping a confident fist in the air. Then, a little sweeter, and accompanied with the appropriate amount of eyelash fluttering, she said, "Anything for my man."

<hr>

She drifted down the pier behind him, two stemmed glasses in her left hand and a bottle of Pinot Noir in her right. She set them atop the tabletop fire pit cover before she sat and flapped open a thick quilted placemat and set it across her lap. Andrew lowered the steaming plate onto her protected thighs as she breathed in the salty aroma. She had never thought of that particular dish as lakefront picnic fare, but she was pleasantly surprised with the outcome. The scent of the butter and garlic blended with the enormous scallops mingled perfectly with the cool evening breeze and the glowing orange and purple sky mirroring off the water.

Andrew filled the two glasses and handed her one. Holding his up, he toasted, "To one of the most beautiful women I've ever laid eyes on."

One of many. We all look the same. Rebecca kept her thoughts to herself and flashed him a shy smile instead. Clinking his glass, she filled her mouth with the wine to prevent her from speaking her mind.

"Wow," he said, his mouth half-full.

"You like it?"

"This is amazing." His eyes were wide as he swallowed.

She giggled at his obvious excitement.

"No, you don't understand. This is one of my favorite dishes and I've had it more times than I can remember at the best restaurants across the country." He took another bite and, once again, didn't wait to swallow. "I've never had it like this."

"Well, I'm glad I can impress you."

"Oh, I'm beyond impressed. What's in here that's different?" He pointed at his plate with his fork.

"A chef never gives away her secrets," she said smugly, hoping he didn't catch the irony of what she had just said.

"I'll get it out of you somehow," he teased.

Rebecca took a bite herself. He was right...it *was* amazing. She washed it down with another sip of wine and changed the subject before she got herself into trouble.

"So, do you have any brothers or sisters?"

"Nope. Just me."

"Where do your parents live? Are they local?" She watched his shoulders tense at her questions.

"My parents are dead."

"Oh, I'm sorry. I didn't know." The awkward turn of the conversation was almost palpable. Not knowing how to retrace her steps, she forged on. "Both of them?"

"Yes. Simultaneously." He stared into his glass, swirling the red liquid. "It was a car accident. A pile-up on Ninety-Five. Some idiot truck driver jackknifed his semi and...game over." He downed the rest of his wine and refilled.

"That's horrible." Rebecca truly felt sorry for him. To lose both parents at the same time without warning was devastating, and she could see it still affected him. "How old were you?"

"I was in college. It was a long time ago...before Spencer was born." His voice was gruff and low.

She had definitely gone down the wrong path. In one quick moment he'd gone from culinary heaven to parentless hell. He stabbed at his food in silence, his brow cinching tighter and tighter. She had no idea how to close the wounds she had just opened...so she empathized with him the only way she knew how.

"I know how you feel."

He snapped his head toward her and gave her a look that pinned her to the back of her chair. "Do you?"

"Yes, I do," she snapped back with confidence. She wasn't going to let him intimidate her. As far as she was concerned, she had lost far more than he had and in a far more horrendous way. "My sister. I lost her too. Very recently."

His brows relaxed and slanted upward in concern. "I guess you do know how I feel." His voice was softer. Understanding. "How did it happen?"

"Like you. A car accident." She wouldn't dare tell him the real story. "She was driving home from work one night and a drunk driver crossed the center line and hit her head-on."

"Did he live?"

"He did. He was in a Suburban and she was in a convertible. No contest."

"Is he at least in prison now?"

"He was...for a little bit."

"How little?"

"Sixty days."

"What? Why only sixty days? A DUI that ends in a fatality is murder!"

"He had a good lawyer. As a matter of fact, he had a great lawyer." Rebecca wasn't necessarily throwing jabs at Andrew and his attorney. It was simply a good example of how people could get away with murder...whether they were the ones in the courtroom or not. People *did* get away with murder all the time. Rebecca's fingers wrapped tightly around her glass, and her blood began to run hot as crime scene photos flashed through her mind. Her sister's murderer had yet to face his punishment. He could have been sitting right in front of her, or he could have been where she had just come from. Whichever it was—whoever it was—he was still free.

Anger rose up inside her as she clutched her hand into a tight fist followed by the earsplitting shatter of glass. In a flash, Andrew was crouched at her feet, taking her hand in his. She looked down at her hand and all she saw was red, streaming down her arm and spattering off the wood decking. She waited for the pain, but it never came. It wasn't blood. It was the red wine. Andrew relaxed when he drew the same conclusion, but continued to wipe her hand and arm with napkins.

"I'm sorry," she said, a little embarrassed.

"Don't be. I completely understand. It's hard to move on without justification, isn't it? When you lose someone you love purely because of some stupid moron's actions?" Her hand was clean, but he continued to wipe it while he continued his rant. "Makes you want to tie them to tree and cut them in half with your car."

"Yes," she said with a satisfied smile. "Vengeance would be golden."

Chapter 23

Rebecca grabbed the handle inside the door to brace herself as the car took the sharp right turn onto Andrew's street. It had been a good weekend. There had been a few awkward and uncomfortable moments, but all in all, a good weekend. As much as she was ready to go home and relax alone, she wished she could put it off a little longer. She was dreading going back to his house to pick up her car, wondering why she hadn't asked him to pick her up at the hospital after a false on-call shift. She hadn't seen the harm in meeting him at his house. They left at the crack of dawn on Saturday, and she knew there would be little chance of encounters with Spencer or Tyler, but she hadn't considered picking up her car when they got back. She wondered if it would be rude to just jump in her car from the driveway without entering the house.

"I can't wait to get back home and sleep for five more hours," she said, prepping Andrew for her upcoming rapid departure.

"Want some company?" He gave her a wink before returning his eyes to the road.

"You know that would defeat the whole purpose of sleeping, right?"

"I guess so." He accepted her decline without a fight. "I need to run into the office anyway."

They turned onto his driveway and began the long journey toward the house. The car slowed as they rounded the bend and the house came into view. Andrew leaned forward in his seat to get a closer look.

"What the hell?"

Rebecca saw it too. A black SUV parked sideways, effectively blocking two of the garage doors. A squad car was parked behind it, blocking the other two. She didn't know if that was their strategy, but it was clear no one was leaving until they did. Her forehead wrinkled, wondering why they were there in the first place. She felt a sick feeling in her stomach as she thought of what kind of trouble Spencer and Tyler had gotten into while being left alone all weekend.

Andrew bypassed the garage and stopped the car at the front door. His face said it all. He was not happy that police were inside his house without his direct supervision. He leaped out of the car, hopped onto the porch, and threw open the front door. Rebecca followed close behind. Standing in the open doorway, he paused for a moment, listening. She heard it too. Voices. Multiple voices coming from the direction of the dining room.

He crossed the marble in three elongated steps and stopped at the archway. From the dining table, the backs of two unfamiliar heads sitting atop cheap suits came into view. One of them scribbled frantically in a small spiral notebook while the other leaned forward on his elbows, staring at the two boys across from them. Standing behind the boys was a uniformed officer, arms crossed and over-acting his authoritative pose.

Spencer's head was buried in his folded arms. His entire body was shaking, while Tyler, his face a mixture of focus and compassion, tried to calm his friend from the adjacent seat. Spencer's head lifted and his red swollen eyes locked onto his father. His jaw clenched and his fingers curled into fists on the table. The suits took his cue and turned around.

"What's going on here?" Andrew said, his voice deep and aggressive.

As the heads turned, Rebecca realized they weren't that unfamiliar after all. She recognized both of them from court. Detective Harmon, the fifty-something, plump and balding lead on the case, and his shadow, whose name she couldn't remember.

"Why are you in my house badgering my son?"

Harmon closed his notebook and stood up. "Ahh...Mr. Donovan. Nice of you to grace us with your presence. We'd like to talk to you too." His tone was laced with smugness as he clicked his pen and slid it inside his jacket.

"About?"

"About the new body we've just added to the Marie Donovan Collection."

"Say again."

"How about I show you, instead?" Harmon flipped open a manila folder and spread half a dozen photos across the table's surface. "Take a look," he said, stepping to the side.

Andrew approached the table and picked up one of the photos. Eyeing it closely, he then dropped it back on the table and picked up another. "I don't know who this is."

"No?" Harmon said with disbelief. "This isn't another one of yours?"

"No," he answered sternly. He then tossed the photo back and turned toward the detective. Standing toe to toe with him, he squared his shoulders and puffed his chest. Harmon matched him and testosterone filled the room.

"Alright, so let's go ahead and get this over with," Andrew said, as he pulled out a chair and took his seat. He sat stiff and motionless, his face full of irritation. He glanced over at Spencer, who was still shooting daggers out of his eyes at him.

"Very well." Harmon looked at Rebecca and motioned to her. "Ma'am," he said, pointing to the seat at the head of the table.

Rebecca trembled as she followed the detective's instruction and took her place at the table. The morning was getting worse by the minute, and she knew it was just getting started. Her anxiety at having to deal with Spencer and Tyler was long forgotten. Her new task was trying to survive a police interrogation...one of the many important things she had overlooked during her planning phase.

Walking around the table, Harmon smoothed his tie and took the seat directly across from Andrew. Shadow, his younger and obviously less experienced partner, slid the notebook across the table into Harmon's reach. Flipping it open, he retrieved his pen from inside his jacket and gave it a click.

His focus immediately turned to Rebecca. His dark eyes sized her up several times before returning to his notes. "Unbelievable," he mumbled under his breath.

His utterance was almost inaudible, but she heard it nonetheless and knew exactly what he was thinking. How stupid she must have looked to them, looking the way she did, after all that had happened regarding Andrew over the past year.

"And who might you be?" Detective Harmon stared hard at her.

She became increasingly more uncomfortable. His eyes were full of suspicion and they shifted with each tiny movement she made. The subconscious hair tuck...the clasping of her fingers under the table as she attempted to minimize the shaking...the repeated crossing and uncrossing of her legs. He was studying her, getting a read on her before she even opened her mouth. The tilt of his head and squint of his eyes made her wonder if he somehow recognized her. He had not been one of the officers that interviewed her, but he had surely at least seen her picture in the case file. More than ever before, she prayed her new appearance was as good as she thought it was.

Events of the last two and a half months flashed through her mind. She had learned so much since then and was uncovering more and more every day, though she still had more questions than answers and it was clear her work was far from done. A wave of strength and obligation washed over her as she realized that she just might be the only hope of finding the truth and exposing it. She certainly could do a better job than the two detectives sitting before her. She was somewhere they could never be. She was inside. Inside the Donovan house and living the Donovan life. New confidence filled her as a feeling of superiority straightened her back and lifted her chin.

"Amanda," she answered with conviction. "Amanda White."

He jotted in his notebook. "And your relationship with Andrew Donovan?"

"We're seeing each other."

"Romantically?"

"Yes. *Very* romantically." The corner of her mouth raised in a subtle smile as she watched the intimidation fade from the detective's face.

"How long?"

"A month or two."

"And did you know anything about him before the two of you started dating?"

"I knew *everything* about him." She gazed at Andrew like a naive schoolgirl as she clasped his hand and interlocked their fingers. She enjoyed taunting the detective, but began to wonder if she was taking it too far. The last thing she wanted to do was paint herself as an accomplice.

"Look, let's just cut to the chase, alright?" Harmon tossed his pen down and leaned forward on his forearms. "You know that this man was arrested for the murder of four women. Four women who he had been seeing...*very* romantically." His tone became stern and impatient as he emphasized his words. "Four women who looked just like you." He leaned back in his chair, chuckling with disbelief. "What am I missing?"

Andrew's fingers tightened around hers, and she knew he was fast approaching his tolerance limit. With her free hand, she gave him a gentle pat. "If I remember correctly, he was acquitted of all charges. You sort of forgot to mention that."

"Lack of evidence doesn't equate with lack of crime." The vein in the detective's temple began to twitch as he fought to control his frustration.

"I didn't say there was lack of a crime. It's pretty damn obvious that a crime was committed. It just didn't happen here." She remained calm and monotonous which, in turn, irritated the detective even more.

"Are you kidding me, right now? Are you really that dumb?"

Andrew shot out of his chair. "That's enough!" He yanked his hand out of Rebecca's and slammed both palms on the table. Leaning halfway across, he looked down his nose at Detective Harmon and lowered his voice to a chilling growl. "Either arrest me...or get the hell out of my house."

Harmon stood, taking away Andrew's higher position. "Where were you on Saturday between the hours of ten a.m. and four p.m?"

"At my lake house...a two-hour drive from here."

"Can anyone verify your location besides Ms. White here?"

"Only my credit card company, the surveillance camera at the gas station, and my phone's GPS." Andrew removed his hands from the table and stood tall, reestablishing his height advantage.

"How is it you always happen to be conveniently out of town when these bodies show up? That can't be just a coincidence, can it?"

"Maybe you should ask whoever's setting me up. He'll probably tell you that he needs me to be out of town so he can break into my house and ransack my knives," Andrew said through clenched teeth.

"Oh, you have it all figured out, don't you?"

From her seat at the head of the table, Rebecca looked in between the two men and toward the other end of the table where Spencer and Tyler sat silently. Tyler's face glowed with admiration. His eyes darted back and forth between Andrew and Detective Harmon as their eyes shot daggers at each other. She knew the immense amount of respect Tyler had for Andrew, and the pissing contest between the two men was fueling his fire.

Spencer's eyes, still puffy and red, were fixed on one of the photos that had floated across the table. From where she was sitting, Rebecca couldn't see the photo, but she had plenty more just like it scattered right in front of her. The men standing above her continued to argue, but she heard none of it. Her finger reached out and dragged one of them closer.

A chill traveled up her spine as she stared at the all-too-familiar scene depicted in the picture. A plastic cocoon, split down the middle revealing the cold, lifeless figure inside. The trademark patchwork pattern indicating the same handiwork as the other four women Harmon was referring to.

Rebecca reached for another photo. It wasn't from the crime scene. Possibly from a passport or driver's license. She looked at it closely and was confident she had never seen the woman before. The picture began to shake as the fingers holding it trembled uncontrollably. *She was new. It wasn't over.*

Her thoughts shattered as Andrew's booming voice echoed throughout the room.

"—not another word without my lawyer present. We're done here."

"Oh, I'm not even close to being done. You contact your lawyer and we'll talk again." Detective Harmon gathered up the array of photos and stuffed them into the folder. "You're not getting rid of me that easily."

Andrew backed up and stopped in the archway. His brows were cinched tightly together as his lips pressed into a thin, hard line. He crossed his arms over his chest and fire spat from his eyes as he watched the detectives pack up their files.

Harmon walked slowly around the table, his shadow and the uniform following close behind. He came to a stop in front of Andrew. A smile cracked his lips as he stared hard into Andrew's eyes.

"You know your way out," Andrew said.

His smile widened and a deep chuckle escaped. "This isn't over." He turned toward Rebecca, still sitting quietly at the table. "Just remember, Ms. White...whether he did this or not, the facts remain the same. Someone is targeting his girlfriends. Someone is targeting Marie look-alikes...which all means that someone will soon be targeting *you*."

Chapter 24

Rebecca could hear the voices coming from the other room. She had hung back after the detectives had left, sitting at the dining room table, completely overwhelmed and unsure of what to do next. This was a family affair, and she was clearly the outsider. However, her involvement by association couldn't be denied. Finally, she rose from her seat and made her way to the kitchen.

"We were here the whole time," she heard Spencer say. "No one came in, no one went out."

Rebecca entered the kitchen but remained hovering in the doorway. Andrew stood at the center counter, facing her, and Spencer and Tyler sat on stools across from him. Spencer heard her footsteps and gave her a glance over his shoulder. The fire she was usually greeted with was absent, replaced by what could have been interpreted as concern. He quickly dismissed her and turned back around. His anger was directed solely at his father. He blamed him for everything that was happening, and Rebecca couldn't help herself from wondering if there was a logical reason for it.

"And my knives?" Andrew looked at Tyler who, in turn, appeared rather bored of the entire conversation. "Ty?"

"All accounted for," Tyler answered.

Andrew released a long drawn-out sigh. "The last thing I need is Detective Douchebag camping out up my ass." He immediately looked over at Rebecca. "Sorry. And I'm sorry you got dragged into all of this."

"She didn't get dragged. She came willingly. And now she's a target." Spencer turned once again and snapped at her. "You did understand that part, right?" His tone was sharp but still lacked the rage she was so accustomed to hearing. Turning back to the counter, he mumbled under his breath. "Shouldn't have come back."

"Enough," Andrew said sharply. "Look, I've got some calls to make so...just keep your head down, and don't talk to anyone." He directed his comment at Spencer. "Can you manage that?"

"Of course." Spencer rose from his stool. "Don't forget...I've done this before."

He shoved his seat back under the counter and motioned to Tyler. The two of them headed for the kitchen's exit. Rebecca stepped to the side as Spencer approached. He gave her a look of complete indifference and continued on his way. Tyler followed close behind him. He sent a slight nod and a wink her way before they both disappeared down the short corridor. Their footsteps pounded on the staircase as they headed upstairs.

She turned back to Andrew to find him staring at her. Not knowing how he expected her to act, her lips began to curl into a nervous smile. She quickly dialed it back as she watched his eyebrows slowly rise. His palms drummed a few beats on the counter and he stepped out from behind it and headed toward her. He paused to plant a quick kiss on her cheek.

"It'll all work out," he said before passing through the doorway. His tone lifted as he continued down the hall. "Spence is right. We have been through this before."

Rebecca took her cue and followed him, catching up to him as he entered the foyer.

"Stamina is vital right now." He crossed the marble floor in long easy strides and stepped through the narrow archway into his office. "Their strategy is to wear you down. Torture you with endless interrogations. Show up at your work. Plaster your face all over the media."

Rebecca's strides were short and quick as she struggled to keep up with him. She entered the office and turned the corner to find him already at the far end of the room. He grabbed the armrest of an upholstered chair and dragged it out from against the wall, resting his hand on its back until she sat. He then stepped behind his massive desk and took his own seat.

"Their goal..." He rolled his chair to the side and pulled the keyboard drawer out from under his monitor. Glancing across his desk at her, he continued, "...is to wear you down so much you simply give up..." He turned his attention back to the large screen and his fingers began typing furiously. "...cop to the crime whether you did it or not. Just to get everyone off your back." His fingers paused as he leaned forward, squinting at the search results on the monitor. "But they should know by now who they're dealing with." Swiveling his head in her direction, he caught her eyes again. "I don't give up. I don't lose."

Rebecca's mind raced as she remained quiet in her seat, listening to his call-to-arms speech. Gone was the gentle, thoughtful, romantic man she thought she had gotten to know in the past months. The gloves were off, and he was, once again, defending himself. Playtime was over. She could see it in his eyes; he was preparing for war.

She hadn't yet said a word, and he hadn't seemed to notice. The clicking of the keyboard broke the silence, which otherwise would have seemed awkward and uncomfortable. She needed the silence. She needed a few moments to wrap her head around the current situation. *Another woman was dead. The killing hadn't stopped even with her close proximity. How accurate was the medical examiner's time of death estimate? Detective Harmon seemed rather confident of it.* Her brain was drowning in new information, speculation, and more and more questions.

"Ah, here we go," Andrew said, moving the mouse across the pad. "Not much up yet." His eyes darted back and forth as he read the lines on the screen in silence.

"What does it say?"

"Pretty much what we can already guess. Saturday evening...body found in Rock Creek Park...same M.O...same victimology."

"Could be a copycat."

Andrew's head snapped toward her and his brows narrowed. "Or...it could be the same bastard who's been doing it all along."

Rebecca kicked herself. "What I meant was...whoever really did it could have gotten scared and stopped. And some other random person, a fan perhaps, could have picked it up."

"Do you think it was me?" Andrew's eyes pierced her and the muscle in his jaw twitched.

"Of course not. You were with me all weekend."

"No, before. Do you think I'm guilty of killing those first four women?" His eyes pinned her to her seat.

Rebecca's eyes widened and her pulse pounded. The seriousness in his voice took her by surprise, and she felt a chill on the back of her neck. She collected her nerves and swallowed hard. "No. I already told you that a long time ago. I wouldn't be here if I thought otherwise."

His cold eyes continued their attack on her senses, penetrating her. They didn't look away. Instead, they held her there for what seemed like hours. Eventually, his head dipped into a slow nod of acceptance, and he returned to his computer. She didn't realize she had been holding her breath until it began to escape her lips. She fought to control it and waited for the keyboard clicking to resume before allowing it to seep out. She tried to control her heart pounding in her chest, but it was no use. It was the first time she had truly been on the receiving end of his paralyzing gaze. With just a look, he had sent her back to those long weeks inside that courtroom. All the confidence and invincibility she had built up as Amanda White, stripped away in seconds.

Her eyes darted around the room, looking frantically for a distraction. She struggled to resist the one area her eyes were trying to lead her to. Instead, she watched him for a moment. His brows were cinched tight and low over his eyes. His breathing was loud and fast, flaring his nostrils with every inhale. The more she watched him, the more her breathing began to match his own. She diverted her attention to the large window behind him. The blinds were half open, giving the dark room some much needed sunlight. She followed their rays to the rows of hardbound books lining the wall to her left.

Finally, she gave in and allowed her eyes their free rein. They immediately shot to the large glass case on the wall to her right. *Tyler was right. All the knives were there.* That didn't really mean anything, though. A killer could stab a person with just about anything. Using one of Andrew's knives was simply what linked them to him...what made it personal. Andrew said he didn't know the latest victim. Maybe it was just a random copycat. A copycat with no access to his knives and no access to his women.

She still didn't feel safe, and Detective Harmon's words continued to ring loud and clear in her head. "Target."

Chapter 25

The door slammed shut behind Rebecca and she leaned back against it, not yet ready to take a second step. Her purse dropped to the floor by her feet with a loud thump. Her eyes closed and her chest deflated with a long, forceful exhale.

"So good to be home," she said to no one but herself.

She had never wanted a few hours to herself more than she did right then. The tension was so thick at the Donovan house she actually felt herself physically suffocating. It was all in her head, but the near panic attack that followed was very real.

Reaching up next to her head, she slid the chain lock into place, before tossing her keys aside and heading for the kitchen. Her fingers rummaged around the drawer next to the sink and pulled out her phone. It was dead, of course, having been shut in a drawer for the past three days. She hadn't dared take her real phone anywhere near Andrew. She had picked up a disposable one for that.

She walked it over to the end table next to the sofa and dropped it into the charging dock. Collapsing on the sofa, she kicked off her shoes and lay there, staring at the ceiling.

A few minutes passed before she powered her phone on. Immediately, a stream of notification chimes began pouring out. Seven missed calls from Lexy, four from her mom, and three from Marcus. Wondering who to talk to first, the phone began ringing in her hand and made her choice for her.

"Hey."

"Where the hell have you been?" Lexy's voice shot through the earpiece.

"Calm down. What's up?"

"What's up? Seriously? Another girl was killed, that's what's up. Where have you been? I've been trying to call you all day. Went by your house, you weren't there." Lexy's words flew out of her mouth like rapid-fire, blending into each other until they were almost intelligible.

"Relax. I just went away for the weekend and didn't take my phone."

"Do you have any idea what I've been through today? Do you?"

"No, but I'm sure you're going to tell me."

"They found another body. Same as the others. They didn't release a name. For Christ's sake, Beck...I thought it was you!"

"Well you can see that it wasn't, so calm down."

"Were you with him? This weekend?"

"Yes, I was. He didn't do it."

"So it was someone else all along." Rebecca could hear the smugness in Lexy's voice, and imagined the smug smile on her face, even through the phone.

"I don't know about all along. I just know he didn't do this one." At that time, Rebecca didn't know what to think, so she thought it better not to speculate at all...at least not out loud. "I'm sure they'll investigate and compare and come out with new—" A firm knock on the front door halted her words in their tracks. "Are you here?"

"No, I'm at home. Why?"

"Someone's at my door." Rebecca's voice lowered into a whisper as her eyes grew wide and pinned the front door.

"And?"

"I don't get unannounced guests at my door...unless it's you." Lexy was silent on the other end. "Hang on...but don't hang up."

"Okay. I'm here."

Rebecca quickly but silently crossed the floor, her phone still stuck to her ear. She reached the front door and cracked it open an inch or three until the chain lost its slack. She peeked out through the small crack and immediately felt the color drain from her face.

"Damn," she muttered under her breath as she closed the door on the visitor. She put the phone to her ear. "Lex, I'll call you back later."

"Well, who is it?"

"No one important." She downplayed her surprise as much as she could. "I'll catch up with you tomorrow." Clicking off her phone and sliding it into her pocket, she unhooked the chain and swung the door open.

"Hello, Miss White...but that's not really your name, is it?"

"No, Detective Harmon, it's not."

"May I?"

She opened the door wider and stepped to the side. With a smug grin he stepped inside. His eyes did a quick sweep of his surroundings as he drifted a few feet further into the living room.

"Nice place," he said as he turned to face her.

She didn't reply. Her heart pounded despite her effort to keep her cool. Her mind raced with possible excuses she could give to explain her dishonesty.

His shoulders shrugged off her silence, and he walked over to the large leather chair in the corner. There he sat...and waited. She still hadn't decided what to say or how to explain herself. Stalling for a few more moments, she closed the door and took a seat on the sofa across from him. They sat in silence, staring at each other with blank expressions, neither wanting to give anything away. Their waiting game ventured into true awkwardness and he finally gave in.

"So...what *is* your name? And don't lie again. I already know your address. It'll take all of two seconds for me to find out for myself."

"And you didn't already check into all of that before you came here?"

"Oh, I did. I was just trying to establish a small measure of trust." He eyed her closely. "But I can see that point is moot now." He took his pen out of his jacket and flipped open his notebook. "Let's see...Rebecca Black. Age thirty. Head chef and co-owner of La Croix D'ior...am I saying that right?" He peered up from his notes, but she remained silent. "It's not important. Oh, and you've got the wrong plates on your car, in case you didn't know."

"How did you find me?"

"I always incorporate high-tech, state-of-the-art location tactics in my investigations." He gave a soft chuckle at the blank look on her face. "I followed you. From the Donovan residence. Looked you up when I got out to my car and discovered rather quickly that you definitely were *not* Amanda White."

"Since you already know everything about me, what more do you want me to tell you?"

"Why? Why lie?" Creases formed in his forehead as his eyes pierced hers. "Did you have something to do with this latest homicide...or with any of them?"

"No, of course not."

Harmon leaned forward, his face drawn taut and serious. "Don't think for one second that I think you're incapable of committing these crimes because you're a woman. The lack of sexual assault on the victims...the attention to detail...the perfectly neat and tidy handiwork. Now that I think about it, a woman would fit these crimes like a glove." He leaned back into the chair, letting his not-so-subtle accusations sink in. "Maybe Andrew Donovan was telling the truth after all. Maybe he was set up by a jealous, obsessive woman that wanted him all to herself. Good theory, don't you think?"

"That's not it," Rebecca said, shaking her head.

"Then what *is* it? If you don't give me something, you're forcing me to make up my own story."

Rebecca thought for a moment. She knew he didn't think she was involved in the killings. He was just trying to scare her, to get under her skin, so she would let some vital piece of information slip. He had to know she was related to one of the victims. If he didn't, he would know as soon as he went back over the files. She was never called as a witness, and she'd never had any facetime with the detective, but it was all there on record. He would find it eventually. It had probably been almost a year since he had gone through the paperwork where her name was mentioned. The differing last names helped, but Rebecca knew it wouldn't be long before his memory came through.

She thought of opening up and telling him the truth, but she wasn't sure if she trusted him or not. She was scared to death every minute of every day. She would love some help, to not have to go through it alone. But she didn't know if he could give her the kind of help she needed, and she couldn't risk finding out.

"I'm being careful," she said.

"Careful?"

"Yes, careful. I haven't been living in a bubble for the last year. I know what he's been accused of. He was found to be innocent, but I'm not naive enough to just pretend it didn't happen." Confidence began to seep into her pores as her story expanded inside her brain. "You said so yourself, Detective. I'm a target. I'm not going to let fear keep me from doing what I want to do or see who I want to see, but I'm also not going to go into it blind."

"Does he know who you really are?"

"Not exactly. A name is just a name. Until the killer is caught, I'd like to keep a bit of anonymity. When I feel it's safe to come clean, I will. But right now, what difference does it make what name he calls me?"

"So you don't think he's guilty."

"No. But I do think it could be someone who knows him. Or it could be a stalker who knows everything about him. Either way, he doesn't come to my house or my work, so anyone who's watching him and targeting me...won't know where to find me," she said with a satisfied smile.

"Unless they follow you. Like I did."

Her smile left just as quickly as it had come. "Yeah, I guess that could happen."

"Not could...will."

Her patience with him was wearing thin. She had a job to do and didn't need him in her head feeding her paranoia. "Detective Harmon, I truly appreciate your concern for my safety, really, I do. But I am a grown woman and I'm free to date whomever I please. I haven't broken any laws here."

"Except lying to the police."

"And I'm sorry about that. I'm just looking out for myself. If you had asked me those questions in private, instead of in front of Andrew, then I would have told you the truth from the beginning. You put me on the spot."

"Understood...I guess." Harmon closed his notebook and rose from the chair. Reaching into his shirt pocket, he pulled out a business card and handed it to her. "Feel free to call me, day or night."

"Thank you. I'll do that." She stood and took the card from him. Shoving it into her back pocket, she went to the door and waited with her hand on the doorknob.

Her hint was clear. She was done talking. He joined her at the door as she opened it, letting the hot July air overcome both of them.

"I mean it. Call me," he said, his eyes full of concern.

"If a reason comes up, then I will," she said with strong conviction. She knew he was just concerned for her welfare, but she couldn't have him popping up and checking in on her every day. She had to draw the line if she was going to finish what she started. He could end up getting her killed if he didn't back off.

The detective disappeared into the bright sunlight as she closed the door behind him. He would be back. As soon as he looked through those old files, and saw her name plastered all over Sara's investigation reports, he would be back; it was only a matter of time. She needed to finish the job before that time came.

Chapter 26

Andrew smiled as the hot plate was set in front of him. He leaned into it and inhaled the aromatic spices riding upward on clouds of steam. Wasting no time, he split the largest scallop in half and devoured it. His eyes closed and a soft moan grumbled low in his throat. He had been craving it nonstop since she had made it for him at the lake. He knew it wouldn't be as amazing as hers, yet somehow it was.

"You okay over there?" said the hulking man sitting across from him.

"You have no idea how incredible this is."

Andrew had known Dominic for over a decade and considered him one of his closest friends. Denver was where he hung his hat, but he had business dealings in Washington and came into town at least once a month. He had wanted to introduce him to Amanda but, as usual, the hospital had priority over her schedule.

"That asshole detective still on your case?"

"More like *back* on my case. I had a few months of peace from him, but now that this new thing popped up..."

"And your girlfriend? Will she vouch for you?"

"She will and she did. That's not going to satisfy him, though. He's on a witch-hunt."

Dominic nodded his head in silent agreement. "So, tell me about this new woman of yours."

"I'd rather show you. How long are you in town for?"

"I leave tomorrow. You know they never give me more than a couple days. In and out...story of my life."

"Maybe next month then," Andrew said with half a mouthful.

"You think she'll still be around a month from now?"

"Why wouldn't she be?" Andrew took offense to whatever Dominic was implying.

Dominic put both his hands up. "I didn't mean anything by that...except that your women...they don't hang around very long. I'm not trying to piss you off, I'm just stating a fact."

"Amanda is different."

"Different how?"

"Just...different. She's not fake. She's not afraid. She doesn't care what other people think of her. She does what she wants to do and to hell with anyone who tries to stop her. It's a great quality, although frustrating at times because I don't get to see her as much I'd like to. But, she's her own person."

"Ah...independent."

"Non-clingy."

"Sounds like you're the one rocking the Velcro."

"Yeah well, she has a way about her. I can't resist it."

Dominic laughed. "The taming of Andrew Donovan. I never thought I'd see the day."

The night continued on filled with the two men's laughter, cleaned plates, and empty bottles of wine. At Andrew's gesture, a young French waiter rushed to their table.

"Are you ready for the check, sir?"

"Yes, and one more thing." Andrew pointed at his empty plate. "This was absolutely divine. I must give my compliments to the chef."

"Thank you, sir. She'll be delighted to hear. I'll pass along your compliments right away."

"Actually, I was hoping I could do it myself. I'd love to know where she learned to prepare this dish in this exact way."

"I'll check with her in the kitchen and see if she has a moment to come out and meet you."

"Thank you."

The boy placed the leather booklet on the table and gathered up the empty plates. He disappeared through the double doors leading to the kitchen.

"What was that all about?" Dominic asked.

"I like to give credit where credit is due, that's all."

"Hmm mm."

Dominic wasn't buying it, but he didn't care. Andrew had his reasons and he didn't feel the need to explain them.

The minutes ticked by as Andrew waited. Finally, the double doors swung open and the young waiter re-emerged. He scurried across the floor to their table with a frightened look on his face. *Frightened because he didn't want to anger his customer or was there another reason?*

"I'm deeply sorry, sir. The chef has sustained a severe burn injury and has left for the night. Her assistant has taken over her duties. Would you like me to bring him out?"

"Did he cook my meal?"

The boy hung his head. "No, sir."

"Then he's not the one I want to see." Andrew had the kid shaking in his black leather shoes and felt a pang of remorse for being so curt with him. "It's okay. I'll come back another time. Hopefully, she'll be recovered by then."

"Yes, sir." Gingerly swiping the booklet from the table, the waiter, once again, scurried down the aisle toward the back.

Andrew drummed on the table with his fingers, sorting through the spectrum of suspicious thoughts running through his mind.

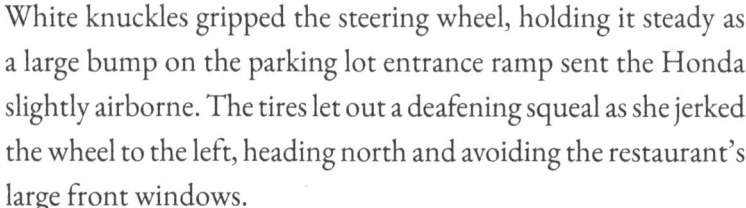

White knuckles gripped the steering wheel, holding it steady as a large bump on the parking lot entrance ramp sent the Honda slightly airborne. The tires let out a deafening squeal as she jerked the wheel to the left, heading north and avoiding the restaurant's large front windows.

How could she be so brainless? Rebecca knew she should have downplayed the meal she cooked for him at the lake. Her pride wouldn't allow it, though. It had always been a hundred percent or zero for her. There was no in-between. The risk involved never entered her mind. She did what she knew how to do, the only way she knew how to do it.

Her dishes were very unique, and he undoubtedly realized that. She could have made up an easy lie, explaining away the duplicate tastes, but no lie would have saved her if he had caught her in that kitchen.

After a quarter mile she took a left off of the main road and onto an empty side street. The car slowed as she pulled up along the curb and parked. She pried her fingers off of the wheel and flexed them repeatedly to get the blood flowing again. Painful needle pricks shot throughout both her hands as her sensation began to return.

Her heart pounded and her breaths came in rapid gasps. Her head fell back on the headrest and her eyes squeezed tightly shut.

The sound of knuckles on glass sent them flying back open. The window next to her head rattled as the knocking continued, echoing throughout the car's interior.

Her eyes remained fixed on the street lamp in front of her, too afraid to come eye to eye with the source of the noise. *Impossible. There was no way he could have caught up to her that fast.* Slowly, her head turned to face her intruder. Her lungs emptied with a long forceful exhale. She reached for the lever inside her door and watched the man come into focus as the window lowered.

"Well, *that* was a close one," the detective said, his smile stretching from ear to ear.

Chapter 27

The door swung open and Lexy's frame filled the entryway. Rebecca reached into the paper bag, grasped the bottle around its neck, and raised it in front of her.

"I have wine," she said.

"Then, by all means." Lexy's smile grew as she waved Rebecca inside. She gave the outer hallway a habitual glance left and right before shutting the door.

Rebecca was already returning from the kitchen with two glasses when Lexy met her at the sofa. She paused to give her friend a once-over.

"Why are you still in your chef whites? And why are you not at work? Did you quit?" Lexy's eyes grew wide with curiosity.

"I might have to," Rebecca said as she filled both glasses.

"What?"

"Not completely." She steadied her voice in an attempt to calm Lexy's rising shock level. "I just need a bit of a break. Maybe a short leave of absence from the kitchen."

Lexy jerked her head as if she hadn't heard her correctly.

"It's okay. I'm fine with it, and it's what I need to do right now."

"It's not easy juggling a busy career and a new boyfriend, is it?" Lexy's eyes popped. "Oh my god! Is that it? Are you seriously quitting your job for a guy?"

"Again, I'm not quitting. I own it. I'm just cutting back a little. Taking a short leave of absence. I'll still keep tabs on the books, and the inventory, and all the other administrative duties. I just need some time. And no, it's not for him—it's for me." Lexy's eyes squinted slightly and it was obvious she wasn't yet convinced. "My family is going through a lot, right now, and I need to be there for my mom."

It disturbed Rebecca how easily the lies came, although some of it was true. Her mother was going through an understandably rough time since her father passed, and she did need to spend more time with her. However, Lexy was right. It was because of *him*. She had almost been caught. She still could be, and she could only imagine the danger she'd be in if Andrew found out she had been lying to him the entire time. He would definitely revisit La Croix at some point, and she had to make sure she wasn't there when he did.

"And how does your partner feel about all of this? About his prized chef just up and deciding to take a break?"

"First of all, he doesn't own me. I own more of the business than he does. I'm *his* boss, not the other way around. And he'll be thrilled to have his son take over for a while. The whole reason he invested in La Croix in the first place was to get Peter's foot in the door. He's counting the days until we'll open another in D.C. and Peter can get one of the kitchens for himself."

The crinkle in Lexy's nose revealed that she wasn't quite buying Rebecca's story.

"Trust me. Peter's ready."

"Wow, I'm impressed. A control freak like you...giving up your kitchen?"

"Well, Peter's the only one I'd trust with that. After all, I trained him and groomed him down to every last detail. What better person to replace me than another me."

It *was* going to be hard giving it up. Much harder than she was letting on. But it was only temporary, and her plan was more important. Lives were at stake. The restaurant would still be there when she was done. A life wouldn't, once it was taken.

"So this decision doesn't have anything to do with the mysterious visitor you had at your house yesterday?"

"What? No, that was no mystery." Lexy sat silently, waiting for Rebecca to elaborate. "It was one of the cops that interviewed me yesterday when we got back. He just had some follow-up questions, that's all."

"So how's he handling it? Being back on the radar?"

"Andrew? Oh, he's handling it like a pro. I haven't seen him since yesterday morning, but he seemed fine when I left. He's getting things in order. Preparing for the onslaught of police attention he knows is coming."

"Okay, enough of the niceties." Lexy reached in front of her and set her glass on the coffee table. She turned to face Rebecca more directly. "Just last week you said you thought it might be someone in his house. Do you still think that, after this last time? How many people are living there? And why the hell are you still hanging around?"

"It's just his son and his son's friend."

"His son's friend lives there?"

"Sometimes. I don't know. He's there a lot, is all I know."

"And you think it's one of those two?"

"I don't know anymore." Rebecca groaned and buried her face in her hand.

Lexy grabbed the bottle and refilled both of their glasses. "Look, it doesn't matter either way. The point is that what you're doing is insane. In fact, it's the definition of insanity. You're tempting fate, and no guy is worth that."

Rebecca resented part of her argument. It *did* matter. However, her actions did sound insane, and it was very dangerous for Lexy to question her motives that much. The time had come for her to come clean to her friend, at least partially.

Rebecca scooted closer and leaned in as if she was about to reveal a deep dark secret. She lowered her voice, almost to a whisper. "I can find out who it was. I can stop it from happening again. I'm on the inside."

"You should be on the inside of a padded room," Lexy said, drawing her head back in shock. "If you have information, why don't you go to the police? What about that cop that was questioning you yesterday? Let him handle it."

"No, that won't work. This guy is too smart. Five murders and he hasn't been caught yet. Unless...he doesn't see it coming."

"So you're an undercover agent, now?"

Rebecca's mouth curved into a smug smile. "In a way." She grabbed Lexy's hand and pulled her closer. "I'm so close. The cops will just mess everything up. Please, let me do this." She squeezed Lexy's hand tighter. "For Sara, I *need* to do this."

"You're out of your mind." Lexy's eyes were wide with disbelief as she jerked her hand away. "This isn't us. We don't do things like this. We are not undercover superheroes. Beck, you're talking absolutely crazy."

"Please. I can end this. If you get the police involved, he'll just hide out until everything dies down, like he did before. I'll still be a target, only worse because I *won't* see it coming."

"But the police are already sniffing around."

"Yes, but they're focused on Andrew. If Andrew is still the scapegoat, then the real killer won't feel threatened and be scared off."

"Let me see if I'm hearing you correctly." Lexy cleared her throat. "You want me to sit back and do nothing so you can act as bait...for a serial killer who butchers women that look exactly like you. Is that about right?"

Lexy might have thought that summarizing it out loud would bring Rebecca to her senses and make her realize how off-the-wall her whole plan was. In fact, it had the opposite effect. Hearing it out loud gave Rebecca a surge of adrenaline that fueled her motivation even more. And she no longer felt so alone. She had an ally. A witness.

Lexy wasn't quite done. "How are you going to defend yourself when whoever it is comes after you?"

"I have a gun," Rebecca lied.

"When did you get a gun? Have you ever even shot one before?"

"I've been going to a range." She hadn't, but purchasing a gun and taking a few shots was sounding like a pretty good idea. She was sure to put that at the top of her to-do list.

Lexy gasped and clutched the center of her chest. "You're planning to kill him."

"No, I'm not. It's just a precaution. My plan is simply to do a little detective work and get him to expose himself. He'll never get close to me. But, if it comes down to it, don't worry...I have no problem blowing his head off."

Chapter 28

Andrew reached over and swept away a lock of hair that had fallen across her eye. In the darkness, he could barely see her, but the full moon cast a beam of light across the bed and that was all he needed. The sheet covered most of her torso, but her exposed shoulders and neck were outlined in a soft moonlit glow. Her features were nothing but shadows across her face, but he had spent so many hours staring at her, it was easy to fill in the blanks. He imagined the emerald brilliance that would have been staring back at him had the room not been so dark.

She really was different. He couldn't quite put his finger on it, but it was there and it drove him crazy. He had only felt that way one other time, and he never thought he would ever find that again. Dominic's words held no meaning for him. She *would* still be around next time he came to town. He would make sure of it.

A low grumble rose from his stomach.

"You can't possibly be hungry again," she said, breaking the silence.

"A little, but I'll be alright."

"That steak you had was enormous. Plus everything else you had with it."

"What can I say, I have a high metabolism."

She punched him in the arm. Playful, yet harder than he had expected. "Lucky you."

He rubbed the spot with tender strokes. "You know, now that we're on the subject of food…" He had been looking for a natural segue into the topic which had been bothering him for the past couple of days.

"We're not on the topic of food. We're on the topic of what a jerk you are for being able to eat whatever you want without batting an eye." She punched him again.

He flinched a little that time but refused to be distracted by her repeated beatings. "Have you ever been to that French place in downtown Bethesda?"

She hesitated for just a moment. "The restaurant?"

"Yeah, the one on Old Georgetown."

She hesitated again. Then, without warning, she bolted upright and her enthusiasm went through the roof. "I love that place! We should go there. This week. We have to go this week." Her words flew out of her mouth quicker than he could understand them. "Oh no, it's too late to go this week." She flopped back against the mattress and let out a groan. "We missed it."

Propping himself up on his elbow, Andrew replayed her frantic rambling in his head, failing to decipher what it all meant. "Missed what?"

She turned her head toward him. "On the cooking show I watch, one of the chefs that's on there sometimes travels around to different cities. She spends a couple days being a guest chef in a restaurant in each city she visits." She turned her gaze to the ceiling fan spinning above them and sighed. "She was scheduled to be in Bethesda Tuesday and Wednesday of this week." Her hands rose and covered her face. "With all the commotion that was going on when we got back...I completely forgot about it. Ugh...it'll probably be another year or longer before she's in this area again."

Andrew paused before responding, not sure if she was done yet. He knew there had to be a logical explanation for what he had experienced the other night. "Is that where you learned that scallop dish?"

"That and pretty much every other dish I make. Everything I know I learned from her."

It made perfect sense and immediate relief washed over him. He had been kicking himself about the doubt he felt. Although he couldn't see her clearly, he heard in her voice how upset she was.

"How about this...find out what city she'll be in next and we'll take a trip."

Her head turned back toward him and he could see her wide smile give off a glow of its own. "Really?"

"Sure." He loved seeing her happy, especially if it was his doing. "We can be food groupies. We'll follow her all over the country."

She laughed.

Suddenly, the sound of the front door slamming echoed through the house. Her laughter faded, and she became still. He could hear her heart pounding in her chest and felt the mattress shake as she trembled.

"Sounds like we're not alone anymore." He tried to make light of the situation but was unsuccessful. It was very apparent that she was growing more and more uncomfortable around Spencer. "Don't worry about him. He's not going to hurt you. That boy can chill your blood as it's running through your veins, but he's not dangerous."

She sat up, drew her knees to her chest, and wrapped her arms around them. "He hates me so much."

Andrew sat up as well and wrapped his arm across her shoulders. "Don't take it personally. It has nothing to do with you. I've told you that," he said, his voice tender and warm.

"You're not even going to deny it? Or lie a little to make me feel better?"

"He doesn't hate you...and I'm not lying about that. He's using you to hurt me. You know how kids of single parents can be. They don't like their world changing, so they try to keep new people out of it." He didn't know what else to say to her. Spencer had been effectively running all of his relationship prospects straight out the front door. But she hadn't run yet...and that was why she was so worth it. "In time, he'll warm up to you, I promise. Right now he's just angry."

"How angry? Angry enough?"

"What is that supposed to mean?" The warmth vanished and his tone became firm and defensive.

She shifted to one hip and turned slightly toward him. The sheet, gripped securely in her fist, was pulled up to her neck. He reached over to the nightstand and switched on the bedside lamp. It was obvious to him that she had something to say.

"Did he have anything to do with the murders? The women before me...that conveniently aren't around anymore and never will be again."

Heat began to spread over his chest and he resisted the urge to react to it. His eyes closed and the fire inside him reduced to just an ember—a useful trick that had come in handy many times before. When his eyes reopened, they were met with the same emerald gems he had been longing for earlier. However, their luster was gone and had since been replaced with distrust and accusation. It broke his heart. "He's just a boy and, as I said before, he's not dangerous."

"Don't brush it off as if my feelings are trivial and unjustified. I have every reason to be afraid of him."

"I'm not brushing it off, and I'm sorry if it sounded that way. You just don't know him like I do. He's all bark and no bite. He's harmless, I promise."

"He glares at me. Yells at me. Threatens me. I shouldn't have to put up with that kind of treatment every time I come over here."

"If you're so deathly afraid of him...why are you still here?"

He regretted his words the second they left his mouth, and her expression revealed that he was right in doing so. The last thing he wanted was to scare her away. Spencer was already hard at work at that job.

"I didn't mean it like that," he said, attempting to pull himself out of the hole he was digging. "I'll have a talk with him. He won't treat you that way again. I—"

"I know, I know...you promise. You're making a lot of promises. I just hope you can keep them."

"Can we not fight about this? Please."

"We're not fighting. We're addressing the elephant in the room... your recent past...and now your present."

His breath caught in his throat. He had avoided the topic for too long. She had, as well. It was one of her most endearing qualities. "Okay, you win. But, can we not get into this right now? Let's sleep on it, and tomorrow I'll tell you everything you want to know. Okay?"

"Fine. Tomorrow, then." She slid down under the sheet and pulled it over her shoulder as she rolled away from him.

"I thought we weren't fighting."

"We're not. I'm just withholding any late-night affection until you follow through. So I guess that'll be tomorrow."

Andrew leaned over and planted a soft kiss on the back of her shoulder before flattening himself on the bed. His gaze found the ceiling fan and its rhythmic rocking as it spun. Questions flooded his mind, accompanied by a plethora of mixed emotions. Why was she still there? That question wasn't meant to be rhetorical. His past worried her, and she obviously thought about it often. And her suspicions of Spencer had grown into a crippling fear. So why was she still there? What sane person would voluntarily enter into a relationship filled with such dangerous uncertainty?

He wasn't pleased with the path his thoughts had taken. Ulterior motive was the only answer he could come up with. He didn't want to believe it, and was hoping she could explain it away like she did everything else, but why did she always have something to explain in the first place?

Chapter 29

Andrew poured a second glass of orange juice for himself, stalling to collect his thoughts. "I have enemies. Some that I know of, but most I don't."

She watched him intently from across the breakfast table, waiting for him to continue.

"I went through months of interrogations, searches, and downright harassment. It was hell. They turned my life upside down and still found nothing...because there was nothing to find."

"What about the knife?"

"The dagger? A dozen places or more have them for sale online. Anybody can buy one and have it within days."

"Whoever supposedly set you up had to have known you owned one."

"Not supposedly. They *did* set me up." His brows narrowed and the irritation was evident in his voice. "And it was no secret that my wife was an art curator and collected hundreds of artifacts over the years. They're posted all over her page. The Phurba Dagger included."

Her head lowered, and she stared at the full plate in front of her. He couldn't tell whether she was ashamed of her attack on him or if she was simply taking a moment to put it all together. Her hand rose and a lock of hair at the base of her neck snaked its way between her fingers. She twirled it over and over and he could see where her mind was going.

"My relationship with those women was long over when they were attacked. What possible motive would I have to kill them when they weren't even in my life anymore?"

"Why are you trying to replace her?" She looked up and her eyes found his again. "It's obvious. Too obvious."

Her question caught him completely off-guard. She was direct, and normally he loved that in a woman, but not under those circumstances. However, she was right. He *was* trying to replace Marie, but that was just human nature...to try to reacquire the greatness one once had. Although he didn't believe she would see it that way.

"It's not obvious, because it's not true," he lied. "I know that's what everyone is saying, but it's simply not true. I'm physically attracted to a certain look, that's all. It's no different than when a person only dates people of a specific ethnicity." His voice rose as he fully committed to his defense. "I have a type. There's nothing out of the ordinary about that. I'm not trying to replace any one person."

Her head tilted slightly, and her gaze remained fixed on him. He searched her eyes for understanding but wasn't sure if he had found it.

"I didn't do this," he added. "The court went over every piece of evidence with a fine-toothed comb and they all agreed. I. Am. Innocent." He was done explaining himself to her. She had her own explaining to do.

"You knew the stories about me when we met. I didn't lie or hide it from you. Not that I could have, even if I had wanted to." He slid his elbows onto the table and leaned in closer. "If you didn't have a problem with this before...why do you now?"

"I don't enjoy people telling me what I should or shouldn't do. Especially people I don't even know, such as the media. I wanted to get to know you and make my own decision."

"And what have you decided?"

"That there are other variables. Spencer, for one." She paused and took a sip from her glass. "And, that I'm invested enough in this relationship to dig deeper into the dirt and know exactly what I'm getting into."

"Aren't you afraid of what Detective Harmon said? Being a target? You definitely fit the description." He gestured at her appearance.

"I could cross the street tomorrow and get hit by a bus." She shrugged and took another sip.

"It's not the same thing, and you know it. You're interrogating me, and you're scared to death of my son. You're living an unnecessarily high-risk lifestyle." She was dodging him, but he remained on-task. "Why are you still here? What's in it for you?"

"I don't want to give up on you. I don't want to give up on Spencer."

It was what he wanted to hear; he just didn't know if he believed it. When something was too good to be true, it usually was. He couldn't deny, however, that he needed a break from the Spencer/Amanda drama as well. It was exhausting and painful watching the exchanges between them.

"How about we spend a little time at your place? You're so on edge here. Maybe Spencer will feel a little less threatened if we didn't always use this house as our home base." Her body jerked and her eyes grew wide. The reaction confused him. "No?"

"Definitely not."

"Why not? We've been dating for months, and I've never even seen where you live."

"I have a roommate."

"So? Don't you think it's time I met some of your friends? You did say you were invested in this relationship."

"She's not a friend...she's a psycho. Crazy." Her finger traced circles beside her temple. "Trust me, it's in your best interest. You don't want to be anywhere near her."

"Maybe I do."

"*I* don't want you anywhere near her." Her statement was firm and final.

Andrew chuckled. "You're afraid of my son because you think he *might* be crazy. Yet you live with a person you *know* is crazy. That logic alone...is crazy."

"Color me crazy, then." She smiled and her emeralds began to twinkle.

Andrew took a left at the end of his driveway and glanced in his rear-view mirror. Her red Honda followed close behind. Returning his eyes to the road, he spotted a familiar tan sedan pulling off to the side in front of him. The driver gave him a quick nod as he drove past, and Andrew replied with a nod of his own.

He had wanted to believe her so badly. There were just too many unknowns about her...and as usual, she had an explanation for everything. Her cavalier attitude about being a possible target was a complete one-eighty from the terror she exhibited regarding Spencer the night before. He had seen two different personalities from her, and unless she was the clinically crazy one, one of them had to be an act. He just needed to figure out which one.

Exiting his development, he made a right onto River Road. As he slowly accelerated, he once again glanced in his mirror. His arm extended out of the open window and gave a wave as she made the left turn and continued in the opposite direction of him. He removed his foot from the gas pedal and coasted for a few seconds until he saw the tan sedan pull out and subtly take its position behind her. Together, the two vehicles disappeared around the bend and out of his sight.

Chapter 30

Sitting in the townhouse parking lot, his fingers drummed on the steering wheel, fueling his nervous energy. It was late, and he had been sitting in the parking lot for over an hour, wondering what to do next. His heart told him to ignore what his eyes were seeing, but his head needed an explanation.

At that late hour, he would much rather have been snuggled in bed next to her instead of sitting in that car. It was her family's turn to have her, though. A birthday get-together in Pittsburgh with parents he'd never met, for a brother he'd never heard of. She had never spoken of her family to him, aside from the brief account of her sister's accident. Nothing about her other family members. He had asked her about them, on several occasions, but she had always remained tight-lipped. It wasn't unusual, though. The loss of a sibling for her, and a child for her parents, was plenty enough to strain family ties. He had never brought them up again until she had informed him of her plans for that night.

Andrew had wanted to go with her. He had begged and pleaded with her to take him...something no one else had ever succeeded in making him do. His pleas were to no avail, though. She wasn't ready for him to meet them yet, and he had no choice but to accept her wishes.

She would be there overnight, depleting any hope of a midnight rendezvous. His friend in the tan sedan had followed her home that morning, so there he sat, alone and obsessed. Stalking her windows and holding out hope that she would forego the overnight stay and return early. At least, that was his initial intention.

Her home wasn't exactly where she said it was. As a matter of fact, not even close. It troubled him that even though he knew she was lying to him, he still wanted her. She had a way of making him disregard his basic instincts about people. The same instincts that had been protecting him his entire life.

He couldn't steer his eyes away from the window. As strong as he was as a man, at that moment, he was overcome with weakness. He picked up his phone instead and dialed her number. She picked up on the third ring.

"I miss you," he said at the sound of her greeting.

"I miss you too, but believe me...it's a good thing you didn't come with me. My brother is in rare form tonight, and not in a good way."

"Does that mean you might be coming back tonight?"

"Maybe if it wasn't so late, but it's already midnight."

"I'll wait up."

"I'm three hours away...and I've been drinking. It's the only way I can tolerate this whole mess. I'll be back tomorrow and we'll meet for lunch."

"Alright, but you can't blame a man for trying."

He ended the call and resumed his nervous finger drumming. He had hoped the conversation would have gone a different way...not that she would jump in her car and drive home, but that she had *already* jumped in her car and driven home. At least that would explain why he had been watching her through her own window for the past hour.

Chapter 31

The glass door to his high-rise office swung open and a slender, distinguished-looking man in his late forties stepped inside. Andrew pulled up a second chair behind his desk and the man sat, tossing a thin folder onto Andrew's lap.

Bruce Mitchell had been a trusted friend to Andrew for years, although, he wasn't just a friend, he also happened to be a private investigator. He had hired him after Marie had disappeared, but he had hoped that would be the last time he would need his professional services. Unfortunately, there they were again, staring into computer monitors and sifting through printouts.

"I managed to lift her wallet from her purse while you two were eating lunch earlier. I took a photo of her driver's license." Bruce took a printout from the folder and handed it to Andrew.

He took it and scanned the sheet with his eyes. "This is her. It's her picture and her name...not the address I was at last night, but it's her."

"It's not her." Bruce slapped his laptop on the desk and opened it.

"What do you mean?"

The screen powered on and Bruce's fingers began dancing across the keyboard. "There are an infinite number of Amanda Whites to choose from. I haven't yet found this particular one, and I don't think I'm going to."

Andrew leaned over to get a closer look as the screen filled with license photos and names.

"The Department of Motor Vehicles has no record of an Amanda White with that address," Bruce said.

"Could the house be in her roommate's name?"

Bruce clicked a few more keys. "Look at these photos. These are all the Amanda Whites registered in Maryland. Not only do none of them fit her description, they're not even in her age range." He leaned back in his chair to give Andrew more room to see the screen. "The address on her driver's license is owned by a David Sanderson. A seventy-two year-old black man. The address you were at last night, the one I followed her to...it's unlisted. But, I'll get that property owner's name shortly."

"Shortly?"

"Yeah. Shortly," he barked.

Andrew backed off. Bruce Mitchell was not a guy to be messed with, even if he was an old friend. He didn't look like much, but looks could be deceiving. "Okay, anything else?"

"Plenty." Bruce picked up the printout of the license and studied it closely. "You can't tell in this picture, but I got a good look at that license when I had it in my hand. The holograms are good, but not perfect. It's a fake."

"She has a fake driver's license?"

"Yep. And that's not all." He rocked back and forth in his chair, waiting for Andrew to respond.

"And? What else?" Andrew was all out of patience. Bruce had a habit of dragging things out for dramatic effect. All it managed to do was waste time.

"The tags on her vehicle. They're fake too." He grabbed another printout from the folder and read from it. "Those tags belong on an '86 Ford Mustang, not a Honda Civic. And they're registered...or they *were* registered to a twenty-two year old white male. That registrant was documented as deceased a year ago."

"Oh my god." Andrew buried his head in his hands. "Is anything about her true?"

"How well do you really know her?"

"Apparently not well at all."

"Well, what does she do? When I followed her yesterday, she went straight home and stayed there the rest of the day. After lunch today, she went home again. Where does she work? Or does she?"

"She's a nurse. She works the evening shift, mostly. I've picked her up there plenty of times."

"What kind of nurse?"

"She's in the OR. A surgical nurse. Cardiac unit, I believe."

Bruce laughed. "A lot of nighttime heart surgeries to be done, I guess."

Andrew spun his chair to face him. "I doubt she just clocks out as soon as the surgery is done. She probably has to wait for them to come out of anesthesia. Check on them in recovery until the next shift comes on. She can't just leave the patients right after they've had heart surgery." It wasn't an issue of defending her. At that point he was simply trying to defend his own intelligence.

"Actually, that's exactly what a surgical nurse does. They're there for the surgery only."

"I've seen her there. Dressed in scrubs and everything."

"They let you watch the surgeries?"

"No, of course not. I pick her up in the lobby after her shift is over."

"Right, the lobby. Because no one can just walk in *there*." Bruce's words were dripping with sarcasm. "Which hospital?"

"Bethesda General."

Bruce took out his phone. He shook his head slowly back and forth as his thumbs made quick work of the phone's keyboard. Finally, he put it to his ear. "Hi, I'm trying to get in touch with a nurse that works there...Amanda White."

As he waited for a reply, he walked over to the large windows that spanned the entire far wall of the office. Andrew's office was on the fourteenth floor and offered a grand view of the city from its height. "Cardiac," he spoke into the phone. "Surgery...okay, thank you."

He ended the call and turned back toward Andrew. Taking long slow steps, he returned to his seat next to him.

"For Christ's sake, man. Come on!"

"Sorry. No one by that name is a nurse or a doctor, or an orderly or anything, on the cardiac floor. Or any other floor, for that matter."

Andrew shot out of his chair and sent it reeling against the wall. In three strong strides he made it to the window and pounded a fist against the glass. His breaths came quick and heavy as his blood burned with anger. He was not one to be made a fool of, but that is exactly what she had done.

His respirations slowly returned to normal as he fought to calm himself. He never made decisions in anger. He was too smart for that. A level head always yielded the best results...in business and in life. His mouth curved into a sly grin, and a soft chuckle escaped his lips. "You know, Bruce...I have a strange feeling that she's a chef."

"Where did that come from?" Bruce looked puzzled. "How did you get from surgical nurse to chef?"

"Apparently she has a love for sharp instruments."

"If you say so," Bruce said with a shrug.

Andrew took a step closer to the window and peered down at the bustling street below. "Amanda White...you really are quite the worthy opponent," he whispered to himself.

Chapter 32

T he deafening chime of the doorbell startled Andrew. He glanced at the digital clock on the stove and then at his watch for a second opinion. With quick feet, he approached the front door just as the chime began to sound again. He opened the door and a touch of surprise washed over him at the woman standing there.

"Amanda? I thought I was going to pick you up at your place?" he said.

"I had some last-minute errands to do nearby. I figured it was silly to drive back home just to wait for you to drive me back here. May I come in?"

Realizing he was still blocking the door, he immediately stepped aside and ushered her in. "You're really trying to keep me away from that roommate, aren't you?"

She didn't respond, and he wished he had kept his comment to himself. He didn't want to get her worked up and defensive. Not tonight. He had thought long and hard about everything he had learned about her in the past few days and had come to a decision.

He pulled her to him and spoke his apology with a deep kiss. "Come." He linked his arm in hers and tugged her along. "Let's go out on the deck. It's a beautiful night."

As she walked with him, she scanned the second-floor landing as they passed under it. Reaching the kitchen, her eyes continued to dart around the large space and toward the adjacent rooms that opened into it.

"He's not here right now."

"I'm not hoping to avoid him. I just don't want to be caught off-guard." Her gaze fell to the floor and she gave her head a quick shake. "I didn't mean it like that." She looked up at him again. "I'm trying. Really, I am."

"I know...and it's okay. You have every right to feel cautious. He hasn't given you any reason not to be."

He clasped her fingers in his and brought her hand up to plant a kiss. Together they walked through the kitchen and out the sliding glass door at the back of the sunroom. It was only 6:00 and the July sun was still high. The deck spanned the length of the house and a table and chair set offered an amazing view for outside meals.

"I wasn't ready for you yet," he said, indicating the unset table.

She followed him as he led her to the right where a free-standing swing stood outside of the adjacent family room. It was plenty big enough for two people and he held it steady as she sank into the plush cushions.

"Wait here, and I'll be right back with some drinks."

He scurried back into the kitchen, returning several minutes later with two tall, ice-filled mojitos, one in each hand. Drops of chilled condensation dripped onto her exposed thigh as he handed her one of the glasses. He slid in next to her and gave the swing a good starting push.

"I'm not used to being able to see you at such a normal evening hour," he said as he stretched his arm behind her neck and along the swing's back. His foot pushed off from the floorboards and kept them swaying back and forth.

She kicked off her flip-flops and brought her legs up next to her. "It feels so good to get some downtime," she said, letting her head fall back onto his arm. "All the new hiring on my floor has been a Godsend. I don't know if I could've survived another week working all those late shifts."

A sly grin spread across Andrew's face. He marveled at how effortlessly she spun her story. It was almost as if she believed it herself.

"Unfortunately, one of the new male nurses is a total bonehead. I, for one, would like to get a look at his degree. I seriously doubt he even has one. He can't do anything."

She continued rambling on and on about her imaginary hospital work life, and Andrew continued nodding his head in agreement at whatever she said. It wasn't long before her voice became a distant white noise as his own thoughts stole his ear.

After Bruce had left his office, Andrew had spent hours thinking of clever ways to call her out on her lies, and twice as many hours wondering if it was even worth it. He didn't know why she felt she needed a false identity to be with him. Most likely it was out of fear and uncertainty of what she thought he was capable of. He couldn't blame her for that. She was acting out of self-preservation.

He admired her extreme level of commitment, and the fact she even attempted to manipulate him through such an outlandish ploy excited him to no end. She would never be boring. Never be complacent. No other woman had ever been that much of a challenge...except one. He had never thought he would ever find that again. Now that he had, he wasn't going to let some petty fabrications take it away. He loved her.

She paused her rant just long enough to poke her straw around the glass, searching for the last remaining drops of rum. She looked up at him and a pair of dimples appeared between her eyebrows. "Can you seriously believe that bullshit?"

"Absolutely not." He had no idea what he was disagreeing with, but it was irrelevant. The way she was in that moment...that was how he always wanted her. Full of fire and confidence. As far as he was concerned, the trembling girl from the other night didn't even exist.

She smiled and nuzzled her head into his shoulder. He waited for her next bout of explosive ranting, but it never came.

"It's okay. I'm done." Her words were so soft he almost didn't hear them.

He gave the swing another push with his foot and pulled her closer to him. It was time to start up the grill, but he knew he wasn't going anywhere any time soon. Dinner could wait.

It was his heart that needed to be fed right then. He savored her warm body pressed against him and knew he had made the right decision. She would not be easy, but his mind would not be changed. He was a strong enough man to handle her, and he looked forward to the opportunity to prove it.

Chapter 33

Rebecca dropped to her knees and thrust both of her arms under the bed. They reached and grabbed aimlessly in a frantic search for the rest of her clothes. Feeling the small mounds of soft fabric, she clutched the pieces in her fists and pulled out her outfit for the morning. Unfortunately, it was the same dress and panties from the night before, as she had forgotten to plan for an overnight stay.

Shooting to her feet, she donned the panties in one quick stroke and wrestled the dress over her head. A digital chime rang from inside the nightstand drawer and she glanced at the alarm clock to confirm the time.

"Damn!"

Andrew had left for work over an hour ago, and she hadn't planned on falling back asleep. There wasn't any place she needed to be, but there was one place that she didn't want to be...in that house when Spencer got home.

She had no interest in facing him. All of the "I'm trying" nonsense she had spewed the night before was simply to put

Andrew's mind at ease. Hers wouldn't be until the killer was caught, and she hadn't found anything to rule anyone out yet.

It was becoming more and more dangerous for her to be there. Andrew had been pushing to be more involved in her life, and she couldn't hold him off forever. She already had a difficult time keeping her lies straight. She managed, but it wasn't easy and it was definitely exhausting.

She swung open the bedroom door and raced down the hallway. Taking the steps two at a time, she crossed the foyer and made a beeline to the dark, narrow doorway of Andrew's office. It was the one area of the floor she hadn't been able to inspect during her bursts of secret nosiness. It was also the one room, she believed, that would reveal his secrets...or rule him out.

The room was dim, but she refrained from switching on the light and revealing her presence to anyone coming up the driveway. The window at the far end let in plenty of natural light. The dark walls and furniture fought against it, but it was still enough to work with. She raced to the window and peered through the slats of the half-open blinds. The exterior of the house projected out and obstructed her view of part of the parking pad in front of the garage, but she could see the front porch and the entire length of the driveway. The coast was clear for the moment.

The window began to fog up as her breaths came in rapid succession. She gave it a quick wipe with her palm and turned to the desk behind her. She had no time. It was already after nine, and Spencer always left to work at the country club at ten. He would be arriving home from Tyler's at any moment to get ready. She looked over her shoulder and took another peek out of the window. She had a great vantage point for his approach from the driveway. She wouldn't be able to get out of the house unseen, but she would, at least, be able to get out of the office.

She turned her attention back to the desk. Rolling Andrew's chair back a few feet, she crouched down and began tugging on drawer handles. They slid open with ease, and she quickly went from one to the other, not even sure what she was looking for. Tidy rows of manila folders with neat handwritten labels stared back at her. Tax returns for the past decade, vehicle titles, insurance forms. Nothing she was interested in.

She stood and leaned over the top surface of the desk. Her fingers rifled through a pile of loose papers. Nothing. Scanning the rest of the area, she was met with her reflection, staring back at her from the dark screen of his computer monitor. She grabbed the mouse and jiggled it. The screen came to life and nearly blinded her with the brightness of the white search engine page. No password was needed. The mouse rolled across the pad and clicked on his email icon.

"Aw, come on," she said as the sign-in screen opened. "Son of a bitch."

She paused for a moment, but decided against the guessing game. She closed the email and clicked on his web history.

"No." The blood drained from her face. Her legs weakened and she slumped into the chair behind her. "No, no, no..."

There it was. Tucked between an array of grilling recipes and European soccer schedules was...her. Only one search result for Amanda White, but half a dozen for Rebecca Black. He knew her real name. He knew she had been lying to him the entire time. How long had he known, and why hadn't he confronted her about it?

A queasiness began to rise in her stomach. He had to have known last night, so why would he leave her unsupervised in his house the next morning? Maybe he really didn't have anything to hide. Or maybe he had an equally deceptive plan for her.

The emotional battle within her brain was interrupted by thumping footsteps at the front door. Keys jingled and the deadbolt retracted with a loud clack.

She froze. Spencer was already home. She had missed him pulling up the driveway because he had already done so, most likely before she even went downstairs. She couldn't see the entire parking pad from the office window, and that mistake would cost her.

She needed to drop to the floor, to hide under the desk or back in the corner. However, she remained motionless. Her body refused to obey her brain's command. She sat as a statue, her heart beating as though it was trying to crash through her sternum.

The footsteps were soft. Slow. She strained to hear them over her own heavy breathing, but they were there—and headed in her direction.

The attack was inevitable, but she couldn't bear to see it. She closed her eyes and waited in the darkness as the footsteps entered the room and came to a stop in front of her.

"What. The. Hell."

Her eyes flew open and it was no surprise to see Spencer standing there, glaring at her with fire in his eyes.

"Are you seriously this stupid? What the hell are you doing snooping around on my dad's computer?"

"What should we do with her?" She hadn't noticed Tyler lurking by the doorway. He leaned against one of the bookcases and folded his arms across his chest. "I, for one, can think of a hundred things to do. Each one more satisfying than the last," he said with a wide grin.

"I—I'm not snooping." As hard as she tried, she couldn't mask the quiver in her voice. "I'm just checking my email before I leave."

"So now I'm the stupid one?" He took a step forward and planted both of his palms on the desk. "Don't, for one second, think I don't know what you're up to. Who the hell do you think you are, anyway?"

"I swear I wasn't—"

"You think this is some kind of game?" His voice became louder with every word. "This is your last warning. Get the fuck out of my house, and don't you dare come back. Ever!"

His voice was as deep and loud as she had ever heard it. It wasn't a warning. It was a threat. She was done tempting fate in that crazy house. She jumped up from her seat and scurried around the desk as fast her legs would allow. She kept her eyes glued to the floor as she passed by him, refraining from any eye contact that could change his decision of letting her leave. As she sped toward the doorway, she glanced at Tyler, still propped against the bookshelf. The signature wink he gave her sent chills up her spine.

Her gait broke into a run when she hit the tile of the foyer. Without breaking stride, she fished her keys out of the glass bowl on the center table and continued on to the front door. Her bare feet slapped against the cold marble, but she didn't care. Her flip-flops were still sitting out on the deck, and she didn't care about them either. She needed to get out of that house as fast as she could.

Throwing open the door, she launched herself off of the porch and raced to the safety of her car. In mere seconds she had the gas pedal pressed to the floor and was accelerating down the driveway...hopefully, for the last time.

Chapter 34

Her phone rang for what seemed like the twentieth time that hour. She ignored it and walked over to the front window and, in the darkness, peeked through the tiniest of slits in the blinds. He was still there, parked in the same spot he had been every night that week.

She backed up into the shadows and slid her phone from her pocket. Yet another voicemail from him, just as she knew it would be. She held the phone to her ear and braced herself for the panic attack that she knew his voice would bring.

"I know you're there. I can see you. Please. We need to talk about this. I told you...I don't care about the fake name thing. I understand it. I'm over it. Will you please call me back?"

Her knees buckled, and she let them lower her into a crouch in the corner of the living room. The phone dropped from her shaking hand onto the wood floor. How could he be over it, just like that? She had lied to him for months. She had stayed in his house, met his family, and shared his bed...all while pretending to be a different person. How could he just let that go?

She knew Spencer hadn't told him what happened that morning in his office. His repetitive phone messages and emails made that clear. He had come home that day to find her search pages opened on his computer. With her shoes still outside and her not answering his calls, it didn't take a genius to put two and two together and come up with the idea that that was why she had left.

The knock came on the door, just as she had expected it would and just as it had every other night. And she continued to sit silently in the darkness, just as *she* had done every other night.

He was getting more and more impatient by the day. His calls were becoming more frequent, and his parking lot stakeouts were steadily increasing, extending well into the early morning hours.

On the second day of her radio silence, he had visited the restaurant. She knew he eventually would. However, the phone call from La Croix still managed to turn her stomach. Peter was on his game, though and told Andrew that she had quit weeks before and hadn't been back since. Hopefully, Andrew wouldn't go back either.

Maybe he would leave her alone if she simply faced him and ended their relationship. How could she face him, though? All of her lies and deception. He said he understood, but he didn't know the whole story—the real reason she was with him. How could she possibly explain it? No. She couldn't talk to him. He would convince her to go back. He would twinkle his eyes and flash his smile, and she would be right back where she knew she shouldn't be. She knew she was being immature but complete withdrawal was the only way she knew how to stay away.

When the sound of footsteps descended down the front steps and faded, she mustered the courage to leave her spot and sneak up the stairs to her third floor bedroom. Her hand went to the light switch out of habit, but she quickly pulled it back, realizing her bedroom was located at the front of the house and visible from the lot. With the hallway light illuminating the room through the open door, she crossed the carpet to her closet. Swinging open the doors, she pulled down the large luggage case from the top shelf and threw it on the bed.

She couldn't take it anymore. She was a prisoner in her own house and she was losing her mind because of it. As she unzipped the top and threw it open, she spotted her other cell phone on the nightstand next to her. Picking it up, she dialed Lexy's number.

"Is your offer still open?"

"Of course," Lexy's voice replied. "Always."

"Okay then. First chance I get."

Any further conversation was halted by another round of knocking on the front door. It was louder that time. He had to have known she was upstairs. Somehow, he was still watching her.

Chapter 35

It had been almost two weeks since Rebecca had left and started staying with Lexy. Since she hadn't been back home, she didn't know where Andrew stood with his stalking habit. However, his phone calls had dwindled and then eventually stopped altogether. The waiting game was over. She had won.

She flipped the lid to the suitcase closed and leaned her weight on it. She was still wrestling with the zipper when Lexy entered the bedroom.

"I'm not sure I should tell you this..." she said, slapping her cell phone repeatedly in her palm.

Rebecca waited for her to continue, but Lexy just stood there, biting her lip and avoiding all eye contact.

"Go on. Spit it out."

"Last week—you had only been here a couple of days—I went to this bar after work for happy hour."

"Yes, I remember. So?"

"I ran into Andrew there." She peeked cautiously at Rebecca.

"What?"

"He recognized me from that time I saw the two of you at The Winslow."

"Why didn't you tell me?"

"You were so freaked out about everything then. I didn't want to make it worse."

"Well, what did he say to you?"

"He just asked me if I had seen you lately and if I knew where you were."

"And what did you tell him?" Rebecca's eyes widened and she felt a knot growing in her stomach.

"I told him that night was the first time we've spoken in years, and that it would also be the last." Lexy puffed her chest and put her hands on her hips. "I told him I'd spit in your face if I ever saw you again."

A giggle escaped Rebecca's lips. "Did he believe you?"

"He seemed to."

"Huh. Well, it's probably better you didn't tell me, anyway. I was going a little nuts, back then."

"There's something else." Her proud stance diminished, and she returned to her former, uneasy cower. "And this is what I don't think I should tell you, but I'm going to put the ball in your court about what to do."

"I'm not sure I want to know now."

"One of my models is a waitress at that bar. She was working there the night Andrew approached me. I, of course, didn't tell her everything, but I did tell her to keep tabs on him for me."

"Does he go there a lot?"

"Enough that she's called me several times since then to tell me he's there."

"Was that her on the phone just now?"

Lexy nodded. "He's there...and he's with someone."

"A woman?"

She nodded again. "A tall, slender woman with short, wavy dark hair just like yours." She gestured at Rebecca's head.

Rebecca gasped. How could he have moved on that quickly? Was that why his calls had stopped? Because he had already found her replacement?

"She's in danger. From Spencer or Tyler, or maybe even Andrew himself." Rebecca's words flew out of her mouth without a single breath in between. "I was able to get out of it, but I was expecting it. Looking for it."

"Don't let your guard down yet," Lexy said. "Sara and those other women had been well out of his life when they were murdered. You still need to keep your eyes open."

"I have to see her. I have to talk to her."

"We can't go there. He'll see you and want to pick right back up where the two of you left off."

"We'll be discreet. It's a Saturday night. The place will be packed." The wheels began turning in Rebecca's mind, and she paced back and forth with nervous energy. "We can slip in, wait until she goes to the restroom, and I'll catch her in there and warn her."

Lexy took a couple of steps back. Her forehead crinkled, and she looked at Rebecca as if she had gone completely mad.

"I have to do something." Rebecca stopped her pacing and closed the distance between them. "I can't just sit here and do nothing when someone else's life is in danger." She grabbed both of Lexy's hands in hers. "It would be my fault. He's angry with me, and he'll take it out on her."

"I would like to go on record and say that this is a very bad idea. But I'm not going to let you go alone so...I guess we're going."

Rebecca dropped Lexy's hands and raced out of the room and into the hall bathroom. "I need a hair tie," she shouted over her shoulder.

Lexy pulled a blue elastic band off her wrist and headed toward the bathroom. "You don't even have enough hair for this," she said, handing it to her.

"I've got enough for a little ponytail." She gathered up her short locks and twisted the elastic around them several times. "It's not a complete disguise, but it'll make me less noticeable from across a room." She looked at Lexy's reflection in the mirror. "Go put your hair up and put on your glasses."

Lexy groaned and gave an overdramatic spin on her heel before stomping out of the bathroom. "Oh my god, I can't believe we're doing this."

Rebecca finished her look with thick, caked-on bands of black eyeliner. Lexy was pulling a bottle of Tequila out of a top cabinet when Rebecca met up with her in the kitchen. She filled two shot glasses and handed one of them off.

"I am not going into this unarmed," Lexy said. She clinked her glass with Rebecca's and threw it back in one swallow.

Rebecca smirked at her choice of weapon, but she was right. They both needed a bit of courage in their back pocket. Unlike Lexy, she spread her shot out over three gulps before slamming her glass back on the counter. Her face twitched and scrunched for a moment as the alcohol burned a trail down her throat.

Lexy was already on the phone calling a cab when Rebecca caught up with her at the front door. Facing each other for a final once-over, they both gave quick nods of approval before heading out. With the door closing behind them, their mission was underway.

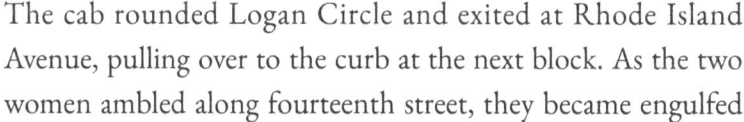

The cab rounded Logan Circle and exited at Rhode Island Avenue, pulling over to the curb at the next block. As the two women ambled along fourteenth street, they became engulfed by the typical Saturday-night, bar-hopping crowd that filled the sidewalks of downtown D.C.

After fifty yards or so, they reached their destination and proceeded with caution, past the pair of oversized bouncers and into a sea of weekend party-goers.

Rebecca's nostrils were immediately hit by an invisible wall of allspice and sweat. The source was obvious. The center of the venue was crammed with young patrons, hopping and swaying to the hot reggae beats that boomed from the overhead speakers. In addition, practically every dining table held steaming plates of jerk chicken and spicy Jamaican patties. Her eyes began to water, as did her mouth, and she realized then that she hadn't eaten since a late lunch nearly eight hours earlier. She buried her hunger in the back of her mind and continued to examine the room.

The restaurant was much larger than the initial street view had let on. Inside, large tiki-torch light fixtures hung from the high ceiling and strings of white lights draped the walls. The room was illuminated to a much brighter level than she would have liked, but the excessive number of people did an excellent job of camouflaging their presence.

The stucco walls were peppered with various hangings of Bob Marley paintings, Jamaican flags, and Red Stripe signs. Lounge sofas squared off to fill the two boxy corner coves on either side of the front door. Large windows gave the small groups lucky enough to obtain those prime seating spots an open view of the bustling street outside. Beyond that, various sizes of dining tables and chairs ran the length of the walls on each side.

The bar itself seemed miles away, situated at the far end of the elongated space. Its large U-shape nearly filled the entire back wall, aside from the kitchen door on the right and a dark narrow corridor that led to the restrooms on the left. A backlit glass-bottle and stucco wall made up the front face of the bar. The array of blue, green, and gold beer and wine bottles emitted a spectrum of radiating light that danced and flickered as a hundred pairs of legs constantly passed in front of it.

Overall, it was an odd mixture of modern swank and Caribbean flair that, for some reason, seemed to work unusually well. The alluring charm of the place was hard to resist, and Rebecca soon found herself swaying along with the smooth island sound. Her Jamaican fantasy was short-lived, however, as Lexy nudged her hard in the ribs.

"There he is," she said, giving a subtle nod toward the far right side of the bar. "And there *she* is, too."

Rebecca's eyes followed Lexy's sightline and landed on Andrew and his female companion. They were huddled together on the side of the bar, right next to the door leading to the back kitchen. His back was to them, but a brief profile shot as he reached for his drink confirmed his identity. He wore his customary white linen shirt which glorified his summer tan. A straw hat and a pair of Ray-Bans was all he would need to be mistaken for one of the restaurant's tiki-bar tourist props.

The woman he was with faced them, and Rebecca swallowed hard at the sight of her. It was exactly what she had been expecting, but seeing it firsthand made her pulse race. Her dark, shoulder-length waves bounced as she tossed her head with an exaggerated laugh at whatever Andrew said to her.

The woman was strikingly beautiful, to say the least. Her skin had a rich Mediterranean tone, and the two of them could have easily passed for a European couple touring The States. A salmon-colored top hung loosely on her shoulders with wire-thin spaghetti straps. It was a beautiful color that seamlessly complemented the beachy theme of the restaurant, but not so much with her dark coloring.

Rebecca spent the next few minutes searching for any other aspects of the woman that she could criticize when her intent became crystal clear. She was jealous. Her career-minded lifestyle and lack of a regular dating schedule had sheltered her from the ugliness and heartache that jealousy usually brought with it. It was an entirely new experience for her, and she didn't quite know how to handle it.

Luckily Lexy was there to bring their goal back into focus. After all, they were there to save that woman, and nothing else mattered.

Rebecca got knocked around a bit as she jockeyed for a better viewing position on the makeshift dance floor. She was losing sight of him as she and Lexy were pushed further and further back by the oblivious dancers that surrounded them. They couldn't stay in their current location; not because of the obstructed view, but because, at that moment, they were on stage. A crowded stage, but a stage nonetheless. Andrew could turn and spot them in seconds. Their so-called disguises wouldn't fool anyone.

She scanned the room and immediately found an optimal viewing spot. On the right, the first table after the window sofas. It was far enough away but close enough to the door for a quick exit if the need arose. It was also situated against the wall and would force him to turn completely around to see them. The centers of the tables created a direct line to his back, and they'd be able to watch him all night without moving an inch.

Unfortunately, the table was already being occupied by a young twenty-something couple. Rebecca looked around a little more for another viable option. As expected, every table was taken, and no one was looking to leave any time soon. Her attention returned to the young couple at the first table.

Rebecca reached into her purse and took out her wallet. From there, she pulled out a crisp hundred dollar bill. She approached the couple and offered it to them in exchange for their table. Not many young drinkers would pass up an opportunity to have their drinks paid for throughout the night, and they were no different. The girl snatched the bill out of Rebecca's hand, shoved it deep into her denim front pocket, and skipped off toward the dance floor with her boyfriend in tow.

Rebecca took the seat against the wall and checked her sightline. Perfect. Lexy flagged down a waiter and ordered a couple of the signature jerk chicken appetizers and a pitcher of margaritas.

"It's to help with our cover," Lexy said. "We would look even more conspicuous if we were just sitting here staring at the bar."

"You won't get any complaints from me. I'm starving."

"How long do you think it took for him to pick her up? Did she come with him or did he just meet her here tonight?"

"I have no idea." The fire of jealousy Rebecca had buried earlier reignited and burned high and hot. "I can't believe he replaced me that quick. Just last week he was camped outside my house eight hours a night, and now..."

"You are so much hotter than her," Lexy said with a smirk. Rebecca's jealousy was noticeable, and it wasn't long before her friend picked up on it.

"You always know exactly what to say, don't you?"

"I've been where you are many times. Too many times."

"Well? Go on." Rebecca had no problem allowing Lexy to make her feel better—even if it was catty and immature.

"He settled for second place because he couldn't get first." Lexy picked up right where she had left off. "Actually, she's more like a ninth." She took another look at the woman. Her brows furrowed and she tilted her head—the way people did in art museums as they critiqued the paintings. "Scratch that, she's not even in the race anymore, because she was disqualified for being too stupid."

They both erupted into laughter. The waiter appeared with their food and drink just as the women calmed themselves into low giggles. He filled two massive margarita glasses and chuckled along with them without the slightest clue why.

"Seriously, though" Lexy took a sip out of her oversized glass. "What are you going to say to her?"

"I don't know. I guess I need to find out if she even knows who Andrew Donovan is first."

"And then what? Tell her she could be sliced up into a million pieces at any moment?"

"I'll just tell her the truth. There is a murderer on the loose that is carving up his ex-girlfriends and she's putting herself in danger just by being with him."

"What if she already knows all of that?" Lexy asked.

"Then she has a death wish and she's an idiot."

"You had a death wish."

"I had a plan," Rebecca said defensively. "It's very unlikely that this woman has that same plan."

The two of them sat in relative silence as the hour passed, enjoying the music, nibbling on chicken, and starting on their second pitcher. The atmosphere was electric and, in the back of her mind, Rebecca wished she didn't have a job to do so she could sit back and enjoy herself. She made a mental note—when it was all over, she would be back.

They both kept keen eyes on the bar and were amazed at how much the woman could drink without visiting the restroom. After three margaritas herself, Rebecca was hoping the woman would make the walk soon.

As if by some miraculous act of telepathy, the woman stood, kissed Andrew on the cheek, and rounded the bar on her way to the dark corridor on the other side of the room. Rebecca shot out of her seat and quickly disappeared into the dance floor crowd. Snaking her way through gyrating hips, flailing arms, and flying sweat, she finally emerged on the other side. Once there, she hit another crowd. Hands in the air, passing money and drinks back and forth, to and from the three bartenders slinging drinks behind the bar. It was organized chaos in the most unorganized sort of way.

She had lost sight of Andrew in the massive crowd and confusion, but she spotted pink salmon amidst the river of people and that became her beacon. Rebecca amped up her aggressiveness and plowed through until she landed in the woman's wake, struggling to stay on her heels as the path tried to close in front of her.

As she rounded the left corner of the bar, the crowd dispersed slightly and she found some breathing room. She let the woman go on ahead as she looked over her shoulder to be sure Andrew was still where he was supposed to be. He was. And he was staring straight at her.

She stood motionless, unable to move as their eyes locked. His face was without expression. There was no surprise, no anger, no suspicion. No jumping out of his seat to chase her down. He simply saw her. The precautions she and Lexy had taken to prevent that one moment was all for naught. He saw her and there was no way around it.

Her mind raced with the limited options she had to choose from. She was caught, and her intent was plainly obvious. She was following his date into the bathroom, and there was no hope to explain it away as coincidence. She could just talk to him. It wouldn't be the end of the world. He wasn't threatening her...he had never threatened her. So why was her gut tying itself into knots? Why did she suddenly have such a strong instinct to flee?

His face was like stone, and his eyes never left hers. They never blinked. They didn't even twitch. She tried with every ounce of strength she had to get her legs moving, but they wouldn't budge; not that she knew which direction to go in. The deafening drum beats pounding out of the speakers filled her brain, blocking out all traces of coherent thought. She fell back into her default position—flight.

Breaking eye contact, she pivoted and ducked into the crowd. She made it across the dance floor and back to Lexy in a matter of seconds.

"We have to go. Now."

"Did you talk to her? What did she say?"

"Now." Rebecca's tone was sharp and cutting.

She glanced back at the bar, thinking it was impossible that he could have tracked her in that crowd all the way back to her table. But it was possible. He had spun a hundred and eighty degrees in his seat and was facing them head-on. Once again, their eyes locked and that same blank expression burned a hole right through her.

"Oh my god," Lexy said as she followed Rebecca's eyes.

He never took his eyes off of her. Rebecca knew he saw Lexy too, but his stare remained fixed, chilling her blood as it raced through her veins.

She rifled through her purse and threw another large bill onto the table. Topping it with an empty glass, she grabbed Lexy by the arm and yanked her toward the door and out onto the sidewalk. She continued, at a quick clip, up to the corner of the block where several yellow cabs were parked and waiting to fill their back seats with intoxicated passengers. Rebecca threw open the door of the first one they came to and pushed Lexy in.

Once inside, Lexy turned to Rebecca, her eyes wide with disbelief. "That was so weird. Did you see the way he was looking at you?"

"Of course I did. Why else do you think I was high-tailing it out of there?"

"It was just so creepy. He looked like a statue, or a mannequin, or something."

Rebecca's heart beat out of her chest. The adrenaline that coursed through her veins at that moment rivaled any thrill ride she could ever imagine.

"What about that woman? What's going to happen to her?" Lexy's face was wrought with concern.

"She'll be fine, for now. Nothing's going to happen to her tonight."

"How can you possibly know that?"

"Because she's with him. The killer never strikes when he's with them. Right now, she's as safe as she could be."

"And if Andrew's the killer? Because, from what I just witnessed from him in there, that scenario seems quite conceivable."

"Will you get it together, Lexy! He saw us. We're witnesses. Even if he was the killer, there's no way he would lay a hand on her tonight. We did our job, so calm the hell down."

Rebecca turned and looked out of the back window. She had almost expected to see him barge out of the bar and sprint up the street after them. But an action such as that wouldn't agree with the side of him she had just seen. It was as if he was a completely different person. Did he have no feeling left for her? Or was he plotting his revenge on her for leaving him the way she did? She didn't know what was going on in his mind and didn't think she wanted to find out.

Chapter 36

Rebecca sat on Lexy's bed hugging her knees to her chest. It was only 8:00 in the morning and she had already declined two calls from Andrew on her cell. She should have destroyed the extra phone as soon as she had left his house that morning or, at the very least, not brought it with her to Lexy's. However, she had been using it to track the frequency of his calls and gauge his remaining interest in her. When his calls had ceased, it had become a source of peace of mind for her. As the calls returned that morning, the phone had done nothing but reignite her fears.

She jumped as the ringtone began again. Finally, she mustered up the courage to answer it.

"Wow, is this really you?" he asked.

"Yes, it's me."

"I wasn't expecting you to answer. Now I don't remember what I was going to say."

Rebecca remained silent. She didn't know what to say either. He sounded like he was back to his old self. He sounded like the Andrew she was actually beginning to have feelings for.

But she couldn't forget the night before. The way he had looked at her...watched her. The memory sent chills racing up her spine.

"I saw you last night."

"I know."

"Why were you there?"

"It's a public place. And they have amazing food. Why wouldn't I go there?" Her words were innocent and logical, but her tone was sharp and biting.

"Come on. Don't be like that." His voice dripped with tenderness and, in that moment, she remembered why she had refused to talk to him before. "Were you there looking for me?" he added.

"Don't flatter yourself. How would I even have known that you'd be there?" She threw in a little sass for good measure.

"Well, I'm glad you were there. And I'm glad you finally answered your—"

"Am I that easy to replace? It's been what...not even two weeks and already you've hooked another? Out of sight, out of mind?"

"You were never out of my mind, and you know that." He paused and she heard a heavy sigh drift out of the phone. "That woman doesn't mean anything to me. I barely know her. I was just trying to get you out of my head."

Rebecca didn't want to believe him but his pain and torment were deafening. The tiniest of cracks formed on her heart and, unfortunately, it was just enough.

"It didn't work, by the way. You're still the only one I want."

She searched her brain frantically for the images from the night before. They had haunted her dreams the entire night, but right then, they were nowhere to be found. The only face she could attach to the pleading voice on the phone was the one that had kissed her with such tenderness all those nights before.

"I need to see you," he said. "Can you come over this evening? Just to talk, I promise. I'll cook for you. The best paella you've ever tasted."

"Well, I do love paella." She did love it, but that wasn't the reason she had accepted his invitation. She needed a resolution. Or closure, if it went in that direction.

Ending the call, she looked up to find Lexy, holding up the doorframe with her shoulder.

"You are *not* going to see him."

Rebecca hopped off the bed and began rummaging through her suitcase, lying open on the floor. "The whole point of last night was to get that woman away from him. If he's seeing me, then he's not seeing her. Mission accomplished."

"You expect me to believe you're doing this for her? That you don't have your own personal reasons for meeting up with him?"

Rebecca didn't answer. She didn't have an answer. Not one that Lexy would be satisfied with. Her fingers curled around a strappy black dress and she pulled it from the case as she stood up and approached the door.

"I've got this," she said as she closed the door on Lexy and the rest of her meddling questions.

———————◆○◆———————

Rebecca sat, her nerves firing on all cylinders as she checked her reflection once again in the glossy sheen of the dining table. Her shoulders twitched as Andrew leaned over from behind her and placed a plate of steaming focaccia bread in front of her along with a small plate of seasoned olive oil.

"This should tide us over until the paella is done. I know I'm mixing Italian with Spanish, but hey...there are no rules here," he said with a grin. "Except how amazing this is going to be, so keep your expert chef critique to yourself until you've tried it, okay?"

He then disappeared into the kitchen and reappeared with two overfilled glasses of red wine. He set one in front of her and walked around the table to take the seat across from her.

"Thank you for coming over."

A trembling hand dropped below the table's edge and traveled to the purse she had strategically draped over the back of the chair. She stroked the exterior leather until she felt the comforting outline of the pistol stashed inside. She had no plans to use it but was ready to, if a particular unwanted visitor happened to grace their presence. Feeling safe, she lifted her glass and gulped down half of her wine in an attempt to still her shaking trigger finger.

"We have a lot to talk about," she said, lowering her glass back down to the table.

"Yes, we do. Starting with you."

Her hand stopped its descent and clutched the glass with a firm grip.

Andrew's eyes held hers tight. "When I found out you weren't who you said you were...I gave you the benefit of the doubt. I assumed you were just being cautious with your personal information, given the horrible things I had been accused of."

"B—but, that *is* why." She wasn't even convincing herself at that point.

"No. It's not." He leaned forward and rested his folded arms on the table. "You didn't want me to know that Sara was your sister."

Her heart stopped, and then started again at a rapid pace. She felt the blood drain from her face.

"How long did you think it would take me to find out, once I knew your real name?" His eyes remained locked on hers, undoubtedly enjoying the torment he was putting her through. "Our meeting wasn't accidental. You were investigating me."

"It may have started out that way, but once I got to know you—"

"Save it." He raised his hand, making it clear he had no interest in her explanation. "It could never work between us. Not now."

His eyes darkened as if a shade had fallen over them. That was the look she remembered from the night before. The look that, had she remembered it during his call earlier, would have saved her from being there at all. His voice had deepened to a low and slow growl that paralyzed her. Even as he reached for his glass and took another sip of wine, his eyes never left hers.

"I have to admit it was pretty entertaining." His lips curved into a smile and released a gruff chuckle. "You were so terrified of Spencer...when all he was doing was trying to save your life."

"No." She heard her voice reverberate throughout her skull.

She needed her gun. Her shoulder strained, but her arm would not budge. She pushed her legs into the floor to stand. They wouldn't move. They couldn't move. They felt disembodied as if they didn't even belong to her anymore. Overwhelming weakness surged through her body and replaced the great strength she once had.

"He tried so hard to drive you away. You just kept coming back. Poor kid. Such a moral dilemma."

Her mouth, void of all moisture, fought hard to release her voice. "But it couldn't be you. You had alibis. And that last girl...you couldn't have killed her. You were with me!" The words slurred into one another, barely understandable as numbness spread to the tip of her tongue.

"Funny thing about 'estimated time of death.' It's only an estimate. There are countless ways to increase a liver temp and throw their entire timing system off," he said, his shoulders bouncing as he laughed.

A deafening gasp escaped her as his laugh came at her from all sides. She squeezed her eyes shut and gave her head a quick shake, trying to rid herself of the cackling onslaught. When she opened them she saw his face blur and split in two. She squeezed them shut and opened them once more. Again, his face multiplied and drifted apart. *What is happening? Get your gun, get your gun!*

She glanced over at the half-empty wine glass and it all made sense. Looking back at Andrew, a dark fog creeped into the surrounding edge of her vision. As it spread further and further across her sight, she knew she only had herself to blame.

She heard his voice in the distance, but couldn't make out anything he was saying. His body was a gray silhouette as it rose and drifted toward her. At last, the darkness engulfed her and the world turned black.

Chapter 37

R ebecca's eyes fluttered open to a blinding wall of fluorescent light. She winced and snapped them shut again. On her second attempt, she cracked them into slits, allowing them to adjust before opening them fully. A sharp pain shot through her neck as she tried to turn her head and get her bearings. Her head pounded as if a stampede of horses was running in one ear and out the other. Her shoulder blades ached as they dug into the hard surface beneath her.

The pain was there, but bearable. At that moment, she welcomed the pain. It felt better than the numbness that engrossed her earlier. *She was still alive.*

She wiggled her fingers and toes. Whatever he had drugged her with had almost completely worn off, and sensation was returning. Her eyes traveled down her body. Without lifting her head, her range of sight only reached her upper chest and the black dress that still covered her. Her eyes darted around in an attempt to identify the room. Bright fluorescent lights. White walls. Stainless steel surgical trays. Was she in a hospital? Had someone saved her? Was it Spencer?

Out of the corner of her eye, she caught a glimpse of movement. Flinching from the pain, she slowly turned her head in that direction. Her vision was still foggy, but she was able to make out a figure, dressed in white, blending into the walls themselves—the only separation being the head of black hair that appeared floating in suspension, bobbing about as the figure moved.

It was Andrew. She could hardly see him, but she knew it was him. She squeezed her eyes shut and then opened them wide, blinking several times. The fog began to lift and the picture became clearer. His back was to her and he was doing something with his hands over a white countertop. She couldn't see what he was working on, but every few seconds he reached for something off to the side and his profile came into view. His mouth was moving, but all that came out was a low, droning sound.

She guessed he didn't know she was awake or that she would wake up that soon. She couldn't see or feel any restraints on her body. Her arms and legs were free. However, she refrained from using them for fear of alerting him to her conscious state. She needed more time to regain her senses but, for all she knew, her time may have already run out.

She could still hear his voice drifting over her from the other side of the room. It remained muffled, as if he were talking underwater, but there were definitely words there. She opened and shut her jaw a few times in rapid succession until she heard a small click. The pressure in her ears released and his voice rang through loud and clear.

"Seriously, I never thought it would ever be you on that table. You were a keeper. At least, I thought you were." He continued to work at the counter with his back to her. He was talking to himself, but perhaps he had also hoped his words would float into her mind through unconscious ears. "You know what was so great about you?" he continued. "You did such a fantastic job of keeping our relationship a secret...of keeping yourself a mystery. No one will even link you to me. Just like the one before you." From his profile, she could see a smile spread into his cheek. "Don't worry, I wasn't cheating on you. I wasn't lying when I said I didn't know her. I thought I was done with all that when I met you, I really did." He let out a loud sigh and shook his head from side to side. "What can I say? I'm weak. I've always had trouble quitting things cold-turkey. But honestly, I was ready to spend the rest of my life with you. Then you decided to go all nuts. And now...there's no other choice but for you to spend the rest of *your* life with me." With those last words, he turned to face her and their eyes met.

"Well, well, well...look who's awake?" He approached the table and stroked the backs of his fingers slowly down her cheek.

He leaned down to grab hold of the leather strap dangling from the edge of the table. Conjuring up every ounce of strength she had, she brought the heel of her hand up and slammed it into the underside of his chin. His teeth clashed together and sent him stumbling backward.

She flung herself off the table. As her bare feet hit the cold concrete floor, her knees buckled and she sprawled out onto her stomach. Immediately, she scrambled to get her legs under her and then pushed herself into a crouch. A glance over her shoulder revealed blue eyes flashing like the flame of a gas burner. Blood trickled out of the corner of his mouth. His tongue emerged to lick it away followed by a wide grin of bloodstained teeth. In an instant, he lunged toward her.

Her feet, damp with sweat, slipped and slid, trying to gain traction. She set her sights on the closed door in front of her. It was the only door in the room and her only shot at getting out of there alive.

She dug her toes into the floor and propelled herself forward just as his outstretched arm grabbed the hem of her short dress. She left him with a fistful of silk as she reached the door and threw it open.

Once outside the room, she bolted across plush carpet, looking side to side to get her bearings. All of it was familiar. The billiards table. The stone fireplace. The large sliding glass door that led out to the patio. She had been down there only once before.

She raced toward the glass door and began pulling on it with all her might. It wouldn't move. She flipped the lock switch, but still nothing. Shoving back the vertical blinds, she saw the secondary lock consisting of a broom handle in the slide track.

His footsteps reached the carpet and were coming at her...fast. Abandoning the door, she dashed around the corner wall and up the steps, taking them two at a time. When she reached the top, his hand clamped down around her ankle and pulled her leg out from under her. She sprawled through the doorway and slammed hard onto the tile floor at the entrance to the kitchen. Pain shot through her knee where it struck the edge of the stair.

She yanked her leg, but his grip was unbreakable, pulling her down the steps toward him. Twisting onto her back, she raised her free leg and kicked her heel into his nose. Warm blood sprayed across her legs and feet. With one more violent yank, her ankle slipped through his fingers and she was free.

She scrambled back up the stairs on all fours. Leaping onto the kitchen tile, the same wet blood that freed her from his grasp suddenly sent her skidding into the doorframe. Down the short corridor she could see the foyer and the front door. She turned in that direction, but stopped in her tracks as he stepped out from the stairway and filled the hall, blocking her escape route. She turned and ran in the opposite direction, further into the kitchen, aiming for the door to the outside deck.

He caught up with her at the sunroom. Grabbing her arm, he flung her back into the kitchen like a rag doll. She crashed into the breakfast table, knocking it over and sending chairs flying against the wall.

He threw his body on top of her back. The full weight of him took her breath away, leaving her gasping uncontrollably for oxygen. He put his forearm onto the back of her head and leaned hard into it. Her face smushed into the floor and she heard her teeth grind into the ceramic. She kicked her legs and threw her fists back, trying to reach him. He released the pressure on her head, but only so he could grab both of her wrists and pin them behind her back. Holding them tight, he sat up and straddled her hips.

"Man, you are spunky."

"Let me go!" she screamed at the top of her lungs, hoping someone would hear her. Anyone.

"Not a chance, sweetheart."

He then flipped her over onto her back, maintaining his straddle, and dropped his weight onto her abdomen. Her breath whooshed out of her. During the transition her arms came free. She flailed them wildly, landing a fist deep into his ribs. Her other hand made contact with the front of his neck and she dug her fingernails into his throat. She raked them down his chest, leaving four crimson gashes in their wake. He let out a deep-throated yelp and slapped her hand away.

"Stop. Fighting. Me," he said as he caught her hands and pinned them beneath his knees. Wrapping his hands around her neck, he lifted her head and drove her skull into the floor. "Stop making me hurt you. It's not my style."

She cried out, feeling like a lightning bolt had just been injected into her brain. The pain was excruciating as it spread throughout her body. His hands tightened around her neck as he dug his thumbs into her windpipe.

"I didn't want to hurt you," he said through clenched teeth. "You wouldn't have felt a thing. My goal has never been to cause pain." He lowered his face to within inches of hers. Drops of blood and saliva pelted her cheeks with every one of his words.

"But now...oh, honey...now you're going to feel all of it. Every slice. No one makes a fool out of me and gets away with it. Not even someone as amazing as you."

She tried to scream but there was no air. She had no voice. Her lungs burned like fire. A sledgehammer pounded in her skull. Pressure built up behind her eyes and she squeezed them shut to prevent them from popping out of her head. Suddenly, his grip loosened and a gush of air flooded her chest. She gasped and coughed violently, taking in as much air as she could, not knowing if he was going to begin again.

"You're not getting off that easy," he said in a low growl.

Her eyes flew open and locked on his. They were cold, blue steel and they penetrated her like two icepicks driving into her eye sockets. She couldn't speak. She didn't know what she would say even if she could. She couldn't think. She had no plan. All she could do was try to survive the next minute, and then the minute after that, and so on. Her thoughts were scrambled and strewn randomly about inside her brain, partly due to head trauma and partly due to shock. But the one thought she could decipher was the one that informed her that there was a likely chance she would die. That night. There, in that house, on that kitchen floor.

She felt his grip tighten again around her throat. No. She couldn't go through that again. She wouldn't last as long as she did the first time. Less than thirty seconds in, her vision began to dim. He became nothing more than a shadow hovering over her. With a second shadow hovering over him. What *was* that?

The loud shattering sound echoed through the house and broken glass rained down on her. Andrew's hands went limp and his torso collapsed on top of her, smothering her with his chest. She inhaled deeply several times and her vision began to clear. She tried to focus on the figure standing over her. She blinked her eyes rapidly to clear the remnants of fog.

For a split second, she mistook the figure for her own reflection. In her concussed state, it made perfect sense. But it didn't take long for her to realize it wasn't her reflection. It wasn't a hallucination, either. It was Marie. She was there. She wasn't dead. She was there...and that quickly, Rebecca devised her plan.

Chapter 38

A ndrew awoke to find himself lying on his back, staring up at the ceiling. He recognized the light fixture—the dining room. The room where, just a short time earlier, he had that Amanda-Rebecca woman nearly pissing herself.

His head pounded. He was acutely aware of the blood pulsing through his brain with every beat of his heart. A warm liquid trickled behind his ear, giving the sensation of hundreds of ants scurrying through his hair.

He tried to raise his hands to his head, but they wouldn't move. Tugging and pulling on his wrists only resulted in a range of motion of an inch or two. His head lifted to investigate the issue, and what he saw took his breath away.

He was lying on top of the dining table, his black silk boxers providing his only cover. Both of his wrists were at his sides, bound with layers upon layers of gray duct tape that extended underneath the table, pinning him to it. His ankles were in the same boat. More strips wrapped across his hips and upper chest. His muscles bulged as he flexed his entire body in an attempt to rip through the tape. No luck. Each restraint point had been wrapped over a dozen times. They might as well have been iron chains bolted through the foundation. He wasn't going anywhere.

He racked his brain, trying to remember what happened last. He was with Rebecca in the kitchen. They were fighting. And then...nothing. *She* did this?

Suddenly, he heard the sound of metal scraping. It was coming from another room, but getting closer and louder every second. He turned his head and immediately found the source of the noise. Rebecca stood in the entranceway to the kitchen. She looked at him, her face void of all expression. Yellow dishwashing gloves extended up to her elbows and, in one hand, she held a large chef knife. In the other, she gripped the long cylindrical honing steel that came with it. With long, slow motions, she scraped the blade along the length of the steel. The screeching made his ears burn, and he squeezed his eyes shut as the throbbing in his head increased.

When he opened them again, the realization of what was happening sent a shock through his system. He struggled violently, desperately trying to pull his limbs free, but it was pointless. His eyes widened as he received his first taste of true fear.

"I think it's sharp enough," a voice called out from the opposite side of the room.

He whipped his head to the other side and his heart screeched to a halt. "Marie? Oh my god, it's you. You came back."

His brain flooded with endorphins and a feeling of warmth spread throughout his body. He could no longer feel the pain in his head or the fear of the knife-wielding woman in the doorway.

"I knew I could make you come back." His head lowered back to the table and a warm smile spread across his face. His eyelids lowered slightly, giving him a dazed, drugged look. "I knew if I could only see you again...talk to you...we could work everything out," he said with a warm tenderness to his voice.

"Is that what all this was about?" Marie asked, walking toward him. "Carving up those women? What was that? Some sick ploy to get my attention?"

His smile never wavered. "You're here, aren't you?"

Her brows cinched together and she grabbed a silver candlestick off of the buffet cabinet behind her. She raised it over her head, rage flashing in her eyes. Her chest heaved with rapid breaths.

"Marie!" Rebecca's voice was loud and firm.

Slowly, she lowered the weapon to her side. "You know what? No. As much as I really want to cave your face in...no." She turned and placed the candlestick back on the buffet. "We have bigger plans for you."

Stepping up to the side of the table, she slid her hand into his. He locked his fingers within hers, squeezing them tight so she could never leave him again. He lost himself in the soft, green pool of her eyes and all his previous anger melted away. Fear, selfishness. Gone. She was his entire world. He had tried to let her go. Tried to replace her. But, he knew that would never be possible. There was only one Marie...and only one way to get her to come back.

"You did get my attention, Drew." Her voice was soft as she gazed down at him. "Watching CNN, reading the news reports. You reminded me what it was like to be with you. Your belief that women were just there to serve your needs, whatever they happened to be at the time." She pasted a serene smile on her face, but her words were laced with sarcasm. "That you could use women in whatever way you saw fit to advance yourself in the world. Your career, your image, your social status. Living with you meant living in fear every day. Not just for me...but also for our unborn child."

"What? We have another child?"

"A daughter. A beautiful, innocent, little girl that I vowed would never know her father. Never know what her father was capable of." The tenderness began to vanish from her voice and the crease between her eyebrows reappeared. "A girl that I would raise to be strong and independent without you filling her life with corruption, slavery, and abuse."

"I would never—"

"You would!" She wrenched her hand away from his. "Look at what you have done already, and you don't even see anything wrong with it."

He watched her eyes flash with anger. Hatred.

"What you did to them is inconceivable. You tortured them, and mutilated them, and dumped them like garbage for the world to see. And the worst part is...you can't even empathize with them. You have no idea what you really put them through."

She leaned down until her face was just inches from his. He could feel her breath across his lips. "You have no idea. But you're going to learn...compliments of your local five-star chef." She grinned and threw a glance at Rebecca.

Andrew's eyes followed hers to the other side of the room where Rebecca still stood, still sharpening that same knife. She took her cue and disappeared into the kitchen, returning seconds later carrying a large silver platter. She took slow steps along the edge of the dining table, giving Andrew a clear view of the platter's contents. She had cleaned out his knife block. Seven knives of all shapes and sizes lined the silver tray. From the small boning knife to the carving knife to the notched Santoku. She set the platter down with a loud clang right next to his face.

"No!" His pulse quickened. He thrashed his head back and forth, and his hips bucked and squirmed as he tried to free himself. It was no use. *It was his turn.*

Rebecca's hands lingered on the handles on the sides of the platter. She looked at Andrew, his eyes glossy, silently pleading.

"Don't do this, Amanda. This isn't you. Don't do this."

A tear emerged from the inside corner of his eye. She tracked it as it ran down the ridge of his nose and off the tip.

"Rebecca." Marie placed both of her hands on the table on the other side of Andrew's head and leaned forward to look deep into her eyes. "You saw what he did to them. You would have been next. Tonight. That's what he was planning to do to you."

Still, Rebecca stood motionless, hands on the handles, staring down into Andrew's eyes, his tears forming a tiny puddle of droplets on the table's surface.

"Don't listen to that psychotic bitch," he said with a quiver in his voice.

"He carved them up while they were still alive, for God's sake."

"She's making you do her dirty work so you can take the fall for it. Why won't she kill me herself?"

"I have no problem killing you myself. In fact, I've fantasized about it for three fucking years."

Rebecca listened to the two of them take turns barking at her until she simply couldn't stand it anymore. She let their voices trail off as she disappeared into her own head.

Murder. That wasn't the way it was supposed to go. That wasn't her plan. And for good reason. She wasn't a murderer. Half an hour before, yes. She was ready to kill him then. When he was squeezing the life out of her. Absolutely, she could have killed him then. But, looking down into his terrified eyes, listening to him beg for her mercy. It wasn't going to be as easy as she had thought.

What would happen if she called the police? If they came and arrested him? Unfortunately, she knew exactly what would happen. Because it had already happened. His expensive lawyers would get him off scott-free. And that was only if he could be brought back into court for it. She would show the police the room in the basement. The room where he did it, all of it. But all they would see was a workshop. The only blood they would find would be his own.

He wouldn't stop. He *hadn't* stopped. She, herself, had been in that room, on that table, just thirty minutes earlier. He had been about to kill her. He was going to slice her up and rearrange her skin, just like he did to the others...to Sara.

She knew how to stop him. She knew what she needed to do, and he wasn't going to be very happy about it.

She released the handles and tore her eyes away from him. She lowered them to the silver platter in front of her. The knives shimmered as the light overhead reflected off their steel blades. It was beautiful. Her fingers brushed over their black handles, one by one. They came to rest at her favorite. The fourteen-inch classic chef's knife. She lifted it off the tray and waved it around in her hand, admiring the heavy weight of it. Satisfied with her selection, she brought her free hand under the tip and held it with both hands like the treasure that it was.

She didn't look at him. Or Marie. She simply walked with quiet steps to the foot of the table where his bare feet hung off the edge. She paused and surveyed the animal in front of her. Then, with one swift motion, she grasped the handle, leaned forward, and with expert precision, flayed his left leg from thigh to calf.

The scream that followed shook the windows, but she barely heard it. She was lost in herself with only one thing on her mind. *Make him suffer.*

Blood poured like a faucet out of the two-foot incision. She had specifically aimed toward the outside of his thigh, careful to avoid the femoral artery. That would have been too quick. He had never shown that kind of mercy to his victims, and she wasn't going to show any to him.

Over the next few minutes, Rebecca worked on the leg. Using every knife on the tray, with laser focus and expert precision, she left a sight that would make even a surgeon proud.

Her eyes were cold and calm as she watched Andrew thrashing about on the table.

"Go ahead. Take a look," she told him.

He did. His eyes bulged and his screaming halted as the gruesome horror began to fully register. Rebecca studied his face and reveled in the pain, terror, and helplessness she saw there.

It was short-lived, however, as she watched his eyes roll back and his head drop backward onto the table like a dead weight. He was out cold. She thought it was remarkable that he had even lasted that long.

"Uh uh. He is not getting off that easy," Marie said as she scrambled around the table and scurried into the kitchen.

Rebecca remained.

She could hear Marie rifling around in the kitchen, opening and closing cabinet doors. A moment later, she re-emerged with a clear plastic bottle of blue glass cleaner. With lightning fast hands she unscrewed the cap and, at the same time, bent down to pick a sock out of the pile of Andrew's discarded clothes.

She doused the sock with the liquid, causing a strong stench of ammonia to fill the room. Next, her hand shoved the wet cloth under his nose. When she received no response, her patience vanished and she resorted to pouring half the bottle straight onto his face.

His head jerked violently as he sputtered and gagged on the liquid that filled his mouth. His screaming returned as a stream of blue seeped in between his eyelids. He threw his head back and forth, squeezing and blinking his eyes in rapid succession. When he opened them fully, they scanned the ceiling behind dilated pupils.

"Great. Now he's blind," said Marie. "Well, when one sense is lost, others are heightened. Carry on."

"Carry on with what?"

"Keep cutting." Marie picked up a knife from the tray and shoved it back into Rebecca's hand. "He's back awake and ready for more."

Rebecca took a step back. Marie's aggressive state felt wrong. Who was she kidding, it all felt wrong. Very. It caused Rebecca to question herself—question her humanity. She wasn't just executing a man. She was torturing him, dissecting him. She had already gone too far, and she couldn't take any of it back. This night was destined to haunt her for the rest of her life. Not just for what she had done to him, but also what he had done to her.

She agreed that he needed to die. As long as his heart still beat, he would still kill. But, she needed this night to be over, for her own sanity. He had to die, but she just couldn't bring herself to be the one to do it. She set the knife back onto the tray, stripped off the gloves, and backed up against the wall. She was done.

"He's a monster." Disappointment rang out in Marie's voice.

"He's human. And so am I."

Marie let out a deep sigh. "Fine. I understand."

She seemed to accept Rebecca's withdrawal and turned back to the barely conscious man lying on the table. Placing both hands on the sides of his face, she rotated his head toward her.

"You broke me, Drew. You broke our son. You will *not* break our daughter."

After donning Rebecca's discarded gloves, Marie picked up the chef knife, still dripping with his blood. Plunging it into the center of his torso, she then dragged it halfway down his abdomen.

Rebecca slapped her hands over her ears to muffle the deafening sound of his agony. Marie however, seemed oblivious to his wails.

After tossing the knife to the side, her gloved hand dove inside and upward until her fingers wrapped around his pulsating heart. Gripping it tight, she ripped it from his chest.

It continued to beat in her palm for another few seconds. When the spasming muscle stilled completely, Marie finished by pulling down his limp lower jaw and ramming the organ into his mouth.

Chapter 39

R ebecca paced back and forth across the kitchen tile in a panic. The reality of Andrew lying dead and mutilated in the other room had fully set in. That she was capable of performing such a gruesome act on another human being terrified her.

"We killed him. We actually killed him," she said as her pacing sped up even more.

"Will you please calm down?" Marie stood at the sink scrubbing Rebecca's lipstick-saturated saliva off the rim of a wine glass. After running a towel around it, she hung it by the stem under a cabinet.

"How can you be so stoic about this? He's dead, and we're both going to end up in orange jumpsuits on the wrong side of prison bars."

"It'll be fine. Trust me."

Rebecca threw exasperated arms in the air and let out a hopeless whimper.

"Here. Take this." Marie shoved a sponge and a spray bottle of bleach cleaner into Rebecca's hands. "Start with that doorjamb. And then anything else that your blood or saliva may have hit. And don't forget the steps."

Rebecca took the cleaning supplies and wasted no time scrubbing down every surface she came across. At the same time, Marie had dropped to her knees with a sponge of her own and worked on the floor.

"How did you show up when you did?" Rebecca was thankful that she had, but she was also a little curious about the perfect timing of it.

"I'd been watching the house. I saw you pull in."

"Then why did it take you so long to come in?"

"I couldn't risk just driving up behind you. I had to park down the street and walk up," Marie said, defending her rescue methods. "When I got here, I couldn't see or hear anything inside. I figured the two of you were probably upstairs, having sex or something, so I waited around the back so no one would see me. It wasn't until I saw you trying to get out of the patio door that I knew you were in trouble. I ran up the deck stairs and came in through the sunroom." Marie paused her scrubbing and met Rebecca's eyes. "I got here as fast as I could."

"I know you did. And thank you. You saved my life."

They both returned to their chores, eliminating every trace of Rebecca's presence. Rebecca disappeared down the stairs and cringed at the spray of Andrew's blood across the handrail.

"So where have you been all this time?" Rebecca called up from the stairwell.

"Cairo."

"Cairo? Egypt? Seriously?"

"There's a lot of work for an art historian over there."

"Then how did you know to come back? You couldn't possibly have heard about all this all the way over there."

"Actually, I did. I've been following the story online since he was first arrested. I can't believe they let him go. And then that other girl..." Marie shook her head in disgust. "I knew it was him, and I knew I needed to get back here and take care of it myself. I got into town two nights ago and have been keeping tabs on him the best I could."

Marie stood and groaned as she arched her back in pain. "I'm all done here. What about you?"

"Yeah. I got it all. But it looks like it's been scrubbed. It doesn't look natural."

Marie walked over to the top of the steps and peered down at the sections Rebecca was referring to. "That's just because it's still wet. It'll dry in a few minutes. Where else were you?"

"Down here."

Rebecca led the way down the stairs and into the massive basement. Turning the corner, she headed straight for the open door at the far end. Marie followed close behind, pausing at the patio door to give the handle and glass a quick spray and swipe.

Stepping into the brightly-lit workshop, the two women immediately halted. Marie's mouth fell open as her eyes took in the room.

"So this is where he does it," she said.

Rebecca stood, unable to move, unable to confirm Marie's deduction. The last time she'd been in that room, her view had been limited, and then she had run for her life. She took several minutes seeing what she didn't see before. The leather straps dangling from all four corners of the exam table. The glass jar filled to the rim with hundreds of thick pads of gauze. The steel tray on the counter he had been working at, and the array of surgical instruments lined up on top of it. Bile rose in her throat as she came face to face with what her fate had almost been.

"Come on," Marie said, stepping over to a cluster of blood droplets on the floor and kneeling beside it.

Rebecca snapped out of her trance and headed to the table. Nearly emptying her spray bottle onto the surface, she proceeded to wash every inch of it until she choked from the rising bleach fumes.

"How did you end up in Cairo, anyway? Why did you leave? You know, everyone thought you were dead."

"That was the point."

Rebecca waited.

"It's a long story."

She continued to wait.

"Okay, fine. I was pregnant. Drew didn't know, but I was getting to the point where I couldn't hide it much longer." She sat back on her heels and squinted up at the wall, as if trying to access parts of her memory she had purposefully forgotten. "It was the day of my twenty-week ultrasound. They told me I was having a baby girl, and I was petrified because of it." Tears began to stream down her cheeks. "He would have accepted a boy. He desperately wanted another boy. Not a girl, though. He made that clear with every fucking word that ever came out of his mouth. But a girl it was, and I didn't even want to imagine how he'd handle it. So I ran."

"But you left your son."

"I couldn't take him. He idolized his dad. He was a teenager, and he and Drew were practically inseparable. He wouldn't have understood why I had to get out of there." She wiped the back of her hand across her eyes. "I knew he would be okay. Drew would take good care of him. Regardless of what a shitty husband he was...he had always been a perfect father to Spencer."

Rebecca thought of shedding some light on exactly what Spencer had become since she had left. A disturbed young man that retreated to his room and cut himself just to take his mind off the knowledge that his father was a serial killer. She decided to keep that information to herself, though. Marie didn't need to know. She was back, and Andrew was dead. That was what was important.

They left the workshop in pristine condition as they shut off the light, closed the door, and headed back upstairs.

"There's something else I need to do," Rebecca said, making her way to Andrew's office in the front of the house.

Once inside the room, she raced behind his desk and booted up his computer. Draping a tissue over the mouse, she clicked into his control panel and did a complete search and delete of anything containing the name of Rebecca Black or Amanda White. She needed to become the ghost that Marie already was.

"Done," she said, trying to forget all the instances that those names had come up in his search history.

"Not quite yet. Give me your phone."

Marie followed her into the kitchen where Rebecca dug into her purse, pulled out her cell phone, and placed it in Marie's open, waiting palm.

"Is this disposable?" Marie asked, examining the phone as she turned it over in her hand.

"Yes."

"And is it the only one you've ever had contact with him on?"

"Yes. I never gave him my real number. And I don't bring my real phone when I'm going to be with him."

Marie smiled. "You're smarter than you look," she said as she ripped open the back, tore out the battery, placed it on the counter, and smashed it to pieces with the bottom of a wine bottle.

"What are we going to do with his body?" Rebecca's forehead crinkled, afraid of the possible answers she might hear.

"Nothing. We're leaving it."

Rebecca's eyes widened and her mouth gaped. "We can't let Spencer find him like that. It would destroy him."

"He won't be the one to find him. We'll get out of here and make an anonymous call to the police. Let them clean up this mess."

"They're going to investigate this. A murder of this magnitude, of this level of cruelty...they're going to be searching high and low for suspects." Rebecca's panic returned tenfold. "The detective...he knows I was dating him."

Marie grabbed her shoulders and stared deep into her eyes. "There is no proof that you were here tonight. They can suspect you all they want, but without proof, all they have is suspicion. Although a valid alibi would be very helpful."

Rebecca thought for a moment. "I can get an alibi," she said. "I have something in mind."

Chapter 40

R ebecca pulled her car into her reserved spot and made her way toward the front steps of her townhouse. Four days had passed since that horrifying night at the Donovan house. She had been pulled into the police station for questioning, but as far as she knew, they had no problem with her alibi. So why was she still a nervous wreck...waiting to be thrown into handcuffs at any moment?

The constant feeling of oncoming dread must have been the universe speaking to her because as soon as her key touched the front door lock, a familiar yet unwelcome face popped up behind her.

"Hello, Miss Black."

She nearly jumped out of her skin as she spun around. "Detective Harmon. What a surprise. Did you need something else from me?" Her voice quaked a little, but he didn't seem to notice.

"Actually, I just have some updates for you. Shall we go inside?"

"Of course," she said as she pushed through the door. Not that she had a choice in the matter.

He walked in behind her and made himself at home in his favorite corner chair, the same one as the last time he visited her. And just like the last time, Rebecca sat on the sofa across from him, a neurotic pile of guilt and anxiety. She adjusted the silk scarf draped around her neck and did her best to appear as calm and carefree as someone who hadn't dissected a live human being less than a week before.

Detective Harmon sat and stared at her as she shifted in her seat and fiddled with her scarf. He continued to watch her for a minute or two more before finally whipping out his trusty notebook and flipping it open.

"Okay, let's see," he said, rifling through countless pages filled with handwritten notes. "A Miss Lexy Laruso confirmed you were with her all weekend in Rehoboth Beach, and she has a number of photographs to prove it. Good thing they were all timestamped. Very convenient and impossible to manipulate." He paused to give her a sideways glance.

"That's right," Rebecca said, holding her ground.

"Your friend is a professional photographer, correct?"

"Yes."

"Mmm hmm."

That simple wordless ejection spoke volumes. It was that 'I know what you did and I'm not going to say anything, but I just want you to know that you're not fooling me' kind of sound.

"What's going to happen to Spencer?" she asked, veering the topic away from herself.

"He will stay under the guardianship of the Maddoxes until he turns eighteen, which will be in a week or so. After that, he'll be an adult and can do whatever he wants."

Rebecca's expression grew sullen thinking about how she had left him an orphan. He had another parent out there, but *he* didn't know that. And it would raise suspicion if Marie Donovan miraculously showed up now.

"He has his father's lawyer to help him through the adjustment of being on his own," Harmon added, noticing Rebecca's worrisome look. "As for you," he said, flipping through his notes. "Apparently, the notes from my earlier interviews with you have mysteriously disappeared. Because of that, there is no record of any Amanda White or the fact that you were living under two different identities, for some odd reason. Your alibi checks out...for the most part." He gave her another sly eye. "All in all, we're done with you, and you shouldn't be hearing from us again."

Rebecca let out a deep sigh of relief. "Thank you, Detective." She stood and extended her hand for an official handshake of closure.

Harmon approached and accepted her gesture. "You know," he added. "I've been with the department for thirty years. It can be extremely frustrating when you know deep in your soul that someone's guilty but the court still lets them go. Thankfully, someone decided to not let him get away with it this time."

His hand reached up to her neck and to the silky fabric wrapped around her throat. He grasped it with his fingers and tugged it downward, just enough to reveal a collar of green-yellow bruising. Sliding it back into place, he gave her a gentlemanly nod and let himself out the front door.

Epilogue

S pencer rolled himself up to the massive walnut desk. It had quickly become one of his most cherished spots. He felt important. Powerful. Free. It hadn't taken him long at all to embrace his new role as man of the house, although, he had to admit he was lonely. But it was a small price to pay for the return of his sanity.

He wasn't heartless. He loved his father with every cell of his being, but it needed to be over. He had ceased to be the father he knew once the bodies began to drop. Spencer had never been sure—not until the end. He had suspected but always had hope that his father was being truthful. That he was nothing more than a victim himself, being set up and targeted by some unknown deranged lunatic.

Nevertheless, Spencer still shouldered the guilt of allowing it to happen more than once. He had wanted to go to the police and unload his thoughts and suspicions. In the back of his mind, he held onto the possibility that a more in-depth investigation might have even proved his father's innocence. But if it didn't, his father would have been gone, and it would have been Spencer's doing. He wouldn't have been able to handle being alone. Not like that.

His fate had already been written though because there he sat...in that massive house...alone. He missed his mother every day, but that day, it was utterly unbearable. His mind wasn't wired the way his father's was. Spencer couldn't simply replace her with a copy. Half of him hated his father for trying to do just that. The other half hated him for dying before ever admitting that he had taken her life.

He leaned forward, folding his arms across the desk and resting his chin atop them. His eyes stung as he thought about her and the five other women that perished beneath his father's hand. He had tried to run them off—tried to steer them as far away from Andrew Donovan as he could. In the end, it didn't matter what he did. They were hunted down anyway.

Tears began to drip across his forearm and run onto the desk. He savored it. It had been too long since he had been able to be honest with himself. He faced the fact that his father was a monster and almost got away with killing all those women. He would have, had Amanda not entered their lives. She was there to do the job that Spencer couldn't do himself. If only he had known her plans. He definitely wouldn't have treated her the way he did.

Through all the regrets and guilt that overwhelmed him every day, he heeded the advice she had given him as best he could. *Let it go.* He couldn't change the past. He couldn't bring them back. It was over. Amanda had made sure of that, and it was time to live his own life.

At that, he lifted his head and wiped his face with the collar of his shirt. Spinning the chair to face the monitor, he powered it up and habitually opened his email. It was flooded, as usual. Condolences from people he'd never met. Requests for interviews on daytime talk shows. Even a batch of hate mail snaked its way into his inbox.

He scrolled for several pages before hovering the mouse over the "delete all" tab. Without an inclination of why, he paused before hitting the button that would send the entire collection into the trash. It could have been fate finally throwing him a bone. It could have been that his eyes saw something that his brain couldn't translate. Whatever the reason, he was thankful, because without that pause he never would have spotted the subject line that contained the pet name he used to answer to. The name that had only ever come from his mother's mouth. Without that pause...he would have still been alone.

END OF BOOK ONE

Keep reading for a preview of the next book in this series:
How Obsession Breeds

Reviews

Please consider taking a few moments to leave an honest review of this book. The review does not need to be long and in depth. Even a simple line or two will greatly help other readers decide whether or not they might enjoy this book. Scan below to be taken directly to the review page for *When Diamonds Bleed*.

For more information about upcoming releases, bonus material, or to follow this author on social media, please visit:
www.ksreidbooks.com

Keep reading for a preview of the next book in this series:

How Obsession Breeds.

About The Author

As the daughter of a nurse, K.S. Reid grew up surrounded by graphic medical journals and surgical textbooks. Her love for blood and guts developed at an early age and led her to a career in sports medicine.

After "retiring," and spending over a decade raising a family, she turned to her love of thriller novels and is now enjoying its creative outlet for her sick and twisted mind.

She currently resides in Maryland where she loves to epically wipe-out in the Atlantic Ocean, run her dog in the Catoctin Mountains, and encounter the occasional rude person that she'll murder in her next book.

Turn the page for a preview of the next book in this series:

How Obsession Breeds.

Prologue

The steel blade glided through the soft skin of her forearm, coming to rest as the diamond was completed. A steady stream of blood flowed across her wrist and pooled onto the wooden surface beneath her. A square of white cloth rushed in to contain the crimson river before it began its final descent over the edge and toward the concrete floor.

With a quick hand, he grabbed a second square to dab and blot the overflowing incision. Content with his measure of cleanliness, he tossed the bloody gauze into the container at his feet, adjusted his stool, and settled in for the part he had been most looking forward to.

He grasped the scalpel with a firm and confident grip, trying desperately to still the trembles that ran through his hands. His cuts were nowhere near as perfect as he would have liked them to be. His diamonds were unsymmetrical and the slices uneven, but it was his first time and he knew that perfection would come with experience. Although, the jumps and jerks of her arm severely impacted his lines, making perfection seem even further off.

His elbow dropped onto hers and his free hand clamped down over the nylon cuff across her wrist, pinning her arm to the table. The muscles of her forearm contracted violently, but to no avail. He leaned forward, adding his bodyweight to supplement the bondage and making even the smallest movement impossible.

Beads of sweat saturated the linen hood that enveloped his head and face. Steam erupted from his cheeks and vented through the mask's eye openings. He took a deep breath and continued to cut.

He struggled to retain his focus and close his mind to the deafening screams that echoed in stereo off the unpainted drywall. *How on Earth did Donovan manage to do this five times?* The trembling in his hands returned and, as a result, his clean slice veered off course.

"Look what you made me do!" His voice boomed, turning her screams into whispers by comparison. "You need to behave, Rebecca. You're just making it take longer, acting like that."

"My name is not Rebecca!"

"Shut up!" He stood and grabbed a fistful of gauze sponges and shoved them into her mouth, preventing her from speaking another word.

He returned to his stool and set the scalpel on the plywood surface next to her bound hand. Interlocking his fingers behind his head, his eyes closed and his chest expanded with a deep inhalation. He had lost control with her. How could he ever hope to control her if he couldn't even control himself?

The screams were still present, but now muffled and less distracting. Her body twisted and struggled against the restraints, but the movement was minimal. He drew another deep breath and his eyes fluttered open.

The horizontal windows high on the walls, although small, let in plenty of natural light for the time being. He had intentionally positioned her in the exact spot where all the streams of light converged and her body gleamed in the sun's rays. The bloody diamond outlines spanned her arms, shoulders, and torso. The cuts were shallow—merely a template for the next stage of skin removal.

His gaze traveled along her naked form to her thighs, still smooth and untouched. He hadn't thought her upper body would take this long. His patience had worn thin long ago, and as hard as he tried to ignore her screams, they were slowing him down and he was running out of daylight. The perfect unmarred skin below her hips drove him crazy, but his project would have to remain unfinished. He had no choice.

Suddenly, a deep retching sound escaped from within her throat. His eyes darted toward her face and he watched clumps of vomit seep from the corners of her mouth. The sound of her muffled cries ceased and her eyes grew wide with panic. Her neck arched as she threw her head back into the table repeatedly, her face turning bright red as the convulsions continued.

"Oh no...you're not going to choke on me. You need to be alive for this part."

He yanked the gag out of her mouth and waited for her airway to clear. The muscles in her neck bulged and the veins appeared ready to burst. The pink tint drained from her face and was replaced with an ashen gray.

"No!" His own panic began to set in as he grabbed both sides of her face and thrust her head to the side. "Spit it out!" Her lips mouthed a silent plea as a hint of blue spread across them. "Damn it!"

He dove across her chest and ripped open the Velcro strap trapping her arm. Grabbing her wrist, he pulled it toward him and rolled her as far as he could onto her side. "Come on!" His palm landed hard between her shoulder blades several times before the coughing began and remnants of her last meal splattered onto the floor.

He emptied his lungs in a sigh of relief. Keeping one hand on her back and a grip on her untethered wrist, he leaned in and positioned his lips an inch from her ear. "You okay? You done? That was a close—"

His words were cut short as her elbow slammed into his windpipe, stealing his breath away. He stumbled backward and dropped to his knees gasping and sputtering, both hands clutching his throat.

With one swift motion she released her other arm from the cuff and sat upright on the table. She hugged the mutilated arm to her chest whimpering in pain.

"No!" His voice was raspy and broken as he struggled to his feet.

She grabbed the scalpel, still lying on the table beside her, and flung it at him. The blade flew past him, slicing into his shirt and taking a small piece of his shoulder with it before skidding across the floor. He winced as he covered the wound with his hand and the warm blood oozed through his fingers. *His* blood.

"So *that's* how you wanna play it," he said as his cold eyes locked with hers.

Her eyes grew wide as a new sense of urgency set in. Her hands flew to her ankles and ripped open both cuffs simultaneously. She swung her legs off the side of the table just as he lunged at her and forced her back down. The breath whooshed out of her as his weight fell on her chest.

Her hands flailed frantically around his head, grasping and yanking on the hood that hid his identity. Catching her wrists, he pinned them to her chest and leaned in further, locking both of their sets of hands between them.

Her legs, strong and free, kicked wildly. Her knee slammed hard into his ribcage and sent him half off the table. With his weight shifted, she rolled onto her side, brought both knees to her chest, rammed her feet square into his stomach, and sent him stumbling backward gasping for air.

Leaping from the table, she raced for the doorless exit, her bare feet slapping on the cold concrete. With two long strides, he caught up to her and tackled her to the floor. He stretched his body atop the length of her, planted his forearm on the back of her neck, and pressed her face hard into the cement.

"Don't think for one second you're going to get away from me, Rebecca. I've looked forward to this for way too long to let you fuck it up," he growled into her ear.

"Please...I'm not her. I don't know her and I don't know you. Please...just let me go."

A smile spread across his face and he tugged off the constricting white hood to let that smile grow. That single word was music to his ears. *Please.* The invincible Rebecca Black begging for his mercy. He never thought he'd see the day and he savored it for all it was worth.

He removed his forearm from her neck and replaced it with his hand, keeping her face buried in the floor. Pushing himself up, he scooted up her legs and straddled the backs of her thighs. With his free hand, he grabbed one of her wrists and wrenched it behind her back as she cried out in pain. Releasing her head, he reached for her other hand, outstretched in front of her.

In that moment, he saw what she was stretching for. Her fingers curled around the steel handle of the scalpel lying in front of her. Without hesitation she swung her arm back and buried the blade deep within the side of his knee.

His scream echoed off the unfinished walls as he clutched his knee with both hands. Free from his powerful hold, she slithered out from underneath him, leaving a slug-trail of blood in her wake.

Toppling back onto his hip, his tear-filled eyes caught sight of the gleaming handle protruding from the outside of his knee.

Taking a deep breath, he grasped the handle and yanked it free from his body as, once again, he filled the room with his screams.

Saliva dripped through his clenched teeth and his eyes turned to fire. "You are so going to pay for that, Bitch!"

But his threat was as empty as that cold, blood-stained room. She was gone.

Chapter 1

R ebecca black paused and soaked in the rhythmic sound of The District's hottest street drummers—battling it out in front of a crowd of onlookers outside of D.C.'s Verizon Center. It was a common sight any day of the week, but especially on a late Sunday night, timed perfectly with the conclusion of whatever concert or sporting event had just occurred inside.

Tonight, it was hockey—the Capitals' first home game of the regular season and the fans were in rare form after watching their team get knocked out of the playoffs back in April. Her friend, Lexy, was no exception. She had been harder to handle than any one of the oversized drunk men that surrounded them. At that moment, she remained inside, trying desperately to find a vendor that hadn't closed its gates yet so she could kick off the season with a bright and shiny new jersey.

Rebecca was glad Lexy was delayed. Although she could genuinely enjoy any sporting event, the rich street culture of the city was what really got her heart thumping. She allowed herself to surrender to the beat as the drumsticks continued to bounce off the array of overturned plastic buckets—each one varying in size and emitting its own signature sound.

After her brush with death just over a year ago, Rebecca had vowed to embrace life and everything it had to offer. Witnessing four teenagers make musical magic right before her eyes was one of those offerings, and she couldn't get enough of it.

She still thought of Andrew Donovan. In fact, she thought of him every day, whether she wanted to or not. She took part in taking his life, and now he seemed to be hellbent on taking over hers—even from his grave.

She vowed to fight it as best she could, and street-band distractions almost always did the trick. Her eyes closed and her head bobbed in unison with the drums. Blonde waves danced around her shoulders. She had completed her reverse makeover soon after *it* happened. Her hair had been colored back to the honey gold she was known for, and it was growing even faster than she had hoped. Little by little, she was returning to her true self and putting that entire hellish experience behind her.

"Okay, I'm ready," Lexy said as she suddenly appeared at Rebecca's side and tugged on her arm.

"*I'm* not."

"Please, I'm starving. We can come back and listen to them after. I'm sure they'll still be here."

Rebecca doubted they would be, but Lexy's pleas won her over. She felt eternally indebted to Lexy. Not because she whipped up an alibi to keep Rebecca out of prison. But because Lexy was the one that had to deal with the traumatized Rebecca immediately following Andrew's dissection and slaughter. Rebecca put her through hell during those first few weeks and she had no problem making it up to her every chance she got.

"You win. I could use a real drink anyway," Rebecca said as she linked her arm in Lexy's and the two headed up 7th Street.

"Amen. A girl can only handle so much beer."

The two strolled another fifty feet and yanked open the brass handle at the entrance of Clyde's.

"Wow," Rebecca said as they entered into a wall of people.

Clyde's was a landmark sports bar containing most, if not all, of the hockey fans they had just left. The decor was primarily dark wood from floor to ceiling, including the walls, booths, and of course, the bar. Bronze sculptures depicting athletes of a bygone era in various sporting poses sat atop most of the booth backs. A grand staircase led to the second floor which housed another bar, and what appeared to be just as large of a crowd.

After realizing the patrons in front of them were all waiting to be seated, Rebecca and Lexy snaked their way through to the far wall.

Available seating was nowhere to be found, but they managed to squeeze into a tight standing space at the back corner of the bar.

"It'll have to do," Lexy said, waving her hand to get the attention of one of the three bartenders.

Moments later, a sodden-faced blonde in her mid-twenties appeared in front of them. "Do you need any menus?"

"Yes. And two margaritas on the rocks to start," Lexy replied.

Rebecca's eyes swept the faces in the room as she waited. It was a habit she found herself doing every time she encountered a crowd of people. She had spotted Andrew's face on more than a few occasions over the past year. She knew it wasn't real, but still...she'd like to know ahead of time if she was going to have to deal with that bastard's ghost all night.

The bartender returned with their drinks and slapped a couple of menus on the bar in front of them. Rebecca wasted no time, grabbing her bowl-like glass and nearly emptying it in one go.

"So, what jersey did you end up getting?" she asked as she wiped the salt from her lips with a napkin and peeked down into Lexy's bag.

"Seriously? What jersey do you think I got?"

"But, you have almost a dozen jerseys of the same guy."

"They can change from year to year. Besides, it's my season-starting tradition."

"Ever thought of trying someone different? Just to, you know...try someone different? What about that Austrian guy? He was cute."

"It's not about cute. It's about total badassery. I invest in the best and only the best."

"I get it. He's your version of *the Big O*."

"Exactly," Lexy said as she giggled and clinked her glass with Rebecca's.

K.S. REID

Rebecca downed the rest of her margarita and gestured for the bartender's return. The girl trudged back over to them, her face drawn tight in annoyance.

"Another?" she asked.

"Yes, please."

As the bartender's arm stretched across the bar and her fingers wrapped around the glass of lonely ice cubes, the cuff of her sleeve rose just enough to send an icy chill down Rebecca's spine. It barely peeked out, but the unique pattern of the scar was unmistakable.

Rebecca snatched the girl's wrist and shoved her sleeve up to her elbow. The scarring continued all the way up her forearm and disappeared beneath the raised cuff. Diamonds. Thick white lines criss-crossing their way over her skin's surface and around, what appeared to be, a full-thickness skin graft. Was the graft performed in a hospital...or in a basement? Rebecca shuddered imagining the answer to that question.

Rebecca's eyes rose and bore deep into those of the young barkeep. What she saw there explained the downtrodden expression the girl permanently carried on her face. Pain, fear, humiliation, self-loathing. She was a survivor...yet she wore the mask of a beaten-down victim.

The girl regained possession of her arm with a hard yank and pulled her sleeve back down until it reached her knuckles. Shooting Rebecca a violated look, she turned and raced to the other end of the bar.

"Wait!" Rebecca called out after her.

The girl gave a quick glance over her shoulder before disappearing behind the towering glass shelves of liquor. Rebecca followed in pursuit from her side of the counter, stumbling through the sea of drunk hockey fans and body-checking several of them to the floor. She reached the other end, ducked under the hinged bridge, and spotted the double doors adjacent to the back bar. Pushing through them, she entered the kitchen and scanned the room for any sign of the runaway bartender.

Her initial search came up empty, and any further searching was halted by an angry white-coated duo ushering her back out. She ducked through the bridge and out from behind the bar to find Lexy there waiting for her.

"What exactly is happening right now?" she asked, waving her hands in confusion.

"That bartender—" Once again, Rebecca was on the run, plowing through the crowd on her way to the doors at the front of the restaurant.

A minute later, Rebecca found herself at the curb amidst the countless number of late diners still strolling the streets at that hour. She set her radar for a blonde ponytail, but there were none to be found. Turning the rounded corner of Clyde's, she headed down the pedestrian promenade hoping for some better luck.

She had only ventured down the brick walkway a few yards before she spotted her target, crouching behind a protruding outer wall on the side of the restaurant. The girl hugged her knees to her chest, stroking her forearm with her palm and staring unfocused at the pavement in front of her feet.

Rebecca approached her with soft footsteps and planted herself directly within the girl's line of vision. Startled, the girl jumped to her feet. She raised her palms and backed herself deeper into the brick cove of the wall.

"What do you want from me?" she asked, her voice shaky and broken.

Rebecca pointed to the girl's arm. "When did that happen?"

"None of your business. I don't know you."

"Did Andrew Donovan do that to you?" Her tone was firm as she took a step closer.

"Andrew Donovan is dead. Now will you please just leave me alone?" She turned her head to the side and squeezed her eyes shut.

Rebecca retreated. She hadn't meant to come off so aggressively and strong. The whole situation was so shocking, her tunnel vision had obscured the fact that this was another human being she was dealing with. She took a deep breath and softened her voice. "I'm sorry for coming at you like that. I was almost one of his victims too."

The girl slowly opened her eyes and turned her attention back on Rebecca, scanning her head to toe. "Do you have scars?"

"No. He didn't get that far with me."

The girl's shoulders relaxed, and she wiped away a couple of stray tears hanging in limbo on her lower lashes. "I still get pins and needles sometimes," she said, kneading her forearm with her fingers.

The girl's barriers began to drop, and Rebecca needed to keep them going in that direction. "What's your name?"

"Hope."

"That's a very nice name. And very fitting, seeing how you actually escaped that lunatic. My name is Rebecca."

"Rebecca?"

"Yes. And I'm sorry for digging this horrible experience up after all this time. It's just that it's quite a shock...seeing you. I didn't know there was a sixth victim. And a surviving one, at that. Why didn't you go to the police?"

"He didn't do it."

"Excuse me?" Rebecca's brows narrowed, confused by what exactly the girl was referring to.

"He was already dead when it happened. Andrew Donovan didn't do this to me. It was someone else."

"Who?" Rebecca's mind raced with questions. *Was there an accomplice? A copycat?* But standing in front of her was a survivor. Someone who could identify whoever was following in Andrew's footsteps. The girl's name truly did fit the situation.

"I don't know who. I never saw his face."

Rebecca's shoulders dropped.

"I heard his voice though."

Her posture regained its perk. "Did he say anything that might give a hint to who he was?"

"He kept calling me by your name. Rebecca. Was that a coincidence?"

Rebecca felt like she had just been punched in the stomach. Her eyes drew to the girl's long blonde waves poking out of a high ponytail. The promenade lampposts cast barely enough light for Rebecca to catch the emerald glimmer in Hope's eyes. "No. I don't think it was a coincidence at all."

Chapter 2

"What've we got, Massey?" Detective Ed Harmon asked as he approached the officer on the scene.

"Something weird, that's for sure," the officer answered, leading the detective across the lot.

Ed Harmon had been on the force for over thirty years and had been quite lucky with the cases he had pulled during that time. Some of the young hotshots around him would call his caseload boring, uneventful, and textbook, but that was exactly how he liked it. Simple gunshot or stabbing homicides were bad enough—there was no need to throw psychoses or freaky fetishes on top of it.

With his sights set on his retirement in the near future, he thought he'd be able to finish his career without ever facing a case that would haunt his dreams for the rest of his life. Andrew Donovan chewed up that possibility and spit it right back in his face. Harmon would be over the moon if he never had to deal with a madman like that ever again. Needless to say, the *something weird* response he received from Officer Massey did not sit well with him at all.

The two continued to weave in and out of the squad cars and emergency vehicles littering the empty mall parking lot. Ducking underneath the caution tape perimeter, they stepped onto the curb and came to a stop beneath the Macy's department store sign.

He glanced at the woman lying supine at his feet. Closing his eyes and bowing his head, the detective whispered a silent prayer.

It was his routine every time he came upon an innocent victim. He gave them those first moments. To see them as the person they were—a daughter, a sister, a wife, a mother. He prayed for them and the families and friends they had left behind. He gave them the respect their attacker didn't.

And when he finished, the doors of his sadness closed. There was so much death in the life of a homicide detective. A man could easily drown within all that pain and suffering if he didn't find a way to make his peace and then close off his emotions.

Harmon had learned that particular coping method from his mentor decades ago and hadn't strayed from it since. His prayer sets their soul free and only then could he turn off his emotions and allow his objective brain to take over.

The detective raised his head and opened his eyes.

Now he was ready to get to work. He fished a small notebook and pen out of his coat pocket and studied the body in front of him.

It was a woman. Late twenties, maybe early thirties. Long blonde hair and wearing nothing but a black bra and panties. A white cloth napkin laid across her upper thighs. The cause of death could have been the eight-inch vertical incision running from the bottom of her sternum down to her navel. A silver coiled wire, similar to the binding of a spiral notebook, looped through the edges of her flesh to close the wound.

He clicked his pen and jotted down his observations before returning his attention to the body. Ligature marks around her ankles and wrists revealed she was bound. Her hands, balled into fists, clutched a silver dinner fork in her left and a steak knife in her right.

"What's with the utensils?" Harmon asked the officer.

"Killer didn't like her cooking? Decided to put an end to it once and for all over dinner?" Massey chuckled until the detective shot him an unimpressed glare. "Sorry." The officer's head dropped, breaking the uncomfortable eye contact.

"Did you call the crime scene unit?"

"They're on their way."

Harmon slowly spun a circle, his eyes scanning the area around the woman. He quickly noticed the half dozen towering lightposts in close proximity. He then turned his attention on the row of glass doors at the entrance to the mall store.

"There are security cameras all over the place," he said. "Collect the footage."

"I'm on it." Officer Massey turned and disappeared into the wall of approaching crime scene techs.

Harmon crouched down next to the lifeless woman for another visual sweep. His eyes darted between the clues that were screaming out to him. The utensils...the napkin...the incision over the stomach. "What are you trying to tell me?" he mumbled to himself.

He jumped as his cellphone vibrated deep within the front pocket of his pants. He stood and backed away from the body allowing the arriving CSU room to work their magic. Fishing his phone out of his pocket, he flipped it open. "Harmon."

"What the hell, Harmon?" An angry voice flew out of the speaker and sent a radiating pain through his ear canal.

He let out a deep sigh. "Calm down, Rebecca. What's going on?"

"Will you please tell me why I'm here talking to a girl covered in ten-month-old diamond scars and why is this the first time I'm hearing anything about it?"

"Look, I—"

"And don't give me some bullshit story about you not knowing what I'm talking about." Rebecca's voice grew louder and even more furious. "She named you as the one who took her statement at the hospital."

"Yes, I knew about it...but I didn't think you needed to."

"Really? How about the fact that her attacker was calling her by my name? She was a surrogate for me, and you didn't think I needed to know about it?"

"I was trying to protect you. There was nothing you could've done about it and I didn't need you running around all paranoid, taking the law into your own hands."

"What's that supposed to mean?"

"You know exactly what it means."

END OF PREVIEW

Reviews

Please consider taking a few moments to leave an honest review of this book. The review does not need to be long and in depth. Even a simple line or two will greatly help other readers decide whether or not they might enjoy this book. Scan below to be taken directly to the review page for *When Diamonds Bleed*.

For more information about upcoming releases, bonus material, or to follow this author on social media, please visit:

www.ksreidbooks.com

THE REBECCA BLACK TRILOGY

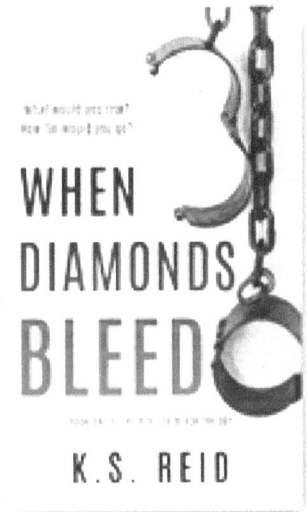

ND - #0236 - 240325 - C0 - 203/133/18 - PB - 9781960632005 - Gloss Lamination